THE GORDONSTON LADIES DOG WALKING CLUB

by
Duncan Whitehead

First published by Dog Ear Publishing
4010 W. 86th Street, Ste H
Indianapolis, IN 46268
www.dogearpublishing.net

ISBN: 978-1-4575-1450-0

This book is printed on acid-free paper.

Printed in the United States of America

As always, for Keira

I would like to acknowledge the following for their assistance, help, inspiration and patience during the writing of The Gordonston Ladies Dog Walking Club:

Rosemary Daniels, Lynette Hendry, Donald and Joan Calder, and above all, Robert Peel.

'The past is not dead. It isn't even past'
William Faulkner

CHAPTER 1

He took one final draw on his cigarette before flicking the wet butt into the hole he had just dug. It was still dark; the sun not due to rise for another thirty minutes. He checked his watch and confirmed the time. He was still on schedule. He turned suddenly to his left, surprised by the rustling noise he had heard in the undergrowth. A grey squirrel peered out from the bushes before rapidly disappearing into the wooded area to the right. Overhead, a woodpecker began to tap against a nearby oak tree. The 'rat-a-tat', like a hammer, echoed through the densely forested landscape.

Satisfied that he was still alone, he re-inspected the freshly dug hole. Ideally, it should have been six feet deep, but four, he thought, would do. It was not the first time he had dug a hole like this, but he wondered though if this one would be the last. He had begun digging the night before and hoped that no one would discover his half-dug hole and half-empty bag of lime salts, which it now appeared, they had not. Usually he would have poured more lime salts into the bottom, to cover the unpleasant smells that would rise from the ground later, but he had decided that the extra bags would be too much to hide. He crouched and leaned over the hole, stretching his arm to full length to pick up his discarded cigarette butt. Unprofessional, he thought. He really knew better than that. He slipped the butt into the packet it had come from, alongside the other nineteen yet unsmoked menthols.

From his vantage point he could see anyone entering or leaving the park. There were three gates, but he had taken the precaution of locking the north and south gates with padlocks, which he would remove and discard once his task was complete. Now the only way to enter the park would be via the east gate, which was the main entrance anyway, and the one he knew would be used that morning.

The recently prepared hole was ensconced just off the well-trodden path that encircled the park; he couldn't have asked for a better spot to perform his task. If only they were all this easy. He picked up his shovel and placed it out of sight in the undergrowth. He would need it later to fill the hole back in. Though he had dug holes like this before, they were usually not necessary. But the instructions he had received were very specific, that there should be no trace of his work for at least one week. He hoped that four feet was deep enough. He considered his surroundings and decided it was.

The park was located in the center of a middle class neighborhood of approximately 300 homes. It was protected by a wrought iron fence and three gates—perfect for his purposes. Signs proclaimed that this was private property, designated solely for the use of those who lived there. At least half the families in the area owned a dog and regularly used the park to exercise them. Not everyone walked his dog in the park. He estimated that only fifty or so people ever ventured where he now stood.

The Girl Scout Hut, an old log cabin-style building that stood in the center of the park, was available for hire for private functions and neighborhood gatherings as well as for residential association meetings. An extensive wooded area, home to an abundance of wildlife, dominated the interior of park. Trees and shrubbery surrounded the perimeter railings, hiding the interior of the park from anyone traversing nearby streets. A children's playground in the northeast corner of the park offered wooden swings and forts. These, along with sliding boards and monkey bars delighted the children of those privileged to play there.

Dog walkers took advantage of the wood-chipped track that circled the park. The path wove around the trees and crossed ditches and natural moats. The occasional jogger who ventured into the park would sometimes make use of the track but would have to watch for fallen trees and avoid the sprawling roots that sprouted from the earth. He pulled another menthol from its packet and lit it. He sucked in the mint-flavored smoke and exhaled it into the early morning air. It was hard to hold the cigarette in his gloved hand, so he removed the leather pair that he wore. He wore the gloves not due to any coldness but as necessary to his task.

The sky was no longer black but a dark blue, the sun now on the verge of rising. The first birds of the morning began their song and the temperature was slowly beginning to rise. The unnatural sound of a car engine straining into life could be heard in the distance. Its owner was probably an early morning worker, beginning his day while most were still enjoying their last few minutes of sleep.

It was going to be another warm day, and air conditioning systems would be on high throughout the city. He considered removing the dark coat that he wore but didn't. It, along with the gloves, was his standard attire when working: an unofficial uniform of his trade. More rustling, this time from the north, made him twist his body and alerted his senses. As before, another squirrel disappeared into the dense wood as the streetlights that illuminated the avenues and streets that ran alongside the park switched off in unison, announcing that daybreak was approaching. Soon bedroom lights would turn on as early risers prepared themselves for the day ahead.

He was conscious of the four homes that backed onto the park on the west side where he waited. He had considered the possibility of being discovered by a dog, released into the morning to relieve himself and to stretch his legs, but had decided that the chances of any animal being able to navigate both a garden fence and the iron railings and still see him through the dense trees were minimal. He was a professional, and he had taken no chances. He never did. The previous morning he had stood in the exact same spot where he was now, at the exact same time, and was confident that neither dog nor man would discover him.

He placed his gloveless hand into the front lower pocket of his jacket and felt the cold stainless steel held snugly there. One final check was required, one final inspection. The last thing he needed was some equipment malfunction.

He removed the Beretta M9/92F 9mm semi-automatic pistol from his pocket and ran his hand along the smooth barrel. It was his weapon of choice for up-close hits, and it had never let him down. For jobs such as this, it was ideal. He checked the safety catch and the clip that contained six bullets. He hoped he would only need one, two at the most. He delved into his other pocket, produced his M9-SD silencer, and caressed the long, sleek black cylinder before attaching it to the barrel of the Beretta. Once again, it was a tool of the trade that had never let him down.

He had always considered silenced, close-up hits to have a personal touch, and strived for perfection whenever tasked with such a kill. It was important to hit the selected vital organ. The quicker a target fell, the quicker one could leave. The heart or the middle of the forehead were his preferred targets, though a well-placed single shot in the center of a chest or the stomach could also result in instantaneous death without the need of a second shot. He considered more than two shots poor form. What separated the best from the rest, he thought, was the swiftness and accuracy of hits. It was easy to kill, but not so easy to kill smoothly, efficiently and quickly, leaving behind no clues or trace as to the identity of the killer. The less blood the better, especially in a situation like this, where instructions demanded the disposal of a body and no immediate trace of a crime.

The sun was rising now and the sky was turning from dark to light. It was going to be another beautiful day in Gordonston, an older but stylish neighborhood where he stood, two miles to the east of downtown Savannah, Georgia, and the Historic District, a five-minute drive at most from the center of the city. He yawned and stubbed out the cigarette before placing into its pack with the other eighteen and the one smoked butt. He put on his gloves and slipped the Beretta with the silencer screwed into the barrel into his pocket.

He could hear voices close by and the barking of excited dogs. Two voices bade farewell to a third voice and the iron gate creaked, opening and then closing as the owner of the one voice entered the park. From where he crouched near to the ground, he could see a dog having its leash removed, then running into the woods. He drew his weapon. His heartbeat didn't quicken, and his breathing didn't rise. He fixed his gaze on his intended target and waited as the darkness gave way to daylight.

A beautiful day indeed in Juliette Low Park, but for one individual, that day would not last long.

CHAPTER 2

"Betty Jenkins said that her light is shining, which I guess means to Betty that the Lord is coming for her."

"I heard that she was on her deathbed and won't make it through the day."

"Young Kelly told me that a priest had been called to administer the last rites."

The three women looked toward the large white house that overlooked the east side of Gordonston Park.

"Poor Elliott," said Heidi Launer, eldest of the three by twenty years. The other two women nodded.

"Yes, poor, poor Elliott," agreed Cindy Mopper, the youngest of the three by a few months.

"Whatever will he do, once she is gone? A man like him needs a wife at his side," added Carla Zipp, the most attractive of the three.

The trio of women stood at the east-facing wrought iron gate—the main entrance to the park—looking out onto the street as more cars arrived at the house carrying friends and relatives of the dying Thelma Miller, who had been diagnosed with throat cancer five years earlier. Given only months to live, she had somehow clung to life longer than anyone had expected. Thelma had been a founding member, along with Cindy, of the Gordonston Ladies Dog Walking Club, and it was her fellow members of this exclusive club that now stood within the railings of the park, discussing among themselves what they guessed was happening inside their ailing friend's home that afternoon.

"I hear he may run for Mayor," said Cindy, throwing the tennis ball that had been dropped at her feet by her Irish terrier, Paddy, into the park. "I heard that from young Veronica, on Kinzie Avenue," she added as her dog disappeared into the wooded area of the park, closely followed by Carla's Bulldog Walter and Heidi's German pointer Fuchsl, all three dogs determined to be the first to reach the ball.

"I think he should definitely run for Mayor," said Carla lifting the red disposable plastic cup that contained her homemade cocktail of gin and tonic, to her lips.

"He's been our alderman for so long now," said Heidi, "and he has always done such a great job. I think he should run. He would certainly get my vote."

The women all nodded in agreement. Elliott Miller, soon to be Thelma's widower, had been alderman for the Gordonston District for the last twenty years. He was a popular man, not just in Gordonston but throughout Savannah. Elliott and Thelma Miller ran a small but profitable real estate agency, though Elliott now devoted most of his time to city politics and Thelma, due to her illness, had not sold a property in months.

"How do you think they've managed?" asked Cindy, "I mean financially? With Thelma bedridden and Elliott caring for her, they haven't sold anything in ages."

"I hear Elliott has family money," answered Heidi. "I know there's no mortgage on that house. Thelma told me once that Elliott came into some money years ago, just after they were married, enough to set her up in business and for him to concentrate on his political affairs."

The three turned from the gates and walked towards the Girl Scout Hut that sat in the center of the park. There they would resume their usual afternoon positions around the wooden picnic table, another permanent feature of the park, each lady with her afternoon cocktail inside a red plastic cup. It was their usual routine. For the past ten years The Gordonston Ladies Dog Walking Club would meet at the picnic table every afternoon at four o'clock, weather permitting. While their dogs roamed the park and played together, the four members—now reduced to three—would sip on their cocktails and pass the afternoon gossiping about their neighbors and friends.

The only rules for membership into the Gordonston Ladies Dog Walking Club were that members had to be female, own a dog, and reside within the boundaries of Gordonston. One other criterion was that members had to enjoy an afternoon cocktail. Not that just anyone could join. Membership was by invitation only. All members had to agree to accept any potential newcomer.

Heidi, Carla and Cindy were all widows. Thelma was the only one with a living husband, and it was not lost on the other members of the Gordonston Ladies Dog Walking Club that she would be leaving him behind, an eligible widower. Cindy's late husband, Ronnie, a successful car salesman had died four years earlier. Cindy considered that he had been a good husband. Carla's late husband, Ian, had not been such a great catch. He had philandered his way through the years, so that when he died of a heart attack in bed with his secretary, it didn't come as too much of a surprise to Carla. The bank that he had presided over for several years had provided for her very well in order to avoid a scandal and ensure her silence.

Heidi's husband, Oliver Marsh, had died over twenty years before. Though she was originally from Austria, Heidi had immigrated to Savannah with her parents just before the outbreak of war in 1939. Oliver had owned several large tracts of commercial real estate in the Savannah area. After his death, Heidi, proud of her European roots, had reverted to her maiden name of Launer.

"Who is going to walk Biscuit and Grits?" asked Cindy, a hint of concern in her voice. "Those poor dogs. You know Thelma dotes on them. They are her babies."

Biscuit and Grits were the Miller's two pet poodles. Since Thelma had become bedridden four months before, Biscuit and Grits hadn't been seen in the park by any of the trio. Elliott would release them in the morning onto the quiet street and let them roam about for twenty minutes before ushering them back inside the house. The two small dogs could be heard barking each day from the street outside, trapped in the house and no doubt missing their three canine friends.

As the women pondered the physical well-being of Biscuit and Grits and the lack of exercise that had befallen them, the gate to the park opened. All three heads swiveled to see who had arrived.

"Ah, that's Doug, Veronica's husband," said Cindy.

"Isn't he Australian?" asked Carla.

"No, I think English," said Heidi.

"That's right," Cindy confirmed. "He is English. I'm sure he used to be some sort of an accountant, in Switzerland or somewhere like that. But he retired so he could be with Veronica and the baby."

The ladies watched as he opened the gate and released his dog into the park. The animal, a German shepherd, made its way speedily towards the other frolicking dogs. Dressed in khaki shorts and a white t-shirt, Doug was pushing a baby stroller, which he wheeled onto the wood-chipped track that circled the park the moment his dog left his side.

"He's here every day," Carla observed, "with the baby and the dog."

"She's a beautiful baby," said Cindy. "She looks like Veronica, I think."

"They have a beautiful house. They've done a lot to it. I remember Thelma telling me that she sold it to them," said Carla as Veronica's English husband and baby disappeared from view, swallowed up by the trees and shrubbery. "She also said they paid cash for it. No mortgage. He just wrote out a check. I guess that's why he can retire so young. He's thirty-five, at the most," said Carla.

"More like forty, I think," said Cindy, "I think he made his money dealing stocks and bonds. Used to work for one of those big international banks, I heard. Veronica told me he was waiting on immigration now to get a permit or something. I don't know; it all sounds complicated."

Heidi agreed. "It is, you know. These days it's not easy being a foreigner over here. I remember when I came over it was very easy. But now, boy they make you sweat."

The women all nodded, as if they were well aware of the pitfalls and red tape encountered by new immigrants to their country. Then each of them took a sip from their red plastic cups.

"Where will they bury poor Thelma? Does anyone know?" Heidi asked as the women returned to the previous subject. "I would have thought Bonaventure Cemetery," replied Carla, "I'm sure that they have a plot there. They're Old Savannah."

"What about her sons? Do you think they'll fly in for the funeral?" Cindy asked. Thelma had two sons from a previous marriage, both highly successful Los Angeles based television producers.

"I would think so," said Heidi, and the ladies all agreed that Thelma's sons would make the trip to Savannah for their mother's funeral.

"You know, they're both queer," announced Heidi, taking another sip from her cup.

"I had heard that, too," agreed Cindy. "Who would believe that two brothers could both be gay? What a cross for Thelma and Elliot to bear. And how sad to think that they could never hope to be blessed with grandchildren, either."

"You know, of course, that Elliott isn't their father," added Carla.

"I knew that," Heidi nodded. "Thelma told me once about her first husband. Died young, she said."

"So Elliott inherited a whole family. What a good man," said Cindy.

"They are good boys though, despite, you know, them not being like other men," added Heidi. "I remember when they were growing up. You would never have guessed."

"Maybe that's why they went into television—they're all homosexuals, those TV people," Carla said, her over-generalization readily accepted by the other two women.

"Poor, poor Elliott," said Cindy again, as all eyes again turned to the large white house that overlooked the east side of the park. Well, let's hope he runs for mayor at least," said Carla. "God knows, Savannah needs a decent mayor!" All three ladies, in unison, raised their cups to their mouths and drank, as if toasting Carla's words.

The ladies were now joined at the picnic table by four dogs, panting and out of breath. Walter, Paddy and Fuchsl were accompanied by Bern, Veronica and Doug's German shepherd. After greeting the trio of women, the four dogs made their way to the water bowl outside the scout hut and gathered round it. The hose that filled the bowl was set to a slow drip, ensuring that no dog playing in the park ever became thirsty or dehydrated. It was a hot afternoon, as it always was in the summer, but like everything else that came with living in such a unique place, the residents of Savannah were used to it. The afternoon temperature hovered just below ninety degrees, though the coastal breeze brought some light relief.

"Bern! Bern!" Veronica's husband was calling his dog to join him at the gate. Bern looked up from the water bowl and sped towards his master. The three ladies waved at the man. "I am not sure what to make of him," said Carla. "My neighbor Kelly told me he was once rude to her, for no reason—trying to be smart," said Cindy.

"I haven't spoken to him yet," said Heidi as she inspected the man who was now waving back to the women. "He looks scruffy. He's always dressed in a t-shirt and shorts. I've never seen him wear anything else."

"I like Veronica, though," said Carla, and the ladies all agreed that they preferred Veronica over her English husband, despite the fact that not one of them had ever spoken to the man or even so much as given him the time of the day.

"I bet he suffers with this heat though," said Heidi. "I know I did when I first got here." They watched as Bern was put on his leash and continued to watch as man, baby, and dog disappeared from view.

More cars were now arriving at the Miller residence, as those wishing to bid a final farewell to poor Thelma came by to do so.

"Should we pay our last respects to Thelma now, all together," asked Carla, "or wait until the relatives have left?"

Heidi and Cindy considered their friend's suggestion.

"You know, I am not sure what the protocol is," said Heidi. "Maybe we should. Perhaps we should knock on the door and see her. I saw her last week, but I think since then she has been in and out of consciousness."

"I think I'll pay my respects at the funeral," said Cindy. "I hear she's incoherent, that she doesn't even recognize poor Elliott. I don't want to remember her that way."

"Poor Elliott." said Carla.

"Indeed, poor Elliott," repeated Heidi as she slowly raised her cup to her lips, a slight trace of a smile developing as she took a sip of her afternoon cocktail.

Again all heads turned to the big, white house. The number of cars outside the Miller residence had begun to dwindle, and Edgewood Road had resumed its normal sedate and tranquil state.

"Look, its Kelly, my neighbor," exclaimed Cindy. At the gate, about to enter the park, was an attractive young woman with blond hair, accompanied by a golden Labrador. As soon as his owner opened the gate, the dog bounded over to where the other three dogs had resumed their playful frolicking in the park.

"Hi, Shmitty," said Carla as the dog sped past the picnic table, oblivious to the seated women and headed into the dense trees.

"You know she could be a model, that girl," said Carla, referring to Kelly. "She must be on her lunch break, just letting Shmitty out for a run." The women watched as the young woman talked on her cell phone.

"She just missed the Englishman. I wonder what he said to her?" said Carla.

"Who knows?" said Cindy. "She must have her work shoes on. I don't think I have ever seen her actually come inside the park. She always just stays outside."

"Maybe we should call her over?" suggested Heidi. "I would love to know what Veronica's husband said to her." The others agreed that it would be good to know.

Kelly didn't join the group, however. She waved and called for Shmitty to come back to the gate before they had the chance to summon her over to the picnic table. The three women waved back as Shmitty once again bounded past them to return to his owner.

She does this sometimes," said Cindy. "She comes home from the mall to let Shmitty stretch his legs for a few minutes. She works at Macy's, at one of the perfume counters."

"Her husband's Tom, isn't he?" asked Heidi. "A lovely boy, just as handsome and good looking as she is." The ladies all agreed that Cindy's neighbors, Kelly and Tom, were a good-looking couple. "Hollywood" was how Carla described the couple.

Kelly and Shmitty disappeared from view. "You know, they are great neighbors," said Cindy. "He's always doing odd jobs for me, very kind. They're a great couple."

As they discussed the virtues of Cindy's young neighbors, the ladies didn't notice an elderly black man enter the park, followed closely by his white Cairn terrier dog. He saw the ladies, though, as he saw them every day at around this time, and he raised his arm to wave at the three of them even though they weren't looking. Then he let his dog off the leash, but unlike the other dogs that had arrived at the park that afternoon, the terrier didn't run to play. Instead the old dog stayed at his master's side as he slowly traversed the park's perimeter path.

Now Heidi caught a glimpse of him. "There's the old man," she said. "You know, he doesn't scoop." The other two women turned to watch as he disappeared behind a clump of trees.

"Maybe we should say something to him. You know everybody else does it. Scoop, I mean. I've seen his dog—Chalky, I think he's called—poop near the swings," said Carla indignantly.

"Do you know his name?" asked Cindy.

"No. I know he lives in Gordonston in the house with the turret. You know he's the only one who doesn't clean up the mess," Heidi complained. The three ladies decided that the best course of action would be to have the Gordonston Residents Association write to the old man reminding him to clean up after his dog.

The three women agreed to meet again, the next day at four p.m., when the Gordonston Ladies Dog Walking Club would reconvene. They finished their cocktails and called their respective dog to heel, each dog responding immediately to his mistress's voice. Once the three dogs were leashed, the trio of women made their way to the gate. As they exited the park they paused across the street from the Miller house.

"Poor Elliott," said Carla.

"Yes, poor Elliott," said Cindy.

Of the three women, Heidi lived nearest to the park, along Kentucky Avenue. She owned a large five-bedroom home, set on the corner where Kentucky Avenue joined Edgewood Road, which made Heidi and the Millers neighbors. As they reached her house, Heidi bade farewell to her friends, "Well, let's all hope Thelma is still with us in the morning," she said, "I'll say a prayer for her tonight." The other two women agreed that they, too, would include Thelma in their prayers.

"And we mustn't forget poor Elliott," added Carla.

"Yes, of course, let's pray for poor Elliott too" agreed Cindy.

Cindy's home was a modest cottage-type bungalow located on Henry Street about five hundred yards from the park. After bidding goodbye to her two friends, she headed eastwards towards her home.

Carla also made her goodbyes and began her short walk home, Walter trailing behind on his leash. Carla's home was situated along Georgia Avenue. Like the Miller residence, her home overlooked the park, on the south side. Like Heidi, she had a large five-bedroom home. Even she admitted that it was far too big for just her and little Walter.

Heidi Launer, though Austrian by birth, had no trace of a European accent. Her dialect was pure Georgia with a distinct tidewater twang. She had arrived in Savannah in 1939 as a teenager, her parents having left Europe just before the outbreak of war. Her father had started a small butcher shop on Oglethorpe Avenue in the center of the city. The family lived in a large house with servants, adjacent to Wright Square.

Heidi met and married Oliver Marsh in 1964. Oliver was a successful commercial real estate entrepreneur and leased his many downtown properties to national companies, who, looking to expand their businesses in the thriving city, opened their restaurants and banks in his buildings. After eventually selling his real estate holdings and retiring on the proceeds, Heidi and Oliver moved, at Heidi's insistence, into the large house in Gordonston. Oliver died soon thereafter, and Heidi became firm friends with Thelma and Elliott Miller and their two sons.

Heidi and Oliver had one child, a son, Stephen, who moved to New York after graduating from law school. He still lived there with his two children and wife, having established a lucrative practice in criminal law. When time permitted, Stephen still returned to Savannah to visit his mother, bringing with him her grandchildren who, though practically adults themselves, enjoyed their visits south.

After Oliver's death in the mid-eighties Stephen had urged his mother to move out of the big house and join him and his family in New York. Unable to pull herself away from the memories of the past, Heidi decided to remain in Savannah, in the little community she knew so well. She had her good friends Carla, Cindy and Thelma and couldn't imagine moving away from them. She had a large home to keep up, but employed a housekeeper who attended to cleaning and cooking four days a week. Fuchsl, her German pointer, was her constant and loyal companion, and over the years she had come to be seen as the matriarch of the small community. As such, she was held in high esteem by her neighbors in Gordonston.

Oliver had amassed a small fortune before he died, so Heidi was well provided for. She was an avid reader and had converted one of the larger bedrooms of her home into an extensive library. Shelves of books adorned every wall, with the complete works of such diverse writers as Dickens, Poe, Twain, and Shakespeare among the many she owned. A true bibliophile, she kept a careful inventory of every book she owned.

The biggest section in her library was her collection of children's books. A keen collector of any story written for the young, from paperbacks to illustrated works, she had hundreds of such titles. If it was available, then Heidi owned it. She had first editions of all of Enid Blytons, Carolyne Keens and even J. K. Rowling's books. Besides these well-known authors, she owned first editions of works by lesser-known and out-of-print authors such as Kenny Wilkes and Brendan Benzie.

Collecting books, walking Fuchsl in the park, enjoying her afternoon cocktails, and gossiping with her friends were Heidi's main joys in life. These activities helped keep her healthy and active. Though in her eighties, she still drove and didn't rely too heavily on neighbors and friends for help. She still hosted dinner parties, her regular guests being other members of the Gordonston Ladies Dog Walking Club, and Elliott. Her housekeeper, Betty Jenkins, was an excellent cook whose dishes were legendary, and she cherished the evenings when she could entertain her neighbors by setting her housekeeper's delicious low country-style feasts before them.

Though she had never returned to her homeland, she vowed she would do so one day before she passed on, taking Stephen and his family with her. She had already begun her search for tickets and planned to travel to the country of her birth the following year. She had organized trips to Austria before, but due to Stephen's heavy schedule and court appearances she had had to cancel more than one of them.

Though proud of her son's achievements as a respected defense attorney, she was a little dubious of the company he kept. She had read in the papers of infamous clients he had successfully defended over the years. Stephen had become the lawyer of choice for any mob boss indicted to appear before a jury. Of course, that didn't make her son a gangster, but she did worry about him and his family. That worry was far outweighed by the pride she felt as he regularly and successfully defended crime lord after crime lord, earning himself a reputation as one of the country's most highly regarded criminal lawyers.

But New York was miles from the tranquil surroundings in which Heidi had decided to spend her twilight years. She was happy with her books, her dog and her regular afternoon forays into the park for cocktails and gossip with her friends. As she entered the cooled house, she could smell the aroma of the dinner Betty was preparing for that night. Fuchsl, now unleashed, made his way into the living room where he promptly collapsed, exhausted from his playful frolics in the park. Betty greeted Heidi with a smile and offered her some of the homemade lemonade she had just prepared. Heidi took a glass and thanked her.

Heidi took this opportunity to ask Betty if she knew the name of Chalky's owner. She wanted to begin the process of drafting the letter of complaint detailing the Resident Association's disappointment in the man's failure to clean up after his dog.

"I know the man who you mean," said Betty. "I've seen him at church." Betty attended the Sunview Baptist church at the edge of the Gordonston neighborhood along Gwinnett Street. Though housed just within the borders of Gordonston, the congregation was mainly made up of African-American worshippers from outside the neighborhood. Betty spent four days a week in Gordonston cooking and cleaning for her employer, but her home was across President Street and in an area known as East Savannah.

"I think he is a widow-man," Betty continued. "He lives just by the park, in that big house on Gordon Avenue. Hardly ever passes the time of day with folks. He's so quiet; I don't even know his name."

Heidi asked her housekeeper to do some discreet investigating on behalf of the Gordonston Residents Association. The park, she believed, was for all the residents of Gordonston to enjoy, and for one user to let his pet defecate without even attempting to clean up the mess, well, that was not going to happen, not if she could help it. Heidi was seen as the unofficial chairperson when it came to matters of etiquette like this one. Betty was happy to do what her employer asked, and promised that when she went to church that Sunday, she would ask some questions.

After thanking her housekeeper, Heidi made her way up the winding staircase to her bedroom. As she reached the second floor, she passed the one room that remained permanently locked. She checked the door, as she always did. It remained tightly shut. Only she had the key; only she would ever enter the sealed room, and then only when Betty was not around. Satisfied that the door was locked, she retired to her bedroom for her regular afternoon nap.

The first thing Cindy did when she returned home with Paddy was open a can of his favorite dog food. Paddy was a large dog, who would be having his usual hunger pangs after an afternoon in the park. After feeding Paddy, Cindy took a seat, kicked off her shoes, and relaxed.

Cindy's afternoons in the park were the highlight of her day. As co-founder with Thelma Miller of the Gordonston Ladies Dog Walking Club, many years before, she had intended the club to be a way for the older female residents to socialize and bond together. The cocktails had been Thelma's idea. It was a pleasant way to spend afternoons, chatting with friends while their dogs ran free. Cindy was active in the Gordonston community, a member, along with Heidi, of the Gordonston Book Club and secretary of the Residents Association. She was also a neighborhood watch block captain and helped organize neighborhood events in the park.

Cindy Mopper had lived in Savannah all her life, the last ten years in Gordonston. She had moved from the south side of the city after her husband Ronnie's death. Ronnie had sold cars for a living and had managed a car lot along Abercorn Street, home to Savannah's two malls and the main shopping thoroughfare for the city and nearby towns. Ronnie's relatively early death, the result of a stroke, had been a shock to Cindy, who threw herself into as many activities as she could to cope with her sudden loss and subsequent grieving.

Cindy and Ronnie had been a childless couple. Cindy's closest relative, in blood and distance, was a brother who lived just outside of Atlanta but whom she seldom saw. She doted on her brother's son Billy, and she looked forward to her nephew's letters and emails. It had been Billy who encouraged his aunt to buy a computer, which she had done. The computer enabled her to produce neighborhood newsletters and fulfill her role as secretary to the Gordonston Residents Association with efficiency. Her newsletters were well-written and her neighbors looked forward to reading them. They were informative; introducing new arrivals to Gordonston and announcing events to be held in the park. Heidi provided most of the information for the newsletter, and Cindy would produce the pamphlets and distribute them to the homes of the area. It had been her nephew, Billy, who had encouraged her to set up an email account. He had also introduced her to the inner workings of the Internet, which Cindy now found to be a tool she could no longer be without. It was the best way to stay in touch, he told her. He intended one day to travel the world, and they would be able to communicate quickly and cheaply, no matter how far apart they were.

Thus, Cindy had become a computer wizard and Internet junkie. She would log onto the Web and surf the Net on a regular basis, reading news articles, browsing home shopping networks, and generally discovering things she had never known before the advent of the information superhighway.

Each day she would look forward to Billy's emails from around the world. True to his word, Billy had indeed embarked on his global adventure, and Cindy would often receive emails and electronic postcards from exotic locations. Billy would update her on his travels and the places he visited, and she would reply with her news from home. He had always been a good kid, she thought, and she missed him—not that he had ever visited her in Savannah.

Cindy was a popular member of the Gordonston community and got on well with all her neighbors—especially her immediate neighbors to the right, Kelly and Tom Hudd. Tom was one of Savannah's finest, a full-time fire-fighter, who often helped Cindy when she needed a strong man for garden or household chores. Tom, Cindy often thought, was the ideal husband, and she thought that her young neighbors were the picture-postcard couple. All they needed was a couple of kids and they would be the all-American family, and Cindy was sure that it wouldn't be long before children joined the Hudd household.

Kelly was an extremely attractive young woman and could quite easily have embarked on a modeling career, and Tom, as well as being a great guy, was just as handsome. She would often spend time with them, enjoying an impromptu cocktail in the garden or chatting over the fence that separated their two properties.

Cindy enjoyed her peaceful and quite life in Gordonston, and though naturally upset by her friend Thelma's approaching death, she had known that it had been on the cards for a while. The mere fact Thelma had survived this long had been a bonus, and some, including Cindy, would even say a miracle. She would miss Thelma. She and the fellow members of the Gordonston Ladies Dog Walking Club were beginning to feel the effects of not having their friend with them for their afternoon soirees. Thelma had always been a live wire; her ability to come up with gossip about anyone in the neighborhood was legendary, and the Dog Walking ladies all missed her, though Cindy felt she would probably miss her the most. Poor Elliott, she thought. He would be lost in that big house by himself; she was sure he would need help in the weeks and months after his wife's death.

As she relaxed in her easy chair, Cindy decided she would take it on herself to provide Elliott with homemade meals and good company. She was sure he would welcome her southern cooking and maybe the company of a woman, once Thelma had passed away. Elliott was an attractive man, and who knew what could happen in the future? Cindy's mind was taking her forward in time. She pictured herself one day as the mayor's wife, she and Elliott together at functions and entertaining guests at City Hall. Thelma surely wouldn't want Elliott to remain a single man for the rest of his life. Elliott would surely welcome, and even need, the support of a spouse, especially if he was going to run for office.

Cindy temporarily dismissed her thoughts of wooing Elliott and turned them to the next Resident's Association meeting. She felt there was room to increase the membership of certain neighborhood societies; the Book Club could do with more members and the Neighborhood Watch Association was lacking block captains. Even the Dog Walking Club could do with one or two very select new members. She considered inviting Kelly to join them, work and job permitting, maybe as a weekend member, though of course she would have to run that idea by Heidi and Carla first.

Her thoughts then turned back to poor Elliott. Poor Biscuit and Grits. Maybe they could make a special dispensation for Elliott. Maybe if she discussed it with Heidi and Carla, they could invite Elliott to join them as an honorary member of the Gordonston Ladies Dog Walking Club. It would be a way of getting close to Elliott, and it would mean Biscuit and Grits could rejoin their friends in the park for afternoon fun.

Cindy checked the time on her watch. It was fast approaching six o'clock, and she wondered if her nephew Billy had managed to find a computer that he could email her from. She hadn't heard from her nephew for over a week, when he had sent her an email from India. She doubted rural India offered many computers, though, and wasn't worried. Billy was always exploring places other tourists seldom visited, and she was sure if there were a computer to be found, Billy would find it. Regardless, she booted up her laptop anyway. She needed to produce some flyers for the upcoming oyster roast that the Residents Association was planning for later that month.

Cindy decided she would make sure Elliott got a hand-delivered flyer. She also decided that tomorrow she would broach the subject of inviting Elliott to be an honorary member of the Dog Walking Club with Heidi and Carla. Cindy smiled as her computer switched on. She had two new emails, and one was from Billy. She would reply with her news before baking the apple pie she would give to Elliott the next morning, Cindy was sure that the poor man hadn't eaten a decent home-cooked meal in months, and of course it was the least she could do for her dying friend's husband.

Carla Zipp had been a High School and college cheerleader and was a former beauty queen, having won several contests in her youth. She possessed a youthful air and her good looks and healthy figure belied the fact that she was in her sixties. Carla was a relative newcomer to the Gordonston area, having arrived five years earlier from Florida. Though born in Savannah, Carla had left the town she grew up in to forge a career as a dancer. Her travels had taken her to Las

Vegas, where she had been hired as a showgirl. There she danced in many reviews and shows and had appeared on stage with such entertainment greats as Tom Jones and even Elvis Presley himself. It was while in Las Vegas that she had met her future husband, Ian Zipp. Ian was visiting Las Vegas for a banking convention; though still relatively young, he had become the rising star of the Floridian banking group for which he worked. Already a manager at the young age of thirty, he was brash, wealthy, and lived life to the fullest.

Carla had met Ian while taking a late night stroll, which she often did after a grueling three-show night. The young man approached her and offered to buy her a late night supper. Though Carla had encountered many admirers during her time in Las Vegas, she was impressed with the clean-cut young bank manager from Florida. Compared to the mobsters who used to send her flowers night after night, declaring their undying love for her, he seemed like a breath of fresh air. Carla always suspected that those men were only after one thing, and once they had it, she probably would never see them again. Ian was different, she felt; he had manners and was romantic, and when his convention in Las Vegas ended after a week and he returned to Florida, he flooded the young dancer with letters every day for a month. He would beg her to visit him, and finally Carla had taken a Greyhound to Daytona to spend a week-long vacation with Ian and his parents. That week turned into forever. Carla, impressed with all that she found in Florida, abandoned Las Vegas and married Ian four days after he proposed to her.

As Ian's career with the bank skyrocketed, Carla found herself in the role of dutiful housewife. Her own career aspirations now ended, her new ambition was to become the perfect wife to Ian and mother to a large brood of children. Ian though was too busy with work to plan a family. It wasn't until much later that Carla discovered her husband had had a secret vasectomy.

The reason for this operation became apparent to Carla when she caught her husband cheating on her on various occasions with various women. With her friends, women he would meet in bars, bank tellers and even customers: Ian couldn't keep his fly zipped.

Carla left him on numerous occasions and headed back to Vegas, only to be convinced to return on the promise that the infidelities would never happen again. Unfortunately they always did, and her fairytale was turning into a nightmare. When Ian eventually became president of the bank, Carla hoped that his days of philandering were now behind him, but unfortunately they weren't. He had secretly embarked on a clandestine relationship with his secretary, who was more than thirty years his junior. At the age of sixty, grossly overweight and bald, he died of a massive coronary attack in his office while in the arms of his younger lover. To avoid a scandal, the bank hushed up the affair between bank president and secretary, and to ensure Carla's silence and continued discretion regarding the circumstances of her husband's death, they offered her a generous pension for life.

Carla wasn't exactly heartbroken at her husband's sudden demise; over the years she had come to detest her cheating spouse while accepting the wealth her marriage offered. She remained in Florida for several years before realizing that her heart actually belonged back in Savannah, and she sold her beachfront home in Daytona Beach and bought the large and spacious home she now resided in, in the picturesque neighborhood of Gordonston.

Carla had many admirers among the men folk of Savannah, though the only male who shared her bed these days was Walter, her Bulldog. It was thanks to Walter that she had met Cindy and Thelma and joined the Gordonston Ladies Dog Walking Club. The afternoon cocktail club had gradually become the highlight of her day.

Though childless, Carla had sponsored several youngsters in third world countries, donating substantial monthly sums to charities, and in return, she received letters of thanks from the children she helped. Some had even visited her. One boy had done so well that he had risen from the slums of India to become a leading pediatrician with a practice in Ohio. He visited Carla in Savannah whenever he could.

Carla was pleased that she was able to help others with Ian's money, and she prided herself on her caring nature. Overall, things had not turned out too badly for her. She loved her home and enjoyed the company of her three good friends and neighbors. Sadly, though, one of those friends would soon be gone, and as she poured herself a glass of sweet tea, Carla couldn't help but reminisce about the fun times she'd had with Thelma. Poor Elliott, she thought as she took a sip of the refreshing tea, how was he going to manage all alone? Elliott was an attractive man and a kind man too. He always had a smile on his face and a kind word for everyone he met. This was probably why he had defended his seat on the city council so successfully all these years, Carla thought. She had heard, just as Cindy had, that it was his intention to run for office at the next mayoral election. If he did, he would definitely have her vote, she thought.

Maybe she would bake Elliott one of her famous apple pies and drop it off in the morning, or maybe even offer to do some of his laundry. He probably hadn't eaten a decent home-cooked meal in weeks—maybe even months—and of course he would need to look presentable if he were going to run for mayor. She would do his laundry, and even offer to press his shirts. It was the least she could do. No doubt the poor man was beside himself with grief, the news being that Thelma probably wouldn't last the week.

Elliott would also need a shoulder to cry on, Carla supposed, to help him through the coming months. Yes, Carla's mind was made up; she would bake him a pie tonight and take it round to him in the morning. Who knew what the future might hold. If he became mayor he would need a companion at official mayoral functions and other civic events. Carla pictured herself arm in arm with Elliott at a charity ball, he in an elegant tux and she in a long, sequined gown and her sable stole, press cameras flashing away. She quickly dismissed the image from her mind. Thelma was not even dead yet, and she was her friend. What was she thinking? How could she even think of becoming involved with Elliott?

Carla rose from her seat and checked her pantry; she had apples and the ingredients for a pie and decided to spend the rest of the day baking. Walter, exhausted from his afternoon of play, was curled up asleep in his wicker basket in the kitchen. She refilled his water bowl and switched on the oven before getting out her mixing bowl and rolling pin. Poor Elliott, she thought as she began to peel the first apple from the pile before her. She was sure a pie would help him feel a little better.

As Heidi rested, Cindy emailed Billy, and Carla peeled apples for a pie, Thelma Miller slipped into unconsciousness for the last time and died peacefully in her sleep, her devoted husband Elliott at her bedside holding her hand. Many relatives and close friends had gathered, including her two sons, Spencer and Gordon, who had arrived just minutes before their mother's death via a privately chartered jet from Los Angeles.

Elliott wiped a tear from his eye and kissed his wife on the forehead. Biscuit and Grits whined softly out of confusion, aware somehow that their mistress was gone. Thelma's eldest son, Spencer, placed a gentle arm on Elliott's shoulder as he knelt by the body of his wife, and the city councilman appreciated the gesture. He rose and smiled at the assembled throng of relatives and close friends who had come to say their final farewells to his wife. "Thank you all," he said to those gathered, and then promptly and unashamedly burst into tears.

CHAPTER 3

It had been a long sad night for Elliott Miller. First the undertakers had arrived and transported Thelma to the chapel of rest, where she now lay in an open casket, made up and attired in the outfit she had selected for the occasion, awaiting the many friends and relatives who would file in to pay their final respects. Elliott then had had the unenviable task of calling close friends and relatives with the news of the death of his beloved wife, lover and soul mate. Gordon and Spencer, Thelma's two sons, had been pillars of support and had assisted Elliott in this heartbreaking chore, as well as in composing the heartfelt obituary that would be published the following day in the Savannah Morning News.

Elliott slept intermittently that night, managing only an hour or two of sleep He tossed and turned, not used to the solitude of the empty house. Despite the fact that Elliott had known for the past few years that this day would eventually come and had prepared himself for it, it didn't ease the pain and heartache he felt. The house he had shared with his wife of thirty years wouldn't be the same without her laughter and larger-than-life presence. Even the diagnosis of terminal and untreatable throat cancer five years earlier hadn't altered her sense of fun and her zest for life. Thelma had always been his stalwart, mate and support, and though his beloved wife had been gone only a few hours, he felt empty inside.

Still, he was lucky, he thought, to live in a community where people actually cared about each other, a close-knit community with neighborhood values and residents who knew and looked out for one another. Only that morning, while releasing Biscuit and Grits into the street to exercise and toilet, he had been greeted by Cindy Mopper and Carla Zipp, both bearing apple pies they had baked for him the previous day. He had told them the tragic and sad news of Thelma's death the night before, and after their initial tears and commiserations they promised to spread the word throughout the neighborhood. Cindy said she would announce Thelma's passing in a special bulletin of the Association newsletter, which she would produce immediately and distribute throughout the neighborhood by nightfall. Carla said she would personally inform Heidi Launer, who she knew was a close and long-time friend to both Elliott and Thelma and who would be just as devastated as they all were by her friend's demise.

There was also much more to do to prepare for Thelma's funeral. Spencer and Gordon had checked themselves into suites at the Hyatt in downtown Savannah, two miles west of Gordonston, despite Elliott's insistence that they stay with him. The men told each other that it was better that Elliott be alone with his thoughts and that it was more appropriate for them to give him space and time alone to grieve. They would be arriving back at the house later that morning to assist Elliott with the preparations for the funeral and wake.

Thelma had left specific written instructions that her wake should be a joyous affair, celebrating her life rather that mourning her death. The gathering at the house the night before Thelma's funeral would be by open invitation, extended to all who knew her, and would be followed by a grander wake after her funeral on Friday, when a jazz band would play and white-jacketed, black-tied waiters would man an open bar. Thelma wanted to be remembered as a fun person with style, flair and a penchant for the finer things, who, though struck down at a relatively young age, had enjoyed life to its fullest.

Elliott had often marveled at his wife's resilience and ability to deal with the illness that doctors had told her would, without any doubt, eventually kill her. Despite the warnings that she only had months to live, Thelma had continued to smoke heavily and partake of her afternoon cocktails. Many who knew her well put her staunch defense against the cancer down to the fact she had refused to just lie down and die. She had laughed at suggestions that she stop smoking and drinking, and waved away the warnings about how her habits might be hurting her.

Miraculously, she had survived the first year after her diagnosis, continuing to work and refusing to let the disease dictate her lifestyle. She had been especially grateful that she had been able to assist young Veronica in securing her house on Kinzie Avenue, and was pleased that at last the husband she had heard so much about was finally going to move to Savannah. It had been her final act as a realtor. She had known that Veronica wanted a good home in a great neighborhood for her new baby, and of course, Gordonston was such a place, the park especially, with its woods and children's play area.

The few months the doctors had given Thelma had eventually lengthened into five years. Despite the chemotherapy and the multi-hued variety of fashionable wigs she wore, it was sometimes difficult to remember that Thelma was actually ill. She maintained her sense of humor and outgoing demeanor until the end. Indeed, the very day before she had become bedridden she had still managed to take Biscuit and Grits to the park for their afternoon exercise and playtime with their canine friends and partake of her afternoon cocktail with the other members of the Gordonston Ladies Dog Walking Club. Despite everything, Thelma still had the energy to gossip about her neighbors and the goings-on within Gordonston.

Elliott Miller took a deep breath as he walked into the kitchen and made himself a cup of coffee. He took the two apple pies that sat on the kitchen counter and put them in the freezer. He would save them to enjoy after Thelma's funeral. It was kind of both Cindy and Carla, he thought, and he wondered if maybe, after the funeral, if he should ask Carla over for a drink, just the two of them. He, like most of the men in the neighborhood, had always found her attractive, and he would enjoy her company. He pushed the thought to the back of his mind. He had other, more pressing matters to deal with, and, of course, it was far too soon after his wife's death to entertain such ideas.

Spencer and Gordon would be arriving shortly to assist Elliott in organizing the floral tributes that were expected at the house, the funeral home and the cemetery. Spencer and Gordon were good men; it didn't bother Elliott that both of them were gay. As far as he was concerned they were his flesh and blood. To both Spencer and Gordon, Elliott was their natural father, Thelma's first husband, had died while the boys were only one and three respectively. Elliott had been the family's knight in shining armor, and both men still referred to him as Dad, even today.

Thelma's funeral service would be held at the Cathedral of St. John the Baptist. Both Spencer and Gordon, as well as Elliott, had prepared eulogies. Thelma would be laid to rest in the family plot in Bonaventure Cemetery, just half a mile from Gordonston.

What he would do next, Elliott had no idea. The house held so many memories he had no wish to leave it. Dinner parties, birthdays, family gatherings, Christmases: it had been a home full of fun and laughter. Elliott sat at the kitchen table with his cup of coffee in front of him, Biscuit and Grits at his feet. He closed his eyes to fight back the tears that welled up.

Elliott had bought the house not long after he had returned from Argentina, just after . . . well . . . just after his three books were published. He smiled to himself as he recalled that time many years ago and many miles away: 1974, in Buenos Aires, Argentina. This was a period in his life that had changed everything and opened for him the path that he had taken. Those few months Elliot had spent in South America had such an influence on him that he could only wonder what would his life have been like had it all never happened, had he not met the one man who had changed his life forever...........

It had been the selection of wines that kept him coming back to the restaurant week after week. Of course he had enjoyed the food as well. Who would not have? There he enjoyed the finest cuts of meat, luscious salads, and the most exquisite and flamboyant deserts—all served by the most attentive waiters he had ever encountered. But above all it was Señor Cardasso's extensive and revered selection of wines that led Elliott Miller to return to La Casa Verde every Thursday evening. As soon as his work was done and he had faxed his weekly report of the company's business to the head office in Atlanta, Elliott would lock up his tiny office and prepare himself for his weekly treat of fine dining and even finer wine.

The young American had discovered the quaint little restaurant purely by accident, hidden away among the many small alley-like, cobbled streets that made up the Belgrano district of the city. It would have been easy for anyone who didn't know the area to lose himself in the labyrinth of crossing lanes, many of them unnamed. If you took the Libertador from where it joins Avenue 9 de Julio and carry on westward for about two miles, passing the Museo Nacional de Bellas Artes and the Law Faculty building, you arrive in the heart of the Italian sector of Buenos Aires. If he were brave enough, or dumb enough, to take a cab through the busy and often hazardous Buenos Aires traffic, then the journey would take fifteen minutes. However, being a fit, healthy young man of twenty-eight, Elliott usually walked the two miles to his favorite eatery, his senses always enlivened by the sounds, sights and smells of the wonderful and vibrant city.

The heat and humidity, which would often leave his shirt soaking with his sweat, was at times virtually unbearable, the night air disguising the fact that the Buenos Aires summer evenings could be as intense as the hottest summer day in Georgia. But the heat of Argentina was different. It was far more humid, and where the coastal breezes that blew into Savannah to cool the air reduced the overall temperature, there were no such breezes emanating from the River Plate, that famous stretch of water which separated Argentina from its neighbor to the north, Uruguay.

The noises were different, too. Though Savannah was also a busy port city, the town itself was not overly crowded. There were open spaces like Forsyth Park, and of course the patchwork of downtown squares where you could walk without feeling crowded. He could forget he was in a city when he strolled through Savannah. By contrast, Buenos Aires was a jostling, lively metropolis, and the noise of the traffic-filled avenues and boulevards would flood Elliott's ears, the continual sounding of car horns, as volatile Latinos fought their way home. This was intermingled with the cacophonous voices of a society notorious for its ability to converse at decibels usually reserved for arguing.

Elliott was employed as the South American representative for a very well known and highly successful soft drink manufacturer based out of Atlanta. Elliott's job included the overseeing of marketing and sales, and he was the link between the company's plant in Buenos Aires and head office. When he first heard he had been selected for the position he held, Elliott had been delighted. It was a good start, the first rung of the ladder to bigger things.

Unfortunately, his personal circumstances had changed, and he pined to be back in Savannah. He had known Thelma Solomon for years; they had been classmates in high school, and he had always felt affection for her. She had married his good friend Charlie Myers, and Elliott had attended the wedding. He had also been a guest at their first son's christening and had considered himself a friend to both. Charlie had died a year before, though, in a tragic hunting accident. Elliott had done what most friends would have done and helped Thelma overcome her grief. He took her bottles of her favorite cola—

courtesy of his job—played with her elder son Gordon, and assisted the young widow with household maintenance.

Neither Elliott nor Thelma had meant to fall in love, but it happened, and he proposed marriage only days before he received word he had been selected to represent the company's interests thousands of miles south.

Thelma had urged him to take the position; it wouldn't be forever, she said, and she would wait for him. They announced their engagement in the Savannah Morning News, and he left for Argentina. He wrote to his bride-to-be every day and called her often, urging her to visit. Though he liked his work and the pay was good, it didn't compensate for being away from the woman he loved. He sent her money and she was grateful, but he knew she needed him home so they could plan their wedding and begin their new life together. The boys, too, needed a father. Elliott spent many a sleepless night worrying and hoping that something, maybe a promotion, would come up to enable him to return to Savannah.

Famed for its Italian architecture, Belgrano was the spot many Argentines gravitated to when it came to selecting a venue for an evening of dining and entertainment. The maze of long, narrow cobbled streets, dubious lighting, and the sounds of tango announced to the visitor that he has finally reached the Belgrano district. Once a poor neighborhood, home to Italian immigrants who had arrived in Argentina at the turn of the century, Belgrano was now a prosperous area to which the children of the well to do flocked. Every bar, cafeteria and dance hall was brimming with the youth of Argentina, drinking Mate, smoking cigarettes, and discussing the issues that youngsters world-wide seem continually to debate: sex, sports, politics, music and sex again.

La Casa Verde—The Green House—was set apart from the main thoroughfares, and unless you knew it well or found it by accident it would have been hard to tell anyone how to get there. Elliott had stumbled on it purely by chance, after becoming lost and disorientated in a maze of crisscrossing cobbled streets, each indistinguishable from the next. The evening he stumbled upon Casa Verde had begun uneventfully when, as he headed back home to his rented apartment he passed by the restaurant's open windows. His nostrils filled with the aroma of cooking meat and spicy salsa and his ears rang with the sounds of the chattering diners. He couldn't help but peer in through the door. He was delighted by what he saw.

The set tables, covered in red and white checked cloth, with bowls of chimichuri, the piquant Argentine sauce of parsley, garlic, olive oil, black pepper and salt positioned centrally, were occupied by chattering and animated *Porteños*. Elliott could also see the *parrilla*—grill—filled with slabs of meat in various stages of cooking; it was from here that the smells that had lured him closer were originating. It was at this parrilla that the finest butchers and chefs in the whole of Buenos Aires prepared and cooked any cut of meat you could desire.

But what really caught Elliott's eye was the vast selection of wines stored horizontally along every wall. There must have been five thousand bottles of wine, maybe even more, waiting unmoved and dazzling—a beauty to behold for a wine connoisseur such as Elliott. The wine was held in racks that Elliott supposed must have been at least fifteen feet high and fifty feet wide. Before his arrival in South America wine had held no special interest for Elliott, but as time progressed wine drinking had become something of a hobby for the young Savannah native. Back home he would have drunk beer with his friends and taken sweet tea with his dinner. He would never have dreamt of ordering wine nor learned to appreciate its taste, texture, vintage and grape. Elliott had gradually evolved into a wine snob, and would now insist on ordering the correct grape and year for the correct dish, which was making dining out an intellectually stimulating adventure. As soon as he saw the selection of wines housed on the walls of La Casa Verde he knew that he had to enter. From that day on, Elliott was hooked.

Every Thursday night was La Casa Verde night. He would deliberately reschedule meetings to avoid any encroachment on his evenings of culinary pleasure. He was a man of routine and would offend clients and staff alike in his determination to maintain his pattern of dining, often leaving work incomplete and causing anxiety at Head Office back in Atlanta, where they were waiting for his weekly report. Every Thursday for six months he took his usual table, conversed with the waiters, soaked up the atmosphere, and engaged Señor Cardasso, the proprietor, in conversations that included wide-ranging topics from politics to the exploits of Superman.

Over time Elliott became recognized as a regular at La Casa Verde and was greeted by Miguel, Sergio, Carlos, or any of the other many waiters, dressed in their black trousers and food-stained white shirts, the same way every evening, "Welcome Señor Miller, your usual table. How was your week? Would you like a menu, wine list? I am sure not—you know everything to be found there. Please be seated." This was their standard greeting, and Elliott enjoyed conversing with the men.

Then, one Thursday in December, during the height of the Argentine summer, due to an unavoidable deadline imposed by Head Office, he had to stay late at the office. He tried his best to keep his regular date at La Casa Verde, but it was impossible. The Head Office was demanding that he double check the production figures he had forwarded the previous week; it seemed production was up and before they announced record-breaking profits, the company needed Elliott to verify his figures. He was frustrated and returned to his apartment hungry and deflated very late that night. It was of no consequence to Elliott that his figures had been correct and that a large bonus would eventually find its way to his bank account. All that mattered to him was that he had not managed to dine at Señor Cardasso's fine eatery, and he would now have to wait another week before he could enjoy the fine wine and great food.

The following day Elliott vowed that he would renew his lapsed acquaintance with La Casa Verde. He cancelled a meeting and rearranged several appointments, and for the first time ever, the familiar face of Miguel the waiter greeted him on a Friday night instead of his regular Thursday. Miguel, his typical Latin features enhanced by a black moustache, joked how Señor Cardasso had fretted so, when Elliott, his favorite customer, had not taken his usual seat the previous evening. Elliott laughed at the thought of the waiters and Señor Cardasso frantically trying to ensure his usual table would not be taken by some other diner, bemused by the fact that though the house full signs were up, a vacant table lay undisturbed.

Elliott ordered a bottle of Luigi Bosca 1970 Merlot and perused the familiar menu. He opted for the morcilla and a piece of morjella, blood sausage and sweetbreads, to begin his meal, and a rare lomo—the very finest cut of steak—as his main course. The wine he ordered would complement the meal; Elliott was pleased with his choices. Miguel brought Elliott's food and wine to the table and Elliott embarked on his evening's pleasure. It must have been around ten o'clock, while Elliott was midway through his main course, when ***he*** walked in.

Elliott had always assumed that he was the most popular and regular diner at La Casa Verde, mainly because of his belief that he was the only foreigner who frequented the restaurant and that he was a generous tipper. However, it seemed he was wrong. Usually a handshake and a wave from the waiters he knew by name would greet him; this made Elliott feel important and would always ensure a large tip for his evening's server. However, Elliott had never been personally greeted by Señor Cardasso himself. Granted, he would sometimes come over to Elliott's table and they would talk, but Elliott had never seen him embrace a customer, like he did the elderly gentleman who had just entered the restaurant.

He must have been in his late eighties, and that was a generous estimate. He was bent over with age, supporting himself with an extravagantly carved wooden cane that possessed an ornate ivory handle that sparkled with jewels. His hair was gone and the wrinkles on his face seemed to continue upwards to the top of his head. He was short, no more than five feet six, Elliott guessed, probably shrunken by age. He was by far the most dapper octogenarian Elliott had ever seen. He was clad in an impeccably tailored, three-piece navy blue pinstripe suit with a slight flair at the base of the trouser; the whitest and crispest shirt Elliott had ever seen majestically complemented the suit. His tie was blue, matching exactly the color and shade of the suit. The old man's shoes were of obvious good quality leather and the shine on them was dazzling.

After Señor Cardasso had embraced the elegantly attired man he clicked his fingers, and Miguel and Guillermo, probably the best two waiters in the whole restaurant, stopped what they were doing and assisted the old gentleman to his table. Elliott noted that the table was positioned in the most delightful little corner, surrounded by greenery and shielded from the other diners. He was mesmerised by the scene. Some of his fellow diners raised their heads and turned to each other, discussing the man's presence. Perhaps they knew who he was, maybe he was a famous old actor, or maybe, like Elliott, they too had never seen Old Cardasso greet a customer in this way.

Elliott beckoned Santiago, the youngest and possibly the brightest of the waiters over to his table with a raise of his hand. "Who is he?" whispered Elliott, tilting his head in the direction of the old man. Santiago nodded, a broad smile engulfing his young face, "Ah . . . that is Señor Kurtze, he too is a foreigner like you, Swiss I think, or maybe Hungarian. He has been coming here every Friday night to dine for the last thirty years."

That still didn't explain why the old man had received such an elaborate reception. Elliott encouraged Santiago to explain why Cardasso himself had greeted him in the way that he had. "He is a very generous man." The young waiter smiled, his affection for the man obvious. "He helps many people. Only last year he paid for me to visit my sick and elderly mother in Chubut. The year before that, he paid for Miguel's youngest daughter to have an operation that probably saved her life. He has done many good things for the people of the city. The poor and needy turn to him for help. He is a Saint, Senor Miller, a true Saint." Elliott saw that Santiago was close to tears. "And if it was not for him there would be no Casa Verde." Regaining his composure, he continued his narrative. "Many years ago, when I was just a young boy, Señor Cardasso was in serious trouble. His wife left him, ran away with his brother, and took all his money. Senor Kurtze, who comes here every Friday, saw Señor Cardasso in trouble and helped him by giving, not lending, him the money to buy the building in which we now sit and stand. You see, the old landlord wanted too much rent, and Señor Cardasso, he almost killed himself. I believe my employer is alive today thanks only to Señor Kurtze."

Elliott was astounded. He had never heard of such generosity before. Elliott called Señor Cardasso to his table and insisted that he be introduced to Señor Kurtze as soon as the old man had finished his meal. Señor Cardasso was initially reluctant to disturb his benefactor and favorite customer, but eventually relented to Elliott's persistent pleas and as soon as the old man had devoured his last piece of meat, Cardasso took Elliott over to his table.

Elliott was presented to the old man as a fellow visitor to Buenos Aires, though it was apparent that the old man was no longer a visitor but a part of the city, at least of the Belgrano District, anyway. As the old man attempted to rise, Elliott insisted he remain seated and shook his hand as Señor Kurtze slowly returned to his seat. The two men exchanged pleasantries and discussed the intolerable heat of the country, the state of the nation, and how they were both looking forward to the Soccer World Cup, to be held in Argentina in three years time. They spoke, as is customary when two foreigners converse in a neutral country, in the language of the host country. The old man spoke no English and Elliott didn't speak Swiss, French, or German, the languages of the mountainous central European country that had been Señor Kurtze's home—not Hungary, as young Santiago had suggested. Elliott liked the old man immediately; it was good to finally meet someone with whom he could converse without the main topic of conversation being the virtues of a certain soft drink.

"So, Señor Miller, what is your business in Argentina?" Señor Kurtze asked, wiping his mouth with his cloth napkin and leaning back in his chair. His manners and ability to listen to all Elliott said, despite Elliott's less than fluent Spanish, which was in no way comparable to Señor Kurtze's, had endeared him to Elliott almost immediately.

"I am the South American representative of an American soft drink company," replied Elliott, trying not to sound to too pompous or self important, "I have been in Argentina for just under eight months now. I have an apartment downtown, in Recollecta, a close walk from my offices," he added as he took another sip of the Chardonnay that Señor Kurtze had insisted he try. He had to agree it was the most refreshing white wine he had ever tasted. The old man clicked his fingers and almost instantly Cardasso himself had appeared at their table with a fresh bottle and two clean glasses.

"I am from Savannah, Georgia, on the American East Coast," continued Elliott. "I'm not sure how long I have left here. My fiancée back in Savannah wants me home, but I am trying to convince her to join me here. I love Argentina, but it's hard for me. She's a young widow and her two boys need a father. Maybe though I can convince her to come for a vacation."

Señor Kurtze nodded his agreement, "You should, my boy. Forget Paris, I have been there, many years ago, but this is the real city of romance and love. You must bring, what is her name?"

"Thelma," Elliott replied.

"Bring Thelma over and I shall be your host. You could stay with me. I have a large house with many rooms and staff. You must be my guests, your fiancée and you, I have a car and driver and I would be honored to have you stay."

Elliott thanked his new friend for the offer of his home and promised he would try to convince Thelma to come and visit and see for herself this amazing country.

"And you sir," Elliott probed, as he raised his glass of wine to his lips, "What brought you to this land of vast contrasts?" Señor Kurtze smiled. It was the kind of smile reserved for those who had seen all of life's rich and diversified tapestries. It was the smile of knowledge, the smile of experience, the knowing smile that only the special among the aged can produce. Mr. Kurtze looked at his watch and nodded.

"Mine is a long story, Señor Miller, a very long story indeed. I think before I begin, we should order another bottle of wine. This time it must be a wine of your choice." Elliott chose a Luigi Bosca, and once again Cardasso appeared immediately when the old man clicked his fingers. The restaurant owner uncorked the bottle and poured a glass for each of them before bowing and returning to whence he came. Once the wine was poured, Señor Kurtze began his story.

Señor Kurtze had arrived with his young wife in Buenos Aires just before the end of the last war. Fearful that the Russian advances westwards would not stop at Berlin, he had left his homeland never to return. He had been a wealthy man when he had left Europe, and on his arrival in South America immediately invested in property and land. His investments paid off and he and his wife lived comfortably in the same large home that he lives in to this day. Tragically, his young bride had died during childbirth along with his unborn son, soon after his arrival in Argentina. He had been devastated. She was the only woman he had ever loved, and he would have done anything for her. Consumed by grief, he saw no reason to return to Europe and couldn't bear to be parted from her grave, which he tended every day with freshly cut flowers. He had a niece, of whom he was fond, but had lost contact with all his family after the war. Elliott could sense the angst in the old man's voice, as he explained how he had no trace of his relatives.

His great passion, the old man informed Elliott, was the telling of children's stories. He would spend hours creating characters and placing them in adventures set in his homeland. The children of the neighborhood would flock to listen to the old man with the strange accent and his amazing tales of witches, wizards, magical forests and dragons. He told Elliott he had always possessed a passion for the arts, he had painted as a young man and dabbled with play writing. His future, though, had not lain in the arts, and he sometimes regretted the fact that he had not devoted more time to his painting.

Elliott asked him about the generous deeds he had done for the people of Buenos Aires and what had motivated him to be so kind, especially to those who weren't even his own countrymen. His answer was humbling. We were all countrymen he had said, countrymen of God. He had no one to share his wealth with and felt that God would want him to do what he could to help others. Elliott wondered whether the old man was trying to atone for something or was just a good man. Either way, Elliott had warmed to his new friend and knew that he was in the presence of a special and charismatic person.

When the old man had finished speaking, Elliott noticed that hours had passed and it was now late. Elliott insisted that he walk his new friend to his home, a short distance from La Casa Verde. Elliott was truly amazed by its size. It had to be the grandest house he had ever seen, even grander than the Mercer House and the other great houses of Savannah that overlooked the squares he missed so much. Elliott bade his new friend goodnight and arranged to meet him again the following Friday at La Casa Verde, where they would dine together and converse further.

Elliott decided in future he would forsake his usual Thursday evening visits to La Casa Verde and instead would now spend his Fridays enthralled by the stories of Señor Kurtze. They would eat and drink, and Elliott would listen to the old man's tales, meant for children, but so wonderfully and masterfully told that even a grown man couldn't help but be mesmerized. Elliott asked the old man if he had ever had one of his stories published. Señor Kurtze replied that he had once been published, many years ago, but unfortunately the only copy he had was printed in German. Anyway, it was not on the same subject of children's stories, which they spoke of now, and he was embarrassed by it. He said it was not much and that it was best forgotten.

Not all of their Friday evenings were spent with Elliott spellbound by Kurtze's tales of magic and adventure. He would often tell Elliott of his fears for Argentina and the rest of the world, how the spread of communism had to be stopped. Señor Kurtze would often, as Elliott walked him to the door of his magnificent home, stop and join in the discussions of the disillusioned young men they could hear arguing in the street and through open bar windows. The young and volatile youths would discuss and argue that the only way forward for Argentina, and indeed the whole of South America, was a switch to the left and the advent of communism.

The old man would put his view across so passionately, so eloquently, that many of the youths would immediately change their opinion. Elliott had never met anyone like him. He had a magnetism that was awe-inspiring. How he cursed that damn wall that split a country in two, dividing families and friends. He said that one day, we would all see how wrong the Marxists had been and that Stalin, Castro and the like preached the politics of evil. One day soon, he predicted, the wall would come tumbling down and the world would see that the communist ideal could never last. He called it a corrupt and dangerous system and was sure that history would prove him right. Elliott thought it amazing to see the old man lecture. He ignored those who heckled him, dismissing their arguments with a flick of the wrist. He was confident and possessed an air of authority that made people listen to what he had to say. He almost hypnotized the crowds that gathered around to hear him speak.

Often, after one of the old man's tirades against communism, the youths would applaud, and bystanders curious about what was happening would join in the debate, agreeing with what the old man had said and listening intently as Señor Kurtze, though weak in body, rose up and convinced others that the way forward was definitely not via socialism. Those preaching the socialist manifesto and viewpoint were always silenced and when Elliott and Señor Kurtze returned to the bars they would be welcomed with open arms. Elliott noticed that the proponents of communism were nowhere to be seen. It was as if the old man were cleansing his beloved Belgrano of those determined to cause trouble for the rest. Elliott often imagined that the would-be revolutionaries were now practising their rehearsed speeches in some other neighborhood, afraid to return and once again be shouted down and outmatched by a man old enough to be their grandfather.

Elliott looked forward to his Friday evenings all week. It was as if he had known the old man all his life, and now, looking back as he sat at his kitchen table with Biscuit and Grits at his feet, he could see now that he, like everyone else who had met him, had become entranced by the old man.

Thelma had never been to Argentina or met Señor Kurtze, and Elliott wiped a tear from his eye as he remembered his happy time there. Of course, Thelma had had the boys from her first marriage, and there was no way she could have come. He knew eventually he would have to leave South America and that if he wanted Thelma, he would eventually have to forsake his career.

Biscuit barked and Elliott's reverie abated as he remembered that he had not fed the dogs yet that morning. He opened a can of their favorite dog food and filled their bowls. He watched as the two poodles, one white, one chocolate, devoured their breakfast. Thelma had loved those dogs and he was sure they were grieving too. He took a deep breath and returned to his memories.

Elliott, knowing that the old man was unique, would often stare into his wise old eyes and wish that he had known his own grandfather.

He imagined that his grandfather would have been just like Señor Kurtze, wise, kind and above all, understanding. The old man had encouraged Elliott to listen to the music of Wagner and urged him to pursue a career in politics one day, at any level. He told Elliott he saw potential in him and encouraged him to stand up for what he believed in, that just one voice could change the hearts and minds of many. It was a lesson Elliott had never forgotten, and in some ways it was thanks to his old friend that he ran for City Council, over thirty years later.

As another Friday evening once again passed all too quickly, Señor Kurtze turned to Elliott as he led him up the steps to the front door of his lavish home and said that if his son had lived, he would have wished him to have been like Elliott. He again mentioned his niece, whom he missed greatly. He had no idea of what had become of her, he said, and this was one his greatest regrets in life. Once again Elliott felt the anguish in the old man's voice. He told the young American that the only family he had now was Elliott. Elliott fought back the tears and wished the frail old man a good night. He turned to watch as Señor Kurtze safely entered his building. Elliott did not know then that this would be the last time he would ever see his friend.

Elliott returned to his apartment; it was late and he was tired, but that still didn't stop him from recording the evening's events in his diary. He also wrote a letter to his beloved Thelma. Every Friday night, after his evening spent with his old friend, he carried out the same ritual. He would memorize the stories that the old man had told him and translate them into English. Elliott would then type them out, rather crudely, and enclose them with his weekly letter to his fiancée. When the letters arrived in Savannah, Thelma would read the stories to her boys, Spencer and Gordon, who loved to hear the tales of wizards, witches, fairies, and magical forests. It was the highlight of the boys' week for their mother to receive the weekly dispatches from Elliott who, though he was far away, would be home soon.

The following Friday, Elliott arrived, as he always did, at La Casa Verde at eight o'clock sharp. He immediately noticed that the waiters had deviated from their usual attire. Each man wore a black band of cloth wrapped around his left arm. Elliott's first thought was that Señor Cardasso had finally succumbed to his diet of red wine and red meat and that his heart had finally failed, but as he entered the restaurant he saw that Señor Cardasso was there, alive and well, though looking somewhat subdued.

"Señor Miller!" cried Cardasso as Elliott entered La Casa Verde. Elliott was confused by the scene and his expression showed that confusion. Cardasso, though, was eager to explain. "We have been looking for you everywhere," the restaurant owner was in an emotional state and clutched Elliott's hands tightly. "I even called at the American Embassy but they told me that they had no address for you." Elliott pleaded with him to slow down. Over the past months Elliott's Spanish had improved considerably, thanks to the patience of his mentor, Señor Kurtze, but not sufficiently enough to grasp the meaning of what the obviously agitated and deeply upset man before him was trying to say.

"I am so sorry, Señor Miller," he said, as the pace of his voice slowed, "but our friend, our great friend, Señor Kurtze is dead. He died yesterday, in his sleep, and was buried next to his wife and unborn child earlier today."

Elliott felt his legs buckle and a wave of despair engulf him. His heart sank to the pit of his stomach. How could this be? How could such a man, a man of so much vitality, be gone? A man with so much love and generosity, that a whole neighborhood would mourn his loss? Cardasso had done his best to find Elliott and tell him the news of his friend's death. Cardasso knew that Señor Kurtze would have wanted Elliott to be at his funeral and that Elliott would be heartbroken not to have been able to say his final farewells.

The funeral, according to Cardasso, had been a lavish and extremely well attended affair. The old man's coffin was carried to the cemetery by a horse-drawn carriage, and over two hundred mourners had followed the slow procession to the cemetery. The streets of Belgrano were lined with those wanting to acknowledge and pay their last respects to the man who had been the area's benefactor for so long. Shopkeepers and bar owners closed their doors as a mark of respect to the old man, and women, some of whom had not even met him but only heard of his charity, wore black and wept. Even members of the ruling Nationalist Party had made appearances at this foreigner's graveside. The head of the Dirección de Inteligencia Nacional, the Argentine secret police force, laid a wreath at the old man's headstone. Years later, Elliott would read how the man who had lain the wreath at the kind and loving man's grave had been accused of being involved in Argentina's so called "Dirty War," in which thousands of political dissidents were forced to jump out of airplanes far out over the Atlantic Ocean, leaving no trace of their passing. Without any dead bodies, the government could deny they had been killed. The victims became known as "the disappeared."

Elliott decided he couldn't eat after hearing the news of his friend's death, and despite Cardasso's wishes that he remain as his guest and drink a toast to their Swiss friend, Elliott declined and returned, saddened, to his apartment. That Friday night, he wept as a child would weep for a father who was leaving on a long journey and might never return. Even though he had known the old man for just three months, Elliott felt as if he had known him all his life.

Elliott penned a letter to Thelma, informing her of the tragic news. Suddenly he felt the need to be home, back with his fiancée in Savannah, close to those he loved, and not alone, thousands of miles away. Though his job paid well, it had meant separation and delay of his marriage to the only woman he had ever loved. The truth was that if it had not been for Señor Kurtze, he would have left Argentina and his job months ago. Maybe now—now that he had nothing to stay for—it was time for him to go home.

It would be hard though, with no job and a family to support, Elliott worried, lying awake that night, the sound of the buzzing traffic filling his room. But the old man had shown him the importance of family. Señor Kurtze had told him how he regretted losing touch with his only sister's daughter, his only living relation. He had no idea where she was and he warned Elliott never to make the same mistake he had. Elliott closed his eyes. He had a decision to make.

Elliott Miller didn't return to La Casa Verde for a several weeks. He felt that the memories of Kurtze would be overwhelming. When he did eventually return, he reverted to his former special evening of Thursday, out of respect for the memory of his old friend and their special evening.

Cardasso hugged and embraced him like an old friend when he returned to La Casa Verde. It appeared that the affection for Elliott's former dining partner had somehow rubbed off on him. As he finished his main course of roasted pork, Elliott noticed an old woman dressed head to toe in black, who seemed vaguely familiar, talking with Cardasso. The stout restaurateur was nodding and touching her hand, and she was holding a package. He bade her farewell after handing her a bottle of his finest white wine, then approached Elliott's table, clutching the package the old lady had given him.

"Señor Miller, that old lady was the housekeeper of Señor Kurtze. She said that he had told her that on the event of his death this package should be sent to La Casa Verde and delivered to the young American who had become his great friend." Cardasso handed Elliott the carefully wrapped package, which had a note attached to it. Elliott thanked Cardasso. His throat tightened as emotion welled up inside him. He took a deep breath and read the note that accompanied the package:

My Dear Friend,

Of all the people I have met, you were the only one who I feel could have really understood me. Thank you for making my last days on earth as pleasurable as they were. I knew I was dying and that my time had come. Maybe my time had come many years before but I just never knew it. I am writing this note as I lie on my bed before I begin my endless sleep, I have had an eventful life, and my head is full of memories. I wish you happiness for your future and luck in your marriage. Your new wife will be a fortunate lady, as will her sons, to have such a man as you in their lives. Never forget me, my dear friend, and raise a glass in my honor when you next dine at our table. You may find the gift difficult to read, though I am sure you could have it translated. It was the only thing I ever had published. Do not judge me for what I was then, but for what I am now. Goodbye my friend and good luck.

Kurtze

Elliott folded the handwritten note and placed it in his jacket pocket. He didn't understand the last line; he would never dream of judging the kind old man. He finished his glass of wine, said goodbye to Cardasso and his waiting staff and returned to his apartment. He sat on his bed and opened the package; it was the old man's book, the one he had published years before, the only one. Elliott opened the front cover and saw that Señor Kurtze had signed it on the second page.

A few weeks later, Elliott contacted his Head Office in Atlanta and informed them he was resigning his post as their representative in Argentina and that he would not be returning to Atlanta. His wedding had been arranged and he would be returning to Savannah at the first convenient opportunity. Reluctantly his resignation was accepted and arrangements were made for his return home.

Elliott made one last visit to La Casa Verde and thanked all those who had served him in the last few months. Elliott hugged Señor Cardasso, who promised him that every Friday he would raise a glass in honour of the Swiss and American men who had become his greatest friends. Elliott felt that Cardasso exaggerated slightly, but nonetheless returned the Argentine's embrace. Elliott took one last look at the wall of bottles that had attracted him to the restaurant in the first place and took a last, deep breath of the rich aroma of cooking meats and salsas. He shook the hand of each waiter who had served him over the last few months. Then he left.

All of that was now well over thirty years ago. Elliott smiled as Biscuit and Grits finished their breakfast and began frolicking in the kitchen. Elliott had returned to Savannah and married Thelma. Elliott had never returned to Argentina and Thelma had never travelled to the places or met the characters he used to describe in his letters. Elliott did not know if La Casa Verde still even stood, or if it was now a fast food restaurant, though he presumed by now that Old Cardasso's heart has finally stopped. He used to wonder what might have become of Miguel, Santiago, and the other waiters, but in time he couldn't even remember their faces.

He also wondered who tended his old friend's grave, but as the years passed and his own life grew long he no longer wondered if flowers still marked the spot where Señor Kurtze now rested.

To the amazement of everyone who knew him, Elliott briefly became one of the world's most successful children's storytellers. His three books sold thousands of copies and ensured his family's financial future, and financed Thelma's real estate business. Elliott's stories of dragons, witches, goblins, wizardry, and enchanted European forests enabled Elliott and Thelma to purchase the house of their dreams overlooking the park in the Gordonston neighborhood they had always yearned to live in. The publishers wanted more stories from Elliott but were disappointed when he told them he was no longer writing. They urged him to continue, explaining that his stories were unique and that more money could be made. The truth was Elliott had no more stories to tell; he had never really had any stories to tell in the first place.

He had decided that his future lay in politics and had aspirations of one day sitting on the City Council, representing the people of Gordonston.

He recalled the old man's wishes, encouraging Elliott to write down the stories he told, encouraging him to retell them to his two boys in Savannah, Spencer and Gordon. It hadn't been Elliott's intention to pass the stories off as his own nor publish them, but finances were tight, and, well, what harm could it ever do?

Eventually the books disappeared from stores, sales dropped, and the name Elliott Miller was forgotten. Elliott's books were now long out of print and the publishing house that had once championed the young writer was long since out of business. He no longer mentioned his writing career, and only a few people actually knew he had once been on the verge of literary fame and fortune.

Often though, after dinner parties when the boys were away at college, Elliott would recount for Thelma and their guests tales of his time in Argentina. He would secretly smile as the murmur of conversation rose, as those disinterested in his story began talking among themselves. Nevertheless, you could almost hear a pin drop when Elliott would reach below the table and place the oldest and only surviving first edition print copy of *Mein Kampf* on the dining room table, signed on the second page by the author.

Elliott Miller had often wondered as to the true identity of the man he had met thirty years before, briefly, in an Argentine restaurant. Maybe the old man had become confused on his deathbed and had simply given Elliott the wrong book, or maybe Elliott had been the victim of an elaborate hoax, perpetrated by Cardasso or one of the waiters. Or could the man he had befriended and become so in awe of possibly have been the most feared and most evil man in history?

The signature on the second page of the book Kurtze had given him was authentic; Elliott had had it verified by experts a few years after his return from Buenos Aires. If Kurtze had not been the author, then where had he gotten the signed book?

Now, Elliott banished the thoughts of Argentina and the past from his head. He had far more important things to worry about, such as preparing the eulogy he would read at Thelma's funeral service. Elliott checked his watch. Spencer and Gordon would be arriving shortly to assist in the funeral preparations and Elliott needed to dress. He abandoned his memories and returned to the present day. As he made his way to the bedroom where he would change into a sombre black suit and tie, he passed the bookshelf that housed his only copies of the books he had written, and the book of the man whose stories he had "borrowed" and passed off as his own.

Elliott had rarely visited the cathedral where his wife's funeral service would be held. Though she attended mass every Sunday before she had become bedridden, he had not. And why would he? Though Thelma's parents were initially guarded about their only daughter's proposed marriage to a non-Catholic, they had eventually accepted that Elliott did not intend to convert their daughter, or either of her sons, to his own Jewish religion.

CHAPTER 4

"That was mighty nice of you, Carla, to bake Elliott an apple pie like you did," said Cindy as she arrived in the park with Paddy for their afternoon of gossiping, cocktail drinking and dog walking. She released Paddy, and the excited dog joined Walter and Fuchsl in a game of chase in the woods.

"Well it was nice of you too" replied Carla, who was already seated at the picnic table with Heidi. "It just goes to show that when a man needs help a good woman will always bake a pie," The two women laughed at Carla's joke. The laughter, though, sounded slightly contrived, maybe even false. It wasn't difficult for Heidi to notice the tension that had materialized between her two friends.

"Well, the big news is that the funeral is on Thursday and that there is a wake straight afterwards at the house," announced Heidi, changing the subject once Cindy had taken her usual seat at the picnic table with her friends. "There is going to be a jazz band and a book of condolence. I hear caterers from Johnny Harris' are doing the food and that there will be waiters serving cocktails. Seems it's going to be open house, too, which means the whole neighborhood will be there, I'm sure."

"Sounds like it is going to be quite an event. I'm sure Thelma had a hand in planning the whole thing, it seems just like the sort of party she would have loved," commented Carla as she threw a stick for Walter to run and chase before raising her cup to her lips.

"Now you be careful," said Cindy as Carla's lips touched the rim of her cup. "Don't you be smudging your beautiful lipstick. Is that a new shade, honey? It's so red it's almost scarlet."

Cindy returned her friend's smile. "Well, why ever not? I think it is important for a lady to look beautiful, even if just walking the dog with her *old* friends." The two of them forced a smile once again.

"I have to say that dress you're wearing is sure mighty pretty," said Carla, commenting on Cindy's figure-hugging outfit and its plunging neckline.

"Oh, this old thing," replied Cindy, "it's something I just threw on." Carla looked her friend up and down as if inspecting a soldier on parade. "And those heels, they must be six inches high. You look like a movie star." Cindy looked down at her impractical footwear and smiled at her friend.

It was Heidi who interrupted the two friends' verbal sparring.

"It's him again. Look." She pointed to the old man who had just entered the park with his Cairn terrier. He saw that the three women were watching him and raised his hand in a wave before continuing along the perimeter path, his small white dog following closely behind. All three women smiled and waved back.

"You know Betty, my housekeeper, found out that he lives in the house with the turret that overlooks the park. The large four-bedroom place, with the pretty garden and the Oldsmobile parked on the driveway," said Heidi behind her false smile and insincere wave. "I think we need to organize a letter for that man, Cindy."

"I think you are right—a friendly letter from the Resident's Association reminding him of the need to scoop his dog's poop," said Cindy. All three women nodded their agreement.

Doug Partridge sat at his computer and read his account balance again. He sighed as he read the figures on his screen and placed his head in his hands. How could this be? How could he, of all people, have invested so poorly? It was hard enough as it was, what with a baby and Veronica having to support them all, but he had thought his investments would pay bigger dividends so he could contribute more to the family budget. Granted, he had paid cash for the house, and that had alleviated some of the burden and strain on Veronica's hospital salary, but he had expected far more income from his dividend payments.

He looked over to where his young daughter played happily with a toy dog on the floor of the den. There was more expense every day: clothes, baby formula and toys. Then there would be school fees and then college to pay for. Doug couldn't help thinking that he had made a huge mistake. Giving up such a highly paid career so he could be with his new family he knew would mean sacrifices, but he had planned well, or so he had thought. How was he to know that the shares he had bought were going to fall short like they had?

Bern stretched his body on the den floor as Katie toddled over to where her father sat. Doug smiled and grabbed his baby girl and lifted her to his knee. "You want to go for a walk," he said in his unmistakable English accent. "Do you want to come as well, Bern?" Bern raised his head and stood on all fours wagging his tail. Doug closed his laptop and sighed once more. If it got too bad he could always go back to work, but there was no guarantee that his position would still be open. There was also the problem of his immigration status. While waiting for his residency application to be processed, he couldn't leave the country or obtain legal employment. It was as if he was stuck in no man's land. Anyway, he thought, as he bounced the giggling child on his knee, how could he leave his family?

Doug and Veronica Partridge had been married for only three months, though their daughter Katie was already fourteen months old. Doug met Veronica while he had been attending a business conference that had been hosted at the Savannah Conference Center. It had been a banking conference, and one evening Doug ventured away from the conference setting for a quiet drink apart from his fellow delegates. He had met Veronica purely by chance in a local downtown bar where she was celebrating the birthday of a friend. They had clicked immediately and vowed to keep in touch after Doug returned to Switzerland and the bank he said he represented. He visited Savannah and Veronica whenever he could, and arranged for her to join him in exotic locations around the world where his work took him. When she fell pregnant he did not hesitate to give up his lucrative career to settle down with the woman of his dreams. Veronica found them a great house in Gordonston, thanks to Thelma Miller's efforts, and Doug had written a check for the full amount of purchase, depleting his savings but ensuring that the young family was not reliant on a regular income to pay the mortgage.

Doug's mind was made up the moment he first set eyes on his daughter and heard her first cries; he would work extra hours, save as much as he could and invest his earnings in shares and stocks, thus ensuring that he could retire early and become a stay-at-home husband and father. He had many friends who advised him on the best way to invest his hard-earned money—so-called experts—and he listened to their advice. He estimated that he could retire and bring up

Katie while Veronica resumed her career as a respiratory therapist at the Memorial Health Medical Center, one of Savannah's two hospitals. While their reduced income would mean no more trips abroad, Doug's financial planning had been good enough to cover Katie's future educational expenses. Katie, who had been born fourteen months ago, would have the best chances and the best education.

Doug and Veronica married shortly after Katie's birth, and he promptly resigned from his position and began his immigration paperwork with the assistance of a local law firm. But Doug was beginning to discover that things were not working out as planned. His investments were not paying the dividends he had hoped, and it was too late for him to pull the money out of the stocks he had purchased without losing a large part of his original capital investment. The financial statement he had just seen, via his online banking and investment account, showed that his next year's projected monthly income would be far below what he had anticipated. He could kick himself—he knew he should have waited before retiring; he could have worked for another three or four years and secured his family's financial future and maybe even allowed Veronica to work only part-time. Now, due to the regulations imposed by the immigration authorities, he couldn't leave the United States to return to his job abroad, nor could he seek employment.

The Englishman placed his daughter on the floor of the den and searched for her shoes. He ordered Bern to fetch his leash, which the obedient and well-trained German shepherd did, returning with it in his mouth. At least he was getting plenty of exercise, thought Doug. He enjoyed taking Bern to the park and strolling Katie along the tree-lined avenues of Gordonston. Sometimes they would stop by the swings and he would push his baby girl, her squeals of delight echoing throughout the wooded park. He felt sorry for his wife. While he spent his days with their daughter she had to work. Veronica was missing watching Katie grow up, but at least she did see her daughter in the evenings and on weekends, more than he would be able to do if he were still working abroad. Though he regretted the timing of his retirement, at least now he could be with his family. Katie, now dressed and with shoes on her feet, was ready for her afternoon stroll. Doug settled her in her stroller, and with Bern in tow they made their way to the park.

"So Kelly told me she saw you at her makeup and perfume counter this morning," said Cindy through a feigned smile, as the three friends continued their afternoon session of the Gordonston Ladies Dog Walking Club.

Carla also fixed a smile to her face, "Oh yes, that's right," she explained, "I was running out of blusher. You know how much I *love* my blusher," she stressed to her two friends.

Cindy, her smile just as fixed on her face as her friends, nodded agreement. "And eye liner," she said, "and not forgetting new perfume, powders, and assorted bath salts, and of course the moisturizer," Cindy took a swig of her cocktail, "Why, you must be stocking up! Kelly told me you spent well over two hundred dollars. Remind me, if I need anything, to see you." All three of the women laughed out loud, though the laughs of Cindy and Carla were now, to Heidi, sounding more and more forced.

The truth was that Cindy would not need to borrow any makeup or beauty products from her friend. What Cindy had failed to mention was that she had also been to her neighbor Kelly's makeup and perfume counter after Carla had frequented it just minutes before. She herself had spent over four hundred dollars on assorted beauty-enhancing products, not to mention the two hundred dollars she had later spent on the new dress and high-heeled shoes that adorned her body and feet. The conversation halted as all three women's heads turned towards the gate.

Doug entered the park and released Bern from his leash. Bern immediately sprinted to where Paddy, Fuchsl and Walter playfully romped. Doug raised his hand and threw a wave to the trio of women. They all waved back. He headed along the path, pushing Katie in her stroller, unconcerned by Bern's antics. Doug didn't mind what his dog did, as long as he didn't poop in front of the women.

"My oh my, she's a real beauty," said the old man as Doug and Katie approached him on the wood-chipped path that circled the park "Just look at them peepers and that big, wide smile." The old man grinned as Katie giggled and bobbed up and down in her stroller. Doug smiled. He saw the man often in the park walking his old Cairn terrier, and they had often nodded and exchanged afternoon or morning greetings.

"I think she likes you," said Doug as the old man knelt beside Katie's stroller.

"You really are a pretty one, aren't you?" said the old man. He looked up at Doug. "What's her name?" he asked as Katie continued to smile and laugh.

"Katie," replied Doug.

"She's so sweet." The old man returned his attention to Doug "You Australian?" he asked turning back.

"English," replied Doug.

"Oh." Said the old man, "I bet you don't get this heat where you come from." Doug agreed that the heat was far more severe than anything he had ever encountered in his homeland.

"Well, nice meeting you, Katie," said the old man as he rose to his feet. "Come on Chalky. Here boy." Chalky dutifully followed his master's command.

"There he is again," said Cindy as the old man reached the gate. "I don't see him carrying a bag, and I didn't see him use the scooper." The Gordonston Residents Association had provided a "poopa scoopa" for the use of dog walkers in the park so that they could clean up the mess left by their animals. The tool was normally kept against the wall of the Scout Hut, under its veranda.

"Maybe he didn't poop," offered Carla.

"Oh, I doubt it!" retorted Heidi, an angry edge to her voice. "That's it. I am composing our letter this very afternoon, and I would be grateful if you could pass it to the association for approval." Her request was directed at Cindy, who agreed it was time something was done about the old man's failure to clean up his dog's mess. While the ladies' attention was focused on the old man, who was slowly exiting the park with his small dog following behind, they failed to notice that Bern had just finished his business less than twenty feet from where they sat and had now rejoined their dogs in a game of chase and be chased.

Doug continued his lap of the park. While Katie was busy talking baby talk to the trees and squirrels, he was lost in thought. Though he hated having less money in his pocket than he had ever had, somehow this made it all worthwhile. The park, the people he met, the fact he was spending time outdoors with his own child—he liked it all. He had never expected that one day he would be a father and this contented. As he pushed the stroller along the path his spirits rose. Maybe he would contact his old employers and see if they had any openings locally or maybe even some contacts he could use. He had always received praise and commendations for his work in the past.

His thoughts were interrupted as he saw Bern shuffle into the crouching position that meant only one thing. Doug closed his eyes.

The dog was pooping right in front of the babble of ladies that were always in the park and seemed to run the place. Doug opened his eyes, and now Bern was romping with the other dogs in the park. The ladies hadn't even noticed. Doug smiled; maybe his luck was changing. He turned his head back towards where the women sat at the picnic table they always seemed to occupy. He noticed that one of them had really overdone her makeup and that another was wearing a dress and shoes that were really unsuitable for the park. He shook his head. Well, this *was* Savannah, he supposed.

Spencer and Gordon had managed to convince Elliott to take a break from his afternoon of funeral arranging and tribute gathering. Why not, they suggested to their stepfather, take Biscuit and Grits over to the park and give them a run around. Elliott agreed that maybe the poodles did need some exercise, and he had led them unleashed on the short trip across Edgewood Road to the park gate.

"I was so sorry to hear of your loss, Alderman," said the old man as he exited and Elliott entered the park. "That's very kind of you," replied Elliott as Biscuit and Grits inspected and sniffed Chalky. "She was a wonderful woman and will be missed," added Elliott as the old man nodded and began his walk home.

"It's Elliott!" cried Carla as the three ladies spotted him entering the park. They all waved at the widower as he closed the gate behind him. Biscuit and Grits ran excitedly towards the women, searching for their canine friends. "Do you think he's coming over?" said Cindy excitedly as she adjusted her dress and stood up. "I think he may," said Carla as she pouted her lips and tousled her hair.

Unfortunately for the two women, Elliott didn't approach the picnic table where the Club sat with their cocktails disguised in plastic cups. Instead, Elliott waved politely in the direction of the women and headed onto the path, walking in a clockwise direction, the opposite way to that which Doug and Katie were walking, so eventually, their paths would cross.

Cindy and Carla both returned to their seats deflated. Heidi had not failed to notice their excitement at the arrival of Elliott or the gentle goading and banter that they had embarked on during the afternoon. Heidi, who was no fool, smiled inwardly at the petty rivalry that was developing between her two friends. Cindy and Carla were following Elliott with their eyes as he traversed the footpath around the park and Heidi instinctively knew what both women were thinking.

"Hi," said Elliott as he approached Doug and Katie.

"So sorry to hear about Thelma," said Doug as he stopped strolling and greeted the recently widowed local politician.

"Tell Veronica thank you. I got your condolence card this morning. Very thoughtful," said Elliott.

Doug nodded, though he had had no idea that his wife had already sent a card of condolence.

"You know the funeral's on Thursday," began Elliott, "I know you didn't know Thelma as well as Veronica did, but you are both welcome to attend." Before Doug could reply Elliott spoke again, "But don't worry if you can't make it. I know you got this little one to watch," he flashed a smile at Katie, who beamed back. "But on Thursday evening we are going to have a gathering at the house, and I would be pleased to see all three of you there." Doug thanked Elliott for his invitation and once again offered his condolences before both men continued their walk along the path, heading off in opposite directions.

Doug reached the east gate and called for Bern to join him. The three women were engrossed in conversation and didn't notice him and Katie leave, even though Bern sped right past them. "You know that she runs three miles a day," said Cindy as the women sat around the table resuming their normal pastime of gossiping and chit-chatting about their neighbors. "Well, she must do something to keep that figure. She is stunning," said Carla.

"Well, he's not half bad either," chimed in Heidi. The three women laughed at the Octogenarian's remark. The focus of their current discussions was Cindy's neighbors Kelly and Tom Hudd.

"Well, if she had any sense she'd stop working behind that beauty counter and enter a modeling competition," stated Carla as she raised her cup to her mouth.

"Well, you know she's an addict," announced Cindy. The other two women sat open mouthed. "Not *that* sort of an addict," laughed Cindy waving her arms. "I mean she is addicted to competitions. She's always entering them. Crosswords, those caption things, puzzles, free give-a-ways, lotteries, anything," she explained. "She's always entering competitions. Just loves them. Totally, totally obsessed with them." The other two ladies looked surprised.

"Does she ever win?" asked Heidi.

"I think that on the odd occasion, every now and then, she does. Maybe a free bottle of soda or coupons," replied Cindy.

"How about money?" asked Carla.

"Not that I know of. I see her walking to the mailbox on Kinzie and Atkinson most days, laden with a pile of envelopes. They're her entries. She is just hooked. Totally," explained Cindy

"I suppose it's harmless enough," Carla stated.

"In moderation," added Heidi.

"Of course," agreed Cindy, "in moderation."

Kelly Hudd had had a good morning and felt she deserved her afternoon off. The fact that two of her neighbors had spent over six-hundred dollars at her counter in less than half an hour had helped. Shmitty, her Labrador, greeted her as she kicked off her shoes and entered the home she shared with her husband, Tom.

"Get down, Shmitty," she said as the dog stood up on his hind legs and struggled to lick his owner's face. "Stop it. *Get down*," she commanded, and the dog reluctantly obeyed.

Kelly and Tom were newlyweds, both in their mid-twenties. They had arrived in Gordonston from South Savannah the previous year and were relative newcomers to the neighborhood. Kelly worked at Macy's in the Oglethorpe Mall selling perfumes and beauty products, while Tom, once a High School football star, was a fire fighter, working for the Savannah Fire Department. The Hudds spent the majority of their spare time doing one of four things. Their most prevalent pastime was making love, their second was, making love, their third was again, making love, while their fourth was exercising together, running, working out in the gym. In between of course, making love.

Kelly was indeed an avid competition 'junky'. She would enter every competition that she came upon that offered prizes. Word searches, fast food give-a-ways, crossword puzzles, prize drawings—anything and everything that gave her the chance of winning. She had been moderately successful in the past, winning a few small kitchen appliances and free groceries on the odd occasion. And it was how she intended spending her afternoon off.

Tom would not be home from the fire station for another three hours at least, and despite the fact that two newlyweds remained in constant touch through text messaging on their cell phones the entire day, she still missed him. The beautiful couple was besotted by each other, which was to be expected of newlyweds, but when your partner was as attractive as Tom and Kelly both were, it was doubly expected. Carla had not been wrong when she had said Kelly could have been a model. She had perfect features and benefited from the skills and the discounted products that came with her profession. Her blonde hair was styled like the young Hollywood starlets of the day and she was always perfectly manicured and turned out. Constant lovemaking and regular exercise maintained her perfect figure, and measuring just shy of six feet never failed to turn heads, either.

Tom was just as good-looking. His rugged, chiseled features constantly drew comparisons to Richard Gere, and he had the body of an athlete. His thick, wavy black hair and constant tan were an excellent foil for his piercing blue eyes. Like his wife, he knew how to dress and wore chest and arm-hugging t-shirts and tight jeans that made the women of Savannah swoon. Not only was Tom a very good-looking man, he was also considered by many of his neighbors and friends as one of the most generous and kind men they could wish to meet. He always offered a helping hand to his elderly neighbors and was always first to volunteer his assistance during the Gordonston Residents Association organized events. It was Tom who had rescued Shmitty from the Animal Rescue Shelter and brought him home as a puppy as a gift for his young and beautiful wife. And it was Shmitty who now demanded Kelly's attention.

"Ok, I'll take you for a walk in a minute," promised Kelly as Shmitty paced the kitchen. "But first you need to let me finish this." Kelly showed Shmitty the papers in her hand and the dog, not sure what they were, duly sniffed them.

They were her latest competition entries. One in particular had been taxing Kelly's mind for a few days. The prize though was wonderful: a four-day, all-expenses-paid trip to a top Paris hotel for two, and twenty-five thousand dollars in cash for the winner. A well-known soft drink company was offering the prize and the competition entailed five questions to be answered correctly and inclusion with the entry of five bottle tops of the relevant soft drink. Kelly already had the required five bottle tops and was now pondering the five questions.

The first had been easy. Which city is known as the City of Love? She had written Paris into the space provided on the entry form. It was either Paris or Michigan she had thought. She was confident her answer was correct, since the prize was a trip to Paris and not Michigan. The second question was just as easy, and the clue was of course the prize. What tall structure dominates the Paris skyline? Once again certain she knew the answer: she had written the Eiffel

Tower. She had toyed with the idea that maybe it was a trick question, but was positive that the Empire State Building was in New York. The third and fourth questions had involved questions about the soft drink. The answers had been Atlanta and Red and White. Of these two answers she was certain; she drank it all the time—well, the diet variety, anyway.

It was the fifth and final question that she found the most difficult. What was the most popular selling soft drink in France? Kelly had no idea where she would find such information. She had racked her brain, and it had caused her to miss several hours of sleep as she had churned the question over in her head over the past few days. She had decided to throw caution to the wind and guessed that it was the same soft drink that had organized the competition in the first place.

She collected the five bottle tops and placed them in the envelope she had allowed Shmitty to sniff and folded her entry sheet and placed it in the envelope along with the bottle tops. "Ok, Shmitty, come on, let's go," she announced as she grabbed Shmitty's leash from the kitchen table. "We'll just mail these letters, then we will head to the park." Shmitty circled the kitchen table excitedly as he realized he was about to embark on a walk and hopefully a visit to the park.

"….And he used to be a High school football player, quarterback I am sure…and she really is not that bright…" The three women had been discussing the virtues of Tom and the brain cells of Kelly. The conversation ended as Elliott came into view. "Should we go over and say hello?" asked Carla.

Cindy eyed her friend suspiciously, and was about to agree that they should, before Heidi spoke. "No, I think we should let him be, the poor man probably needs to be alone." Heidi was not sure she was prepared to watch her two friends make fools of themselves in front of the recently widowed alderman, which she was sure they would. Elliott saw the women watching him and felt it was probably appropriate to go and speak to them. They had all three sent cards of condolences that very morning, which along with Veronica's card had made him suspect that his neighbors had probably been prepared for Thelma's death as much as he had, hence the speediness of their printed commiserations.

"Good afternoon, Ladies," said Elliott as he approached the picnic table and the seated women.

"How are you bearing up?" asked Heidi, while Carla and Cindy adjusted their respective clothing and hair. Heidi warmly placed a hand on Elliott's arm and he patted her hand.

"Oh, not so bad, Heidi," replied Elliott. "It's all a bit of a haze at the moment, but the boys are here and they're pillars of strength." Heidi nodded that she understood.

"If there is anything, *anything*, I can do, you know my door is open," offered Carla.

Cindy wondered which door she meant. Her bedroom door? She was shameless; Thelma wasn't even in the ground yet.

"And of course, Elliott, you know that I am only a phone call away," said Cindy as she joined the throng of women vying for the widower's attention.

Huh, thought Carla, just a phone call away, from what? Why, Thelma's still warm and the woman is practically throwing herself at the man.

Elliott passed on the details of Thelma's funeral arrangements to the ladies and all three promised they would attend both funeral and wake. Biscuit and Grits joined Elliott as he walked towards the gate after bidding the ladies a good afternoon.

"Well, he is doing very well," announced Carla.

"Of course, he's a politician; he knows how to act in public. He is a true gentleman," said Cindy as she tore her eyes away from Elliott and faced her friends.

"Well, I may need to buy a new outfit for the funeral," announced Heidi "so if you two will excuse me and Fuchsl, I will go check my wardrobe," The ladies agreed to cut short their afternoon session of their club and return to their respective homes to check wardrobes and plan outfits.

Kelly arrived in the park with Shmitty five minutes after the ladies had left. She missed Cindy by just a few seconds as she was mailing her latest competition entry while Cindy was returning home. What she lacked in brainpower, Kelly made up for in looks, and as she crossed Edgewood Road and entered the park, a passing car slowed and the male driver admired her figure and features before accelerating. She let Shmitty off his leash and he charged into the park. Kelly waited by the gate, and didn't follow her dog. Kelly, while she enjoyed the park, didn't feel like messing up the shoes that she wore, even if she stayed on the concrete area that led from the scout hut to the east gate she still might dirty them. Instead she watched as two trucks pulled up outside the Miller house, one containing a tent and the other containing various foods, wines, liquors and beers—the party planners and caterers had arrived.

As Elliott supervised the alcohol delivery, Gordon, Thelma's eldest son, supervised the erection of the tent on the lawn of the big white house. Kelly wondered if she should offer her sympathy but thought better of it. She would wait until the wake; she had heard through the neighborhood grapevine that it was going to be a party to remember. Anyway, Elliott looked like his hands were full, because, appearing at exactly the same time, both Carla and Cindy had arrived from separate directions, each bearing recently-prepared chicken casseroles that had been cooking and simmering gently throughout the morning.

CHAPTER 5

Thelma Miller's funeral and wake were well attended. Over a thousand signatures filled the book of condolence that was opened at her funeral service and then continued to be filled at her wake. Mourners flew in from all across the United States to attend both events.

Her two adult sons each read a eulogy, as did Elliott. The eulogy written by Elliott was poignant yet humorous; Thelma was well known by all to posses a fantastic sense of fun and humor, and Elliott told many stories that highlighted his wife's sense of fun. He recalled the time Thelma had erroneously boarded the wrong aircraft while attempting to visit her sons in Los Angeles—not only was she on the wrong flight but she had convinced a complete stranger, also L.A. bound, to join her. It was only when they touched down in Phoenix, and both Thelma and her fellow passenger were hailing cabs that they realized they were not only in the wrong city but also the wrong state.

The assembled mourners laughed as Elliott told the famous story of Thelma's confusion, caused by an afternoon of cocktails in the park, while preparing a dinner at home for Elliott and some of his political backers. Elliott had planned the dinner party for months. However Thelma, disorientated by her gin and tonics, had confused the days and not only had she not prepared food for her guests, she had greeted her husband at the door wearing only a smile. Instead of being embarrassed in front of Elliott's potential backers, she had simply acted as if everything was normal and that was how she always greeted dinner guests. It was Cindy and Heidi who had saved the day,

Elliott recalled, each woman rustling up food in record time as Thelma, dressed only in her night gown and running shoes, had spent the rest of the evening playing the piano and singing songs from Broadway musicals. The backers, whose support Elliott thought he had lost, all said it was probably the best evening they'd had in years.

There was hardly a dry eye in the cathedral, though, as Thelma's coffin was led out to the sound of Bette Midler warbling "Wind Beneath My Wings," Thelma's own selection and favorite song. The service, bar Elliott's eulogy, and the subsequent burial, were sedate, dignified affairs, and though the mood of those present was somber, there was an underlying sense of relief that at last Thelma's suffering was over. The grief felt by her widowed husband and two grown sons was shared by her friends and relatives, and among the floral tributes was a special wreath from her fellow members of the Gordonston Ladies Dog Walking Club, who were at the graveside and in the cathedral, along with her relatives and other friends. Both Cindy and Carla had sobbed gently during both the service and burial, while Heidi was more composed, wearing a stern and somber look that she had maintained throughout the day, in contrast to the overall theme of Thelma's final farewell.

Heidi had decided not to splurge for a new outfit for her friend's funeral but instead wore the same mourning outfit she had worn twenty years earlier at her husband's funeral. Carla and Cindy, however, had arrived at the cathedral dressed elegantly, and some would even say, provocatively. Carla's figure-hugging dark trouser suit had received a lot of attention, especially the trousers, which were so tight that you could have been forgiven for thinking they had been painted onto her behind. Cindy's outfit had also gotten comment and attention, and though the plunging neckline and the raised hemline of her skirt were not totally inappropriate, they were a little risqué. The fact that both women wore five-inch heels, which obliged both of them to clutch the arm of a nearby gentleman mourner as they teetered their way across the treacherous gravel and seashell path to Thelma's grave, did raise a few eyebrows from those congregated at both cathedral and cemetery.

The wake quickly became a party, and was anything but sedate. As promised, a jazz band was in attendance and the musicians played continuously through what only could be described as the festivities, and the drink flowed nonstop until the most exuberant mourner could drink no more. An outsider would have been forgiven for thinking that those inside the big white house overlooking the park were celebrating a wedding or a birthday and not mourning a death. Laughter spilled out into the usually tranquil Gordonston evening as the party lasted through the night and into the following morning. Practically every homeowner in the Gordonston neighborhood arrived at the Miller home at some point during the evening, and twice the party ran out of beer, resulting in two emergency deliveries from Johnnie Ganem's downtown liquor store.

The caterers had done an excellent job with the food, providing all the local favorites: fried chicken, Brunswick stew, Tybee shrimp and individual pecan pies. For some revelers it would be rated the highlight of their social year and many lapsed acquaintances were renewed. Elliott had, as expected, been the perfect host. While he didn't appear down or morose, he provided an air of decorum, while respecting his wife's wishes for a lavish and fun-filled sendoff without diminishing her memory and his love for her by partying on with the rest of the crowd. Though he had danced with several ladies throughout the evening, he had made sure that none were single and all were chaperoned by either husbands or lovers. This had caused a minor incident that didn't go unnoticed by Heidi Launer. Carla Zipp and Cindy Mopper had left the festivities early, and some would gossip that they both left in a huff, after watching Elliott ask several other ladies to join him on the dance floor. At one stage both Cindy and Carla had physically shoved aside an assortment of women who either encircled Elliott or blocked the ladies' line of vision of their party host. Heidi shook her head in despair at the antics of her two friends.

The main event of the evening, though, was Elliott's announcement that he would be running for mayor in the next election. Cheers and congratulatory whistles met his announcement, as well as handshakes and pats on the back from his neighbors. Spencer and Gordon uncorked a crate of champagne that they had secretly ordered and toasted their stepfather, and those still present raised a glass to a successful campaign. Though it would mean that the district would lose him as alderman, should he be elected, Elliott promised should he become mayor he would ensure that a watchful eye be kept on the neighborhood and his neighbors were ensured of his continued support for all of Gordonston's committees, clubs and associations.

Doug and Veronica Partridge left the festivities early, just before Elliott's announcement. But they would hear about his intentions the following morning through the neighborhood grapevine. Katie, who had accompanied them, had done well for an hour, but a meltdown had occurred just after the band played "When the Saints Go Marching In" for the third time. Elliott thanked the couple for attending, and kissed Veronica on the cheek and Katie on the forehead, which didn't help her mood. Doug shook Elliott's hand and offered to take Biscuit and Grits on walks around the park, should Elliott find himself needing a hand. Elliott thanked the Englishman and said that he appreciated the offer, but both Carla and Cindy had already both offered to dog-sit whenever they were needed.

Tom and Kelly Hudd also missed Elliott's announcement that he would be running for mayor. Due to their regular gym class they had arrived late and learnt of Elliott's mayoral ambitions from Heidi, who had no intention of leaving Thelma's wake just yet. Kelly and Tom enjoyed some food and danced to the jazz music, provoking admiring glances from many guests. Tom especially enjoyed the undivided attention of both Spencer and Gordon, who told the young firefighter that he really should think about a modeling career and that if he were ever in Los Angeles he should look them up. Kelly, who didn't usually drink, became tipsy just before midnight, compelling Tom to make their excuses and take her home. As they left, an old colored gentleman, taking his old and loyal Cairn terrier for a late-night stroll, passed the Miller house and delivered a card of condolence into Elliott's mailbox before returning to his home just across the park.

Heidi Launer had surprised even herself by her ability to last the night. She remained at Thelma's wake until the small hours of the morning partaking of cocktails, catching up with seldom seen neighbors and at one stage even dancing to the strains of "When the Saints Go Marching In," played for the eighth time that evening. But she had spent most of the evening as if she were looking for something or someone in the big house. Both Gordon and Spencer had taken the time to share childhood memories with their former neighbor and she had insisted on a tour of the house and the chance to relive memories by having Thelma's sons produce photo album after photo album so she could peruse them at her leisure. Spencer had the distinct feeling that Heidi was searching for something by the way she scanned through the albums and inspected every nook and cranny of the house, but dismissed the thought as the evening progressed and the old lady seemed to relax.

Elliott felt it had been a successful evening, and as he took a draw on the cigar Gordon had given him, he reflected on the day's events. Thelma would have been pleased with her send off and would have enjoyed that so many had turned out to bid her a final farewell. As Elliott stood at the front door to his home, blowing cigar smoke into the early morning air, he collected the letters from his mailbox. He opened and read the old man's recently deposited card of condolence and reminded himself to personally thank his neighbor for his kind words. Gordon and Spencer were both leaving the following day, again on a privately chartered jet, and he marveled at just how successful his stepsons had become. He was proud of them, as Thelma had been, and was pleased that his writing efforts had helped enable them to pursue such lucrative careers. It was funny, he thought, how things turn out, and as he stared into the park he wondered just what fate would have in store for him next.

Elliott broke away from his thoughts and turned his attention to more mundane matters. He had organized a team of cleaners for the following afternoon to assist with the clearing of the evening's festivities, and he must remember to call Spencer and Gordon at their hotel in the morning to say goodbye. Actually, he thought, the house wasn't in too much of a state anyway. He'd put most of his personal items in the cellar, including his collection of books, including his own three and his rare signed copy of the book he had received over thirty years before, leaving the nooks and crannies free for his guests to deposit empty plates and glasses.

CHAPTER 6

Exactly one week after Thelma Miller's funeral, Kelly Hudd decided to take a well-deserved day off and spend it pampering herself and generally relaxing. She was due vacation time anyway, and as she had worked six days a week for the last month, her department manager was very happy to accommodate his pretty sales assistant and consultant.

After a long lie-in, during which Tom had brought her breakfast in bed of strawberries and melon, freshly squeezed orange juice and whole grain toast, Kelly indulged herself in a long, luxurious bath. She had soaked herself for just under an hour, experimenting with the various free samples, courtesy of her profession, which she often tried out at home. Shmitty, who had crept into the bathroom, was lying on the floor next to where his mistress soaked, and if dogs could smile, he would have probably been doing so.

Kelly had no plans for the day apart from maybe catching up on a few of her favorite daytime soap operas and watching Oprah. Maybe that afternoon, once the heat had abated, she would consider a stroll in the park with Shmitty. She was not quite ready to join the three women who congregated around the picnic table and as she was not a drinker—in fact she never touched hard liquor—the cocktail hour would not be of any interest to her. She was still getting over Thelma's recent wake anyhow, where she had drank too much of the red wine served by the bow-tied waiters. She had become tipsy, and at one stage during the evening had become jealous of the attention Tom was receiving from Thelma's sons. Luckily, though, Heidi had cornered her, rambling on about some books or something, Kelly really had a hazy recollection of the evening and was glad that Tom had taken her home when he had, before she was able to get the chance to embarrass herself or him. She wished she could remember what Heidi had been talking about, but like Kelly, the older lady had drunk far too much and by the end of the evening was incoherent.

Kelly daydreamed as she lay in the tub and her thoughts turned to her favorite fantasy, modeling. Kelly had always aspired to being a model, she knew she had the body and the looks for it and in her younger days she had toyed with the idea. She had never pursued her dream, though; somehow she had thought that her career as a beautician and sales assistant would only be temporary and that one day she would be discovered.

That discovery never came, and while she had no regrets about her life she often wondered what it would have been like had she fulfilled her fanciful teenage aspirations. As she lay in the relaxing water, she imagined herself walking catwalks, lounging on exotic beaches, attending movie premieres and other celebrity functions. She saw herself on magazine covers and blazoned across billboards; this was a recurring fantasy that she played out in her head repeatedly. Of course, Tom was at her side in all of these fantasies. She didn't substitute Brad Pitt or Tom Cruise for the man of her dreams. She had her own hunk, and as far as Kelly was concerned he was better than any Hollywood superstar.

After her extended and relaxing bath, Kelly switched on the TV in her bedroom and inspected the garments hanging in her closet. She liked to keep up with the latest fashion trends, and working in a department store meant she usually had the first pick when it came to new stock. Though Kelly and Tom were not top-end salary earners, between them they made enough to afford their small house, run two cars and indulge themselves in designer label clothing. Not that it really mattered, as both of them could look good in anything. Even the simplest of outfits on Kelly looked like it had originated from an Italian or French fashion house.

As always during summer months in Savannah, it was a glorious day, and Kelly, once she had dressed, took a seat in her small garden with a copy of Vogue—her favorite magazine—and a glass of iced tea, sweetened artificially. Cindy called sweet tea the "house wine of Savannah," and Kelly liked the phrase. It was true, she thought, and she smiled as she took a sip of the refreshing drink.

Shmitty had followed her into the garden, and after sniffing the azaleas that grew against the side of the fence that separated the Hudd's garden from Cindy's neatly trimmed and manicured lawn, he joined his mistress under the sun-screened porch.

The magazine engrossed her, as it always did. Kelly was fascinated by the articles she found there and would spend hours thumbing its pages each month. Her concentration, though, was broken by the siren of an emergency vehicle. Kelly rested the magazine on her lap and looked up. The siren was not close but belonged to a vehicle traversing Pennsylvania Avenue, which bordered the Gordonston neighborhood. Kelly wondered if she had ever seen an emergency vehicle, police, fire truck or ambulance ever in her neighborhood and decided that she had not. That wasn't because the police didn't keep up regular patrols in the area, far from it. Elliott had ensured a constant and regular police patrol of Gordonston, day and night. It was just that nothing ever happened to warrant the need for police. There had not been a fire in the neighborhood since 1978, when the old Carter house was gutted due to an electrical wiring fault, and the last time an ambulance was seen in the streets of Gordonston was when young Sam Cooper fell off the swings in the park and cut his head open.

The siren, though, reminded Kelly that her husband was constantly in danger. She worried about her husband, working as a fire fighter, and the sound of the siren had sent shivers down her spine. Despite this constant concern, Kelly loved her life. Yes, of course she would have liked more money, who wouldn't? Nevertheless, she enjoyed her work, loved her neighborhood, couldn't have wished for a better husband and her pastimes of sex, exercise, sex and competition entries were harmless and gave her immeasurable pleasure.

Kelly's only real regret in life was that she had not pursued a modeling career, but so what? She didn't care. Maybe another regret would have been not attending college and very nearly flunking high school. It wasn't that she was dumb. It was just that she had other priorities. Looking good was one of them, the other was snaring the man of her dreams, the High School Quarterback Tom Hudd. She had succeeded in both.

Kelly returned to the glossy pages of her magazine. She was currently absorbed in an article discussing the love lives of several Hollywood stars. It seemed to Kelly that even the most apparently stable Hollywood marriage ended in divorce, and she couldn't understand the way these beautiful people squandered their marriages. Maybe she and Tom were just lucky; maybe they had something other couples didn't have. She certainly didn't envy the couple on Kinzie Avenue with the baby. They always looked tired, especially the husband. Not that she cared. She didn't really like him anyway, he was foreign and spoke funny and once he had been rude to her. No, for the moment, children were not on the Hudd's immediate agenda, it would play havoc with her figure and she couldn't see Tom pushing a stroller around the neighborhood.

The midday sun forced Kelly indoors, and she called Shmitty to follow her into the air—conditioned house. It was a good time to catch up on her soaps, she thought, and she picked up the *TV Guide* to see what shows were airing and on what channel. She also took the opportunity to text message Tom on her cell phone, who, she expected, was at the fire station doing whatever firemen did when not putting out fires.

'I Luv U' typed out Kelly on her cell phone keypad and sent the message to her husband's phone. Beep Beep. Her cell phone shook and lit up two seconds later.

'I Luv U 2' came the reply from Tom's cell phone.

She grabbed her phone and pressed the buttons quickly *'C U L8R'* and pressed send.

Beep Beep. *'OK 2 Nite xx'*

Kelly smiled and held her cell phone tightly to her chest. She had been with Tom for over fourteen years, including the time they dated in high school, and every day felt like it was the first day they had met. Kelly could not imagine being happier than she was now. She selected a television channel and slid onto the sofa with Shmitty at her feet. She had found a show she liked and was soon engrossed in the simple plot and exaggerated story line. Within twenty-five minutes both Kelly and Shmitty were sleeping soundly in the den with the TV providing accompaniment to both the woman's and the dog's gentle, contented snoring.

It was Shmitty's barking that woke her. For an instant she wasn't actually sure where she was, but as her eyes adjusted to the daylight she remembered she had fallen asleep watching TV. The screen now filled with Oprah discussing the virtues of some silly book or other. Kelly sat upright and looked at Shmitty before patting the Labrador gently on the head. "It's only the mailman, silly dog," she patted Shmitty's head once more and rose from the sofa. She stretched and yawned. She tousled her hair and slowly walked to the front door, Shmitty at her heels, collecting an empty glass that she had on a side table on her way.

The weather was still glorious; the mid-afternoon heat was a little less torrid than at midday, and a gentle breeze cooled the air. Kelly checked the time on the clock in the hallway leading to the front door and saw that it was just after three. She had slept for two hours and felt good for the rest. She opened the door and delved into her mailbox. The mailman who had just delivered the lone letter turned and waved at Kelly who waved back.

"Good afternoon," he cried. "Have a great day!"

Kelly smiled at her mailman. "And you too, have a wonderful day," said Kelly, with a smile. The mailman continued his round, stopping next door at Cindy's home. Kelly took a deep breath of fresh Savannah air and felt the sun on her face before returning inside her cooled home.

The mailman could have had no idea what the letter he had just delivered to Kelly contained. If he had taken the time to inspect the envelope, he would have seen it was postmarked as being mailed from Atlanta. On further inspection he would have noticed the well-known logo, unmistakable the world over, emblazoned on the fold of the envelope. The mailman, though, would never have suspected that his friendly comment of "have a great day" was exactly what Kelly Hudd was about to have. In fact, Kelly's day was about to be greater than any other day she had ever had, and it was all due to the letter she had just received.

Kelly placed the empty glass she had carried all the way from the den, through the kitchen and hall to the front door and then back through the den into the kitchen, placing it on the small kitchen table. She placed the envelope at its side and opened the fridge to retrieved the jug of iced tea she had prepared earlier. She poured herself a drink from the jug into the well-traveled glass and inspected the envelope now in her hand. Like her mailman, she didn't notice the postmark but did notice the logo on the envelope. She expected it was some sort of promotional material advertising the company's well-known product, which she enjoyed in its diet variety. Kelly opened the envelope after taking a sip of tea and read the letter that it contained.

At first she thought she had made a mistake, so she read it again. Maybe she had misread it or maybe she was still asleep on the sofa in the den, and this was a dream. Kelly actually pinched herself, just to make sure she was awake, which of course she was. She began to tremble as the reality of what she had just read began to dawn on her and she put her hand to her mouth as if to stifle a scream.

"Oh my God," she said in a hushed whisper. "Oh my God!" she said again, this time slightly louder. "Oh my God!" she said for a third time, this time screaming the words. Kelly was bobbing excitedly on her bare feet and Shmitty began wagging his tale and barked at his mistress's raised voice. "Oh yes!" she cried and clenched her hands and raised them in the air as if she had just made the winning touchdown in the Super Bowl. "Yes, yes, yes, and yes!!" she screamed. Shmitty barked again and wagged his tail and Kelly crouched down and placed her arms around the excited dog's neck and kissed him on the top of his head. "Oh Shmitty," she cried, the confused dog looked at the bouncing woman in front of him and tilted his head to the right, "I have done it! I have done it! I won! WE ARE GOING TO PARIS!" screamed Kelly, and Shmitty barked again.

The letter that had produced so much elation in the young woman was brief and to the point. However, that didn't really matter, it was the few words that were printed on the single page that counted and for the heck of it Kelly read it again:

Dear Mrs. Hudd,

We are delighted to inform you that your recent entry in our "Paris: City of Love" promotional competition was successful. You correctly answered all five questions and sent us the required number of bottle tops.

You are requested to call Judy Callaghan at the telephone number indicated on the letterhead of this official prize-winning notification. Judy will be pleased to finalize details of your trip to Paris and organize travel and an appropriate hotel. A check for $25,000 is enclosed.

May I take this opportunity to express our heartfelt congratulations.

Yours Faithfully,

The letter was signed by an Alistair Hamilton, who according to the letterhead was head of promotions and publicity for the Atlanta-based global giant of a company.

Kelly looked at the check she held in her hand and screamed with delight. Twenty-five thousand dollars, she had never even seen a check written out for that amount before, but to see the check made out to *her* was even more remarkable. She picked up her cell phone and called Tom, but his phone went straight to voicemail. He must have been out in the fire truck or in a poor reception area, guessed Kelly. Okay, thought Kelly as she sat down at the kitchen table, calm down and concentrate, this needs some serious thought. She dialed the number indicated in the letter and after three rings Judy Callaghan answered the phone.

Judy, who sounded very nice, thought Kelly, went through the details of the prize Kelly had just won. Kelly had a selection of three dates that were on offer for her trip to Paris. The dates of the trip to Paris were unchangeable, the trip could only be taken on one of the dates offered, and once a date was selected and the hotel informed, Kelly would not be able to alter it. Kelly selected the first option, which was less than a week away. Judy asked Kelly who would be accompanying her on her trip to Paris, and Kelly, without hesitation announced it would be her husband Tom. Judy advised Kelly that she was making the necessary arrangements as they spoke, via the Internet, and that the trip, including hotel reservations and flights, was now booked and confirmed for next Thursday.

Kelly and Tom were booked on a flight, first class from Savannah to Paris, through New York, and they needed to be at the airport in Savannah by nine in the morning. They had a luxury suite reserved at the five-star Bonaparte Hotel located in the center of Paris for Thursday night through Monday. They would be departing Paris at six in the afternoon local time for an overnight flight, and were due to arrive back in Savannah sometime Tuesday afternoon; like the trip to Paris the return would be first class.

The schedule was confirmed and all relevant tickets were being processed. It was totally unchangeable and non-refundable, which meant it could only be Tom who accompanied Kelly on her trip. Kelly indicated she understood this and that it would not be a problem. All hotel costs would be met, including all meals and room service, including use of the spa and other hotel amenities. Furthermore, to be dispatched with the tickets would be traveler's checks totaling one thousand dollars that they could use as spending money while in Paris. Judy congratulated Kelly and wished her a fantastic trip.

Kelly couldn't believe her luck! Finally, she had won a major prize! After all the years of entering competitions she had finally won a prize worth something. She decided there and then that she would make this a trip that Tom would remember forever and already had a plan forming in her head. Kelly opened the front door to her home, crossed the unfenced front lawn into her neighbor's garden and knocked on Cindy Mopper's front door. Cindy answered the door with a smile on her face. "I have some great news!" screamed Kelly, a grin covering her pretty face.

Cindy beckoned Kelly into the house, but Kelly insisted that Cindy come over to her home, she had some beer in the fridge and the occasion warranted a drink. She had news and she needed help with a plan she had devised only seconds before. Cindy shut her front door and followed the excited Kelly into her home. The Gordonston Ladies Dog Walking Club had not convened that day, Carla had had a Doctor's appointment and Heidi had needed to travel into the city for an appointment with her bank manager. It meant that Cindy had plenty of time to indulge her pretty neighbor. Cindy, intrigued by Kelly's excitement, said she would join her young friend immediately.

"Read this," Kelly handed Cindy the letter and a bottle of one of Tom's low calorie beers from the refrigerator. Cindy read the prize-winning notification letter as Kelly raised another of one of Tom's bottles to her mouth. After Cindy had read the letter, she herself took a swig of cold beer.

"Well, congratulations. Twenty-five thousand dollars! What are you going to spend it on?" Cindy sounded delighted for her young neighbor and clinked her bottle against Kelly's.

"Nothing," said Kelly.

"Nothing?" repeated Cindy.

"I'm going to save it, keep it in my own private account. I'm not even going to tell Tom about it," said Kelly, defiantly as she took another drink of beer.

"Why ever not?" asked Cindy, surprised by her young neighbor's announcement.

"I'm going to save it and get myself a modeling portfolio done, by a professional photographer. I'm going to use the money to follow my dream. I'm going to try and become a professional model," explained Kelly triumphantly. "It has to be a sign, I was thinking about it just this morning. It must be fate!"

"Well good for you, girl," cried Cindy and she clinked her bottle against Kelly's once again. "What about the trip to Paris? It sounds fantastic. When are you going?" Kelly explained that the trip to Paris had been organized, and that she and Tom would be departing next Thursday morning. Cindy said she would be more than happy to have Shmitty over with her for the few days the young couple was out of the country and that Paddy would enjoy the company. Kelly then explained to Cindy her plan, which she had concocted just minutes before.

"Do you think that will work? Are you sure he can get the time off work?" Cindy asked, a little worried that maybe Kelly hadn't really thought through her intended plan and her voice had a trace of concern in it.

"Oh don't worry about that," she scoffed. "Tom has plenty of vacation days, and the fire chief has always liked me. Once I explain it to Captain O'Hare he'll understand. I'll pack Tom's suitcase without his even knowing. It will be the biggest surprise of his life."

Cindy agreed that Tom would be surprised the following Thursday when told that he wasn't going to have to go into work but instead he was headed for a five-star, first-class trip to Paris. Maybe Kelly's idea would work.

"I know my Ronnie, though, hated surprises. I hope you know what you are doing," said Cindy.

Kelly waved away her neighbor's concerns and took a swig of the cold beer. Cindy promised she wouldn't breathe a word of Kelly's win or trip to anyone, not even her dog walking friends. The last thing Kelly wanted was for Tom to get wind of the surprise she had in store for him.

"So what's wrong with your friend Carla? Why is she at the Doctor's?" asked Kelly as she led Cindy to the front door of her home.

"You know, I am not sure," replied Cindy. "I think it's probably her age. When they get to her age it could be anything." Cindy smiled and Kelly nodded as if she agreed with what Cindy had said. Kelly, though, was a little confused, as Carla was about the same age as Cindy and in truth looked much younger; in fact when Kelly had first seen Carla she had mistaken her for an attractive forty-something. Kelly shrugged and watched as Cindy crossed the lawn and disappeared into her home.

As Kelly and Cindy were discussing her health, Carla was just coming out of surgery. The operation had been a success and the surgeon was pleased with the results. Three day's bed rest followed by a couple of days taking it easy and Carla would be back to normal in no time. As for the procedure, it went perfectly and though expensive, was well worth the price. The plastic surgeon was confident his patient would begin to appreciate her enhanced breasts the moment she awoke from the anesthetic.

CHAPTER 7

Veronica and Doug stared silently at their half-eaten and now cold dinners. Not that it mattered that their food was cold. They had both lost their appetites anyhow. They both hated arguing, but it was becoming more and more regular. It seemed each week that there was some issue or other that prompted a heated debate and raised voices. The majority of issues stemmed mainly from one thing: money. Veronica tried to ease Doug's worries, telling him that they were fine and not to worry that his dividends were not paying as much as he had hoped. She tried to reassure him that sooner or later his immigration paperwork would be cleared and he would be able to find work locally, that companies were always on the lookout for bright and intelligent staff.

Despite Veronica's reassurances Doug was still worried. He felt bad that his wife had to work the long and hard hours she did at the hospital while he spent his days playing with and caring for Katie. It wasn't that he was a chauvinist—it was just that he wanted the best for his family and with the meager contribution he was making, financially at least, despite the fact they owned their home outright, he felt like a failure.

"But if you go back to work means that I would have to stop working," argued Veronica, "and if I didn't stop working that would mean added childcare costs."

Doug shook his head in disagreement. "No, it wouldn't. You could stop working. I can earn enough so you don't have to work. You know I used to make a *lot*," countered Doug, his voice rising slightly.

"But you're missing the point," said Veronica. "We'd be back to square one. You would have to abandon your immigration application and start all over again, and what about Katie?" The two adults turned to face the baby girl playing with her food in her highchair. She enjoyed sitting at the kitchen table with her mom and dad. What she didn't enjoy was the tense atmosphere. She smiled at her parents then slung some food towards the kitchen floor. Bern caught it in his mouth before it hit the ground.

"She's used to you being here now. She needs you. Can't you see how much you two have bonded? Surely you would miss her. I am not prepared to see you like it was before—once every two or three months, and then no idea when you would be back. No. I'm sorry, but I don't want you going back to work. Not abroad, anyway." Veronica was adamant and Doug knew that she was right. But he still couldn't help feeling dejected, and maybe even slightly depressed.

"It's hard for me here," he began, scratching his head, "I know it was my decision but I am worried. What if we can't pay bills, what if something happens to you and you can't work?" Veronica sighed, but Doug continued to speak. "Don't you see what I'm saying, I think I made a mistake. I think that maybe I should have waited a few more years before retiring. For God's sake, I am only thirty-nine. I feel useless."

"You are not useless, don't say that," said Veronica, concerned for her husband. "You have done so much already, missed so much. Look, its fine, everything's okay. I would prefer you home and us poor than you away again and us rich." She smiled sweetly at her husband.

"Well, that's all well and good, but how can we survive? College, school, all those things?" asked Doug, a slight hint of desperation in his voice. Veronica touched his hand gently, which led to squeals of delight from Katie.

"Okay, how about this, why don't you contact your old boss and see if there's anything you can do over here. Maybe you could open an office in Savannah for them. Remember the conference? Maybe there will be another one this year and maybe you could see some of your old contacts and friends. Maybe they'll have something for you."

Doug smiled but shook his head. "I doubt they would have the conference here again, not after what happened." Veronica looked puzzled at first, then, recalled what had occurred during the conference.

"That poor man," she said. "Imagine being shot for your watch. What he was doing in that part of downtown still puzzles me. What an idiot."

Four years previously, during the banking and finance conference that Doug had attended at the Savannah conference center—which had brought him to Savannah in the first place—a conference delegate had been mugged and killed for his expensive watch while exploring the industrial docks near downtown Savannah's riverfront. The news had been big at the time and had attracted media attention from not just across the US but internationally as well. The victim was a high-powered Cayman Islands banker, embroiled in a multi-million dollar lawsuit against former investors who some claimed were directly linked to the Russian mafia. His death had led to the collapse of the lawsuit, and to the Russian mobsters saving millions of dollars. His murder had been high profile as was the Savannah Police Department's failure to apprehend his killer or killers. Since then, the banking conference had convened in Chicago, Montreal and most recently Las Vegas. Doug was right, thought Veronica. She doubted they would ever return to Savannah.

"Listen, I don't want to argue. I hate it, and so does she," Doug gestured to Katie, who was banging her spoon on her highchair tray. "I'll send an email next week, just to let them know I am still alive and just saying hello. Maybe I'll just mention that if there is anything in the pipeline or on the horizon in the States then maybe they could consider me." Doug felt that this was a good compromise; hopefully his email would remind his former employers that he was available and open to offers.

"Okay," agreed Veronica, flashing him the same smile that had made him stay in Savannah in the first place. Veronica turned to Katie, "Come on Baby Toots, eat up or we will feed it all to Bern!"

Heidi Launer was not enjoying her evening meal. Not that Betty Jenkins had done a bad job in preparing the fried chicken. Betty Jenkins' fried chicken was famous throughout Savannah, and it was divine. No. It wasn't the chicken. It was something else that made Heidi move her plate to one side, her food hardly touched.

The old woman stood up from the table and Fuchsl, who had been lying under his owner's dining table, rose to his feet at the same time. She had seen the bank manager a few days earlier and had him release funds that were tied up in one of her savings accounts, an amount sufficient for the work she needed. Though she was no expert; she had guessed an approximate cost but would call someone she knew who could confirm the exact amount she would need later. That she had waited all this time for what she intended to do was her own fault. She cursed herself in her native tongue for her delay. Soon, though, it wouldn't matter; at least now she was ready, and soon she would be able to sleep a little easier.

Apart from Heidi and Fuchsl the large house was empty. Betty, once the chicken had been served, had returned to her smaller house to prepare a lesser dinner for her own family. Heidi climbed the stairs, Fuchsl following slowly behind her. She paused at the locked bedroom door and delved into her purse, which she had carried up the stairs with her. She pulled out the key that would unlock the door and slowly inserted it into the keyhole. The door creaked open and Heidi entered the room that remained locked nearly all the time and only ever entered by her and her alone. Even Fuchsl hesitated at the door before following his mistress into the still and quiet bedroom. As she entered the bedroom Heidi gasped out loud. She always did. The images on the walls always left her breathless, especially those on the north wall. She gazed at the cloth that adorned the wall, mesmerized by its colors and significance. It always had the same affect on the her. Whenever she saw it she could feel her heart thumping in her chest so hard she thought it would burst out from within her. She breathed in deeply and calmed herself. Slowly her heartbeat returned to normal and she smiled broadly, staring, transfixed by the item gracing the wall before her.

The only pieces of furniture in the room were large glass-fronted display cabinets, positioned randomly around the room, and Heidi, once she had pulled her eyes away from the north wall of the bedroom, moved over to the cabinet positioned in the center of the room. She marveled at its contents and opened the glass door, slowly releasing the catch and then gently removing one of the objects contained within. She held it up to the ceiling before lowering it to her chest; she cradled the object as if cradling a baby, gently rocking herself from side to side. Fuchsl gave a low whine and slowly backed out of the room, pausing at the door. He sat and watched as his mistress performed the routine she did each night. Heidi smiled to herself and replaced the object back in the cabinet, took one last look at the walls and left the room, as slowly as she had entered, locking the door behind her.

Carla was delighted with her enlarged and improved chest. When she had seen Cindy in the figure-hugging dress with the plunging neckline at Thelma's funeral, revealing her ample bosom, the ex-dancer and cheerleader had become obsessed with the size of her own breasts. She had always wanted cleavage. Even all those years ago in Las Vegas she had envied the well-endowed girls in her dance troupe. Not that it had made much difference. She was a very attractive young woman back then and had her pick of men, and the truth was that she had a perfectly fine cleavage anyway. Now though, it was great.

Carla often wondered what would have happened had she not married Ian Zipp. She had known a lot of men back then and had fond memories of many, most of all Gino, son of the casino owner who had given the young dancer her first real break. She wondered how different her life would have been if she had continued dancing and married Gino. He had loved her, he had told her often enough. The bewitched man would send flowers, cards, gifts of jewelry and furs, and had been utterly devastated when Carla had never returned to Las Vegas from her vacation in Florida. She still kept in touch with him, though he was now married with children of his own. He would write to her frequently and would sometimes even call, and Carla knew that deep down he still pined for her. Well, who knew what could have been, thought Carla. One thing was certain: she had major voluptuous cleavage now, and she was still attractive. If this didn't snare her man nothing would.

Kelly smiled as she watched Tom in the gym. From the treadmill she could see Tom bench-pressing weights. The man's sweat-glistening body was like a machine, and his muscles moved as if they were pistons. He *was* a machine, thought Kelly, her very own sex machine. He had the physique of a Greek god and her heart skipped a beat when he caught her eye and waved. How lucky she was. Twenty-five thousand dollars in the bank and a modeling portfolio photo shoot booked in two weeks, an all-expenses-paid first class trip to Paris with the man she loved, who still had no idea that he was about to embark on the trip of a lifetime.

The best thing, though, was that Tom had the time off and didn't even know it. Kelly had spoken to Captain O'Hare that morning. She had explained everything, and the Captain was only too happy to switch some shifts and give Tom vacation time. He thought it was a great idea, her surprising him like that. Kelly waved again at her oblivious husband as he stretched. She gazed at his firm tight buttocks and smiled. Tomorrow they would be in Paris.

Cindy Mopper was fuming. She couldn't ever remember being this mad. She was so angry she had been shaking the best part of the day and even now she couldn't eat. That bitch, that nasty, nasty little tramp. Who the hell did she think she was? Did she have no shame? She was acting like a two bit hooker, the Jezebel! Cindy had been speechless when she had seen Carla that afternoon in the park. Along with Heidi, she had stood opened mouthed as Carla had removed her jacket to reveal her new bosom.

"Oh, just a little self indulgence," she said giggling and laughing, her breasts jiggling for all to see. Self indulgence! She was nothing but a whore, thought Cindy, that's all she was. No doubt she had been a whore in Vegas, too. Well this wasn't Vegas, this was Savannah, and as far as Cindy was concerned, war had been declared.

Cindy would have loved to say that her friend had looked ridiculous, but the truth was she didn't. She looked good. She looked twenty years younger than Cindy. That's what hurt most. It was obvious what Carla was doing. She wanted Elliott and was going to get him no matter the cost. Cindy knew that it wasn't just a coincidence that Carla had had her boob job just after Elliott announced he was going to run for office.

Cindy knew that Carla was going to go all out to snare the widowed Elliott. She knew that she would continue to bake pies and prepare chicken casseroles. She knew that she would continue to dress provocatively whenever Elliott was around, exposing more and more flesh each time she saw him. She knew that Carla would flirt and laugh at Elliott's jokes and take every opportunity to be near him. And how could Cindy know this? How could she be so certain of her friend's future actions and intentions? How could she possibly know what Carla was thinking? Well, because it was exactly what Cindy intended to do herself, and she was thinking the same thoughts she suspected her friend of having.

Elliott knew that running for mayor was not the same as running for a city council seat. For a start, there would be a citywide focus of attention on him. Of course the stakes were much higher, and being mayor would bring on added responsibilities. Just like the presidential elections, certain tactics could be expected in the race to the mayor's office such as the digging up of dirt, the raking up of past indiscretions, mind games and the attempt to slur the good name of opposing candidates.

Elliott smiled. He had nothing to worry about. He was squeaky clean. He raised his cocktail of whiskey and water to his lips and took a sip. He nestled into his chair and watched as Biscuit and Grits snuggled next to each other in front of the television set. There was the question of his books, though. It wasn't general knowledge that he had once been a writer, and he certainly had never advertised he had been a writer. Should this be brought up in a debate or other forum, he was sure it wouldn't be a problem. He had shunned interviews just after he had been published when he had been semi-famous. Though he had never been asked what the inspiration for his stories was and how he knew so much about the Bavarian region, especially its forests and many small villages, he felt confident he could handle any difficult questions. He would do what any decent politician would do in his position: he would lie.

Doug Partridge kissed his sleeping wife on the forehead. She was shattered. It had been a long day for her at the hospital, and he felt guilty. He had ruined dinner by arguing with her and hated himself for adding more stress to his wife's life. Just tonight, Katie hadn't gone to Veronica, instead choosing Daddy over Mommy for a nighttime cuddle. Doug knew that this had upset his wife though she had said nothing. She had had just smiled, like she always did, and got on with things. He stroked his wife's face, and she smiled in her sleep. He gently brushed her hair from her face and kissed her again; he loved her and he wanted the best for her. She deserved it. He went over to his baby's crib and marveled at his beautiful child, sleeping peacefully, a smile across her flawless face. It was perfect, his life, and he knew that he should be grateful for what he had. If only he could find some way of securing their future.

Doug had written off his investments, for the time being anyway, and though he had told his wife the truth, he still felt the need to maybe just put some feelers out. Who knew? Maybe his old boss could find him work in Savannah. It wasn't beyond the realm of possibility. He quietly shut the bedroom door so as not to disturb his sleeping wife and child, then he opened up his laptop, careful not to make any noise. It took a couple of minutes to warm up and then a few seconds for him to click onto the wireless Internet network. He hadn't logged into his roaming email account in such a long time he could barely remember his password. He paused for thought, as if composing the email he was about to write in his head. Once satisfied he knew what he wanted to say, he wrote the message.

Once the email was finished he clicked the send button. He then returned to the bedroom and peered around the cracked door; Veronica and Katie were both sleeping soundly. He returned to his laptop and opened the folder that he had protected with a password, he paused, checking that no sound came from the room where his wife and daughter slept, then began to type.

The old man switched off his television set. The news was always grim, be it local, national or international, and though the names and places changed, the headlines were always the same: murders, killings, wars, and terrorists. The old man sighed. He was tired, and it seemed to get hotter every year. Chalky, who lay at his feet, was exhausted too. The old man wondered how many summers his faithful companion had left—and for that matter, had many did he himself have?

He stood, walked to the window, and looked out onto Gordon Avenue. It was quiet, tranquil even, and the old man smiled at the nighttime scene. So this was home, he thought, and he chuckled to himself. *Home*. The word was empty. Home wasn't a building, it was a state of mind, and since his wife had passed away this was no longer home. He turned back to watch his dog slowly rise to his feet. Maybe a late night walk, just so old Chalky could stretch his legs before bedtime, thought the old man. He grabbed his dog's leash, though he never needed it, and the Cairn terrier trotted to the front door for his evening foray into the quiet Gordonston night.

CHAPTER 8

Kelly Hudd had hardly slept at all. She couldn't remember being this excited in her whole life. It had reminded her of when she had been a child, at Christmas, waiting for Santa Claus to come down the chimney to leave gifts. She had stayed up all night one Christmas Eve, unable to sleep due to her excitement. Well, this morning felt like Christmas morning. She looked over to where Tom lay next to her, sleeping peacefully, blissfully unaware that he would be soon jetting off to Europe and the weekend of a lifetime.

The alarm clock was due to go off in the next five minutes, and Tom would wake thinking he was going to work, that it was just another normal day. Kelly could hardly wait. She was tempted to wake him before the alarm went off, but decided she would let him sleep; he looked so peaceful and content and a smile on his lips. She wondered what he was dreaming about. She hoped that his dream included her.

Just after he had fallen asleep she had secretly packed his suitcase and prepared his toiletries for the trip. The tickets had arrived yesterday via FedEx—two first-class tickets through New York in both their names. The thousand dollars worth of traveler's checks was also enclosed, plus an unlimited voucher for use at the hotel, including a top quality suite that had been reserved in Kelly's name. Kelly again thought about waking Tom, though this time in his favorite way, which would really give him something to smile about, and noticed that she had only one minute before the alarm went off. What the hell, thought Kelly, as she lowered the volume of the alarm clock and slid down her husband's body.

"I just had the strangest dream," said Tom, three minutes later, yawning and rubbing his eyes.

"Oh really," smiled Kelly, a mischievous look on her face.

"Yeah, I was dreaming about meeting Arnold Schwarzenegger. It was weird, sort of, well, embarrassing really. We were in a gym, working out together, we were bench pressing, you know, when suddenly, and for no reason, he . . . ."

Kelly raised her hand, indicating that Tom didn't need to continue with his story. She didn't need to hear how his dream had ended. She wiped the blonde hair from her face and adjusted it so it stopped falling forward onto her pretty features. "Well you had better get ready or we'll be late," she said, hoping that her excitement didn't show. She closed her eyes and grimaced, realizing that she had said "we" instead of "you." Kelly crossed her fingers hoping that her husband had not noticed her slip of the tongue.

Tom checked the time on the alarm clock with the time on his watch and sighed "Oh well. I suppose another day, another dollar." He smiled and kissed Kelly on the lips before exiting the bed. "Have you been eating peanuts?" he asked her. "I taste salt on your lips." Kelly shook her head and tried her best not to laugh.

The first clue Tom got that something was not quite normal was when he couldn't find his shower gel, nor could he locate his razor or shaving foam. He called out to Kelly from inside the shower but she did not hear him. It mildly irritated him when she moved things around like that. Luckily, there was soap and shampoo in the shower, so he had used those. In fact, there was a lot of every type of toiletry product in their bathroom: shampoos, conditioners, scrubs and cleansers, all perks of Kelly's job. He had found an old razor, one of his wife's that she used on her long legs, and shaved with that.

The second clue Tom got that something was not as it should be was the fact that Kelly herself was already out of bed and dressed. "Are you not showering?" asked Tom as he dried his hair with a towel.

"I have already. Before you got up," she said. "I've laid out the clothes you need to wear today. They are on the bed." Tom looked at the clothes on the bed: designer jeans, designer polo shirt—this was not the uniform of a Savannah fire fighter.

"Are you nuts?" he said, and playfully flicked the towel he had used to dry his hair in the direction of his wife's well-formed bottom.

"I can't see Captain O'Hare being too happy about me wearing *that* uniform at roll call," he laughed, pointing at the clothes laid out on the bed and imagined his fire chief's face on seeing one of his men dressed this way.

"Oh, I wouldn't worry about Brian. I have spoken to him, and he's fine about it," said Kelly attaching an earring to one ear.

"Oh, *Brian* is it?" joked Tom. "Well, it's Captain O'Hare to me, and that's very nice of you, but somehow I don't think so."

Kelly looked at her husband as she fiddled with her second earring before finally inserting it into her earlobe. "Call him if you don't believe me," she said, rising from the chair in front of her dressing table. She motioned to the phone on the bedside cabinet. Tom looked at his wife and tilted his head, in a way not too dissimilar to that of a dog confused or perturbed by a strange and unfamiliar object or situation.

"Are you serious? You spoke to the captain. O'Hare said I could have the day off?" Tom looked at the clothes on his bed and then at his wife.

"Not exactly," she replied. "More like *five* days off!" she cried and ran into his arms, which he opened. Still confused, he embraced his charging wife, lifted her off the ground and spun her around, confused by her excitement.

"Five days?" said Tom. "He gave me five days off. I don't believe it!" Tom swung his wife around one more time. "Are you serious? This isn't a joke is it?" he asked, suddenly concerned his wife was playing a practical joke on him.

"No, silly, I promise," smiled Kelly as she kissed her husband's still-wet lips as shower water dripped from his muscular body onto the floor. "Well," he said, as he removed the towel that was previously covering his manhood, "we should make the most of this and go back to bed." He gnawed playfully at his wife's neck.

"No!" she cried. "We can't. We haven't got time. Come on, hurry up and get dressed. Cindy will be here in a minute." Tom did as he was told, though he was still none the wiser as to what was going on. Cindy? Their neighbor? Why would she be coming over at this time in the morning?

As Tom finished dressing he could hear the sound of female voices coming from the kitchen. He looked for his favorite socks but couldn't find them—in fact he noticed that a lot of his clothes were missing.

"Good morning Cindy," he said as he walked into the kitchen. Cindy smiled at the handsome young man and instinctively adjusted her hair.

"Good morning to you," she replied, a smile spreading across her face. He poured himself a coffee from the pot made earlier by Kelly. As he walked to the table he noticed something different in the hallway. Two suitcases. Maybe Cindy was coming to stay; maybe there was something wrong with her house.

"You moving in, Cindy?" he asked as he pointed towards the suitcases by the door. He hadn't noticed that they were the suitcases he and Kelly had used for their last vacation to Florida.

"Oh no," laughed Cindy. For a moment she imagined living under the same roof as Tom, and she suddenly felt hot and flushed. She pushed the thought out of her head as quickly as it had entered. "I think they're yours." Tom looked at Kelly for clarification.

"That's right, Tom. They are our suitcases. I think you'd better sit down for a minute."

"Okay, I'm sitting down . . ."

"Listen, I wasn't joking before. Captain O' Hare has given you the green light. You have five days off. Well, six actually, but we only need five. Tom, I have a surprise for you."

Tom sat patiently at the kitchen table, anxious to hear his wife's news. "Cindy is going to take care of Shmitty, so you needn't worry about him." Tom looked at Cindy who nodded and smiled at the still-confused fire fighter. "You don't need to worry about spending money or hotel costs or anything like that because it is all taken care of." Kelly was smiling broadly, hardly able to contain her own excitement. "Tom, we are going to *Paris*," Kelly screamed. She jumped up and down and clapped her hands in exactly the same excited way she had done when she had discovered she had won the trip. "Oh my God!" she cried elatedly. "I'm going to Paris!" She placed her hands over her mouth as if curtailing a scream of delight.

Tom didn't respond. He raised his cup of coffee to his mouth and took a drink. He lowered his cup and then looked over to where the two packed suitcases sat. Ignoring his wife's uncontrolled whoops of delight and Shmitty's excited barking, brought about by his mistress' excitement. He shook his head slowly. He raised his cup once again to his mouth and took another sip of coffee before he spoke.

"There is only one problem," he said, raising his cup of coffee to his mouth. "I don't have a passport."

CHAPTER 9

Kelly cried all the way to the airport, all the way through check-in and during the flight to New York. She stopped crying long enough to board her flight to Paris, before she cried again. She was inconsolable. The stewardesses on both flights had tried their best to cheer the pretty but forlorn woman, but it was to no avail. She was inconsolable. What a disaster. It was a disaster of the largest magnitude. Kelly couldn't think of any other disaster worse than this. It was simply awful.

Tom and Kelly had spent at least half an hour arguing over whether or not she should go to Paris alone. She had said that there was no way she was going to go, without her husband, the man she loved. That was the whole point. It was why she had planned it this way: as a romantic surprise. How could she go alone? She would be miserable the whole time and would miss him too much. She would rather spend five days with him in Savannah than one day in Paris without him.

Cindy had agreed with Tom. It was the chance of a lifetime for Kelly. She had always dreamt of visiting Europe, especially Paris. She loved French fashions, French perfumes, French fries and was quite fond of Elliott's French poodles.

Tom told Kelly he was fine with her going alone, that it would be an absolute waste for her not to go. Cindy promised she would make sure Tom ate well and waved her off. Kelly's tears had started the moment Tom switched on the car engine and began the twenty-minute drive to the airport.

During the drive Tom had reassured his pretty bride. She was the one who had won the prize in the first place, and really, it wasn't a big deal. He told her he would be more devastated if she didn't go. In fact he said he would be more upset if she missed out on the trip of a lifetime because of his failure to own a passport.

She managed to stop crying at check-in, going straight to the front of the line, courtesy of her first-class ticket, but had burst into tears as soon at the girl at the check-in counter had wished her a great trip. Tom did his best to console her, and at one point while they were waiting in the atrium of the Savannah airport, prior to Kelly's security check, he considered taking her home. But he persevered through her sobbing and breathed a sigh of relief as she disappeared through the metal detectors of the security check area and into the area for those who possessed a boarding card.

Kelly's tears finally stopped as the Paris-bound aircraft took off. She had drifted off to sleep in the comfortable and spacious first-class seat. Her dreams had been filled with catwalks, photographers and flashing lights. The flight attendant assigned to Kelly's seating area in first class, placed a blanket around her and marveled at the smile on her face. Kelly's smile grew larger once she was gently awakened and informed the flight was entering French airspace and asked if she would like a drink.

It was at that moment that a young boy crept up from coach class and asked the flight attendants if he could get the autograph of the famous model who was sleeping in first class. Kelly had heard the young boy's request and watched as he was led through the cabin. Kelly sat up in her seat, trying to see where the model was. Wow, she thought, a famous model on the plane, I wonder who she is?

The small boy stopped when he reached Kelly's seat. He handed her a pen and a little red autograph book. "Could you sign it please?" he asked Kelly, a smile nearly as wide as the Atlantic itself spread across his face.

"Me?" said Kelly surprised. "Oh dear, I'm no one special, I'm just, well, me." Kelly smiled sweetly at the small boy. He didn't move. Instead he just pushed the pen and book further towards Kelly. She shrugged her shoulders and signed his book. She simply signed Kelly. He looked at her signature and his smile grew wider.

"Thank you," he said, and ran back to his section of the aircraft to show his most recent autograph to his parents.

That was just the start of it. The rumor spread around the first-class cabin that "Kelly" was on board. One passenger said he had read somewhere that she was a model off to Paris on a photo shoot. Another had heard she was on the way to Paris to film a commercial for jeans. Eventually Kelly even signed autographs for the pilot and co-pilots. A French passenger took her photograph and the flight attendants flitted around her for the last few minutes of the flight. When the aircraft eventually touched down on French soil, the air-crew arranged for her to leave the aircraft first, so she could avoid the crowds. She was ushered quickly through immigration and her bags were the first on the carousel. She was asked if the airline could provide a car for her, but Kelly had told them no, that would not be necessary. The prize had included a complimentary limousine transfer to the hotel from the airport. This added to the illusion that Kelly was a celebrity when the sleek black Mercedes pulled up to the curb. Kelly could hear the clicking of cameras, all aimed at her.

Kelly had to admit she was enjoying the attention. She hadn't lied to anyone; they had all just assumed that she was a famous model. Though her fans couldn't recall ever seeing Kelly in anything specific, they just knew she was famous. Flying first class, limousine at the airport—it all seemed to fit. Kelly was no longer crying. For the past hour she had forgotten about Tom and that he had no passport. After placing her small bag and suitcase in the trunk of the Mercedes, the limousine driver welcomed her to Paris. He said he hoped that she enjoyed her stay and remarked that the facilities at the Hotel Bonaparte were the best in the whole of Paris.

The drive from the airport to the Hotel Bonaparte took just under an hour. Kelly watched as suburban Paris turned into the city she had read so much about. It was a far cry from Savannah and Gordonston, though the tree-lined avenues reminded her a little of her neighborhood. Her limousine driver, Jean-Paul, pointed out various sights and places of interest during the fifty-five minute drive: the Eiffel Tower, the famous museums, and other monuments. Kelly smiled, but again her feeling of loneliness returned, and she fought back tears when she thought of how Tom would have loved to have seen what she was now seeing.

The Hotel Bonaparte was far more luxurious than Kelly could ever have imagined. The entrance seemed to Kelly to be more like that of a palace than a hotel. The tall columns that rose skyward to support the intricately painted ceilings seemed to come from below the marble-encased tiled floor. Plush red carpets led to the large reception desk. Antique-style furniture—chairs, sofas and chaises lounges—was sporadically but tastefully placed throughout the foyer. The hotel was vast, with signs pointing to restaurants, cafés, spas, and shops. There was even an Olympic-sized swimming pool housed within the walls of the gothic-style building. Kelly stood open-mouthed as bellboys attired in military-style uniforms carried bags and escorted guests to various locations within the hotel.

The reception area was alive with people. Elegantly dressed ladies, men in business suits and dinner jackets, and camera-laden tourists of all nationalities paraded through the reception area. Kelly breathed in her surroundings. She could smell the aroma of exquisitely cooked food coming from the hotel's three restaurants, one of which was the best in Paris. In one of Kelly's guidebooks it had even been touted as the best restaurant in the world. Even Conrad Brown, the famous food critic, had given the food five of his coveted stars. To her right, as she traveled along the red carpet towards reception, she could see boutique windows that formed a parade of hotel shops, selling jewels, watches, designer clothes and handbags. Goods with names that she recognized from magazines—Hermes, Rolex, and Cartier—were on display at prices that only those who didn't have to worry about paying the rent every month could afford. She had never seen such a place before. There was certainly nothing like it in Savannah.

Jean-Paul had informed Kelly that he would ensure that her bags were sent to her room and that all she needed to do was present herself to reception. She thanked her driver for his welcome and for the tour he had given her en route. He bowed and wished her a happy stay in Paris. Before he left her he told Kelly the hotel was expecting her and they were honored to have her as a guest.

The pretty receptionist who greeted Kelly spoke perfect English, and her smile seemed painted on. "But where is Monsieur Hudd?" she asked, a hint of concern in her voice, as she handed Kelly her room key and various pieces of literature containing information about the many amenities the hotel had to offer. Kelly fought back the tears and composed herself before replying. "I am afraid he couldn't make it," Kelly took a deep breath, she could feel herself about to cry. "He didn't have a passport, so I'm here all on my own."

Kelly burst into tears as soon as the words had left her mouth. The receptionist looked concerned and left her position behind the reception desk and joined Kelly in the reception area. She placed her arm around the crying American.

"Oh please, Madame, please don't cry," said the concerned receptionist. Kelly blew into her handkerchief.

"I am sorry," Kelly said. "It's just that I miss my husband so much, and I am so sad he is missing all this." Kelly once again blew into her handkerchief as she indicated with her other hand the hotel scene.

"Can I be of any assistance?" Kelly looked to see where the voice had come from. The man wore a blazer similar to that of the receptionist, who still comforted her. "My name is Henri Dubois, and I am the head concierge of the Hotel," announced the large man. Henri nodded at the receptionist who returned to her post behind the reception desk. "Please, allow me, Madam," said Henri, offering Kelly a fresh handkerchief, the hotel's motif of a crown entwined with roses stitched into the cotton.

Henri was an older man; probably in his late fifties, supposed Kelly. He reminded her of her Uncle Rick. He was tall and large, not fat, just big, and he looked friendly. She knew straight away he was her friend.

"Would you care to explain to me why such a beautiful young woman as you, Madame, in the most beautiful city in the world, at the most beautiful hotel in the world, is so distraught?" asked Henri kindly. So, Kelly told him. Henri listened to her story intently. Nodding and shaking his head, smiling and looking up to the sky, Henri followed Kelly's story. After Kelly had finished her tale of woe, she wiped away her tears with the handkerchief Henri had given her. She offered it back to him but he shook his head.

"Please, keep it," the Frenchman said smiling.

Just talking about Tom and how she missed him, had made her feel better, and she blew her nose into her new handkerchief

"Your husband is a very lucky man indeed," announced Henri once Kelly had finished speaking, "to have such a beautiful and caring wife such as you." Kelly flashed a smile at Henri. "But, I am sure he would be heartbroken if he knew that his pretty bride was so sad. I think the best tribute to your absent husband is for you to make the most of your time in our wonderful city and enjoy all it has to offer." He smiled kindly. "I will make it my personal mission to ensure you enjoy your stay in Paris," continued Henri.

Kelly smiled back. Henri was right. Tom would be distraught if he knew she was crying like this in front of total strangers, even if they were the nicest strangers she had ever met. She vowed then and there that she would forget about Tom's passport and just enjoy herself.

Henri clicked his fingers and a bellboy arrived. "Françoise will take you to your suite." Henri informed Kelly, "You have a beautiful suite, and I just know you will enjoy your stay with us here at the Hotel Bonaparte." Kelly thanked the concierge, who made her promise again that she would not cry anymore while she was a guest in his city. He told her that if she needed anything she should see him, and if he she couldn't find him then to send one of the bellboys to find him.

Françoise led Kelly to the elevator, and as she waited for the elevator doors to swish open she waved at both Henri and the friendly receptionist. Henri looked across to where the receptionist stood; he shrugged and winked at the pretty girl who smiled back at him as Kelly disappeared behind the closed elevator door.

The suite was spectacular. It had four rooms, and was the best the hotel had to offer. As soon as Kelly walked through the door she was in a spacious sitting room. Antique furniture and ornately decorated objects were elegantly placed throughout the room, and there were sumptuous rugs underfoot. Original artwork painted centuries ago filled the walls, and a large crystal chandelier hung from the ceiling. Françoise led Kelly through the sitting room and showed her the rest of the suite. The bed was the biggest she had ever seen; it could have slept Tom, Shmitty and her three times over. It had a canopy fit for a princess, was made up with silk sheets and adorned with fluffy soft pillows. Kelly ran her finger along the sheets and then pushed down on one of the pillows; it was the softest she had ever felt. The bathroom was also enormous, five times the size of the one in her home in Gordonston. The gold taps sparkled as Françoise switched on the light and he explained to Kelly how the whirlpool in the corner bath worked. He showed her where all the switches were and told her that instructions were printed in English in her welcome documents, which she would find in the top drawer of her dressing table. The bath was the biggest she had ever seen, and Kelly estimated at least four people could have bathed together in it. A smile formed on her lips as she imagined herself, Tom and Shmitty, all splashing around in the bath.

François could see that the young woman was impressed but had saved the best for last. He led Kelly back to the sitting room and flung open the double doors that led onto the balcony. The view was breathtaking. From her balcony she could see the whole of the Paris skyline. It had to have been one of the best views of Paris, and it was hers. Kelly put her hand to her mouth. "Oh my God!" she said. "This is fantastic."

Françoise nodded, indicating that he agreed with her statement. The balcony had a small table with two chairs in the corner. "It is a great place to take breakfast," he said. "You can smell Paris from here, feel its character, hear the traffic and enjoy the hustle and bustle of the streets. It is the best room in the hotel." François handed Kelly the keys to her room and bid her goodnight. As he was about to leave the room her bags arrived, courtesy of a second bellboy. She told them both goodnight and offered them five dollars each as a tip. They smiled at her gratefully. "Madame," said François, "please, your gratuity is not needed. It is my pleasure to have been in the company of such a beautiful woman. It is I who should be paying you."

Kelly thanked François for his compliment and once again bade him and his fellow bellboy goodnight. Kelly's mood had improved greatly, in part due to the kindness of the hotel staff. But her spirits had been lightened most by the room. She felt like a queen. She hadn't noticed before, but a bottle of champagne sat chilling in a silver ice bucket on one of the tables in the sitting room area, along with a basket of delicious looking fruit. She read the note that accompanied the bottle of chilled champagne. "Welcome to our honored guests, Mr. and Mrs. Hudd. Enjoy your stay at the Hotel Bonaparte."

A few minutes earlier Kelly would have burst into tears if she had seen a note welcoming her and Tom to the hotel. It would have reminded her that Tom was missing their romantic trip. It surprised her when she realized the welcoming note hadn't made her feel sad. She was here and Tom wasn't, there was nothing she could do about that now, and she was determined to make the most of her trip.

Kelly had no idea what time it was in Savannah. In Paris it was nearly ten, and she was tired. She took a shower; she would wait to use the bath until morning when she could soak without fear of falling asleep. She climbed into bed and picked up the phone on the bedside table. The phone rang for what seemed ages before a tired and confused sounding Tom picked up.

"Hello," he said.

"Hello, honey," Kelly said.

"Hey. What time is it there?" Tom asked.

"Eleven. Why? What time is it there?"

"Five in the morning," said Tom. Kelly heard a click in the background, which she guessed was Tom switching on the bedside light. "Yeah, it's five," he said yawning.

"I'm sorry," said Kelly. "Did I wake you?" It was obvious that she had, and Tom ignored her question.

"How is it? How was the flight? And how's the hotel?"

Kelly explained to Tom about the flight and how she had been mistaken for a model. She also described the luxurious hotel and her room. She told him about Henri and François and how kind everyone had been to her.

"Well, that sounds great," Tom said, pleased that his wife was having such a good time.

"I wish you were here, Tom," said Kelly, sadness filling her voice.

"I know, honey," he said, "but the fact you are having such a good time makes me feel great. You know it means more to me, you being happy, than anything else."

Kelly smiled. "I know. And I promise I will have fun."

"Good," said Tom. "Make sure you do."

Kelly said goodnight, even though it was morning in Savannah, and Tom promised to take Shmitty on a long walk in the park later. She told him she loved him and fell asleep minutes later.

Kelly slept in until ten the following morning. When she awoke she headed to the bathroom and began to fill the enormous tub with warm water. François had told her it took fifteen minutes to fill so she decided she would take breakfast on her balcony. She called room service and ordered coffee, orange juice and toast to be delivered to her room. It arrived quickly, and the waiter placed the tray of food and pot of coffee on the balcony table. She thanked her waiter and signed the slip of paper he put in front of her indicating she had received her breakfast, and then Kelly sat back in her seat and took in the Paris view.

François had been right. The sounds of the Paris morning filled her balcony, not loudly but as if a background tape were playing street sounds. It was a gentle sound, car horns, the ringing of bicycle bells, and the chatter of voices. This was how she had always imagined Paris would sound. The temperature was milder than Savannah's. It was a beautiful day, and she felt that she was the luckiest woman alive.

After eating her breakfast, Kelly took a two-hour bath. It was the most fantastic bath she had ever taken. She had taken a Jacuzzi, too. She felt exhilarated. The hotel had provided the best bath salts. Kelly recognized the brand name, one she sold herself, but one that, even with her store discount, she couldn't afford.

After her bath she unpacked her suitcase and chose an outfit for the day. She then pampered herself with moisturizers and other products she had brought with her. The hotel had provided a hairdryer in the room and she did her hair. The outfit she had chosen for the day was simple but sexy. It didn't matter what she wore. She looked good in most things, especially in this pair of figure-hugging dark trousers, with a slight flare at the bottom, matching sandals and a pink blouse.

It was already three o'clock in the afternoon by the time she made her way down to the reception area. The same receptionist who had been on duty the night before greeted Kelly. Today Kelly's mind was clearer, and she noticed the girl's name tag. Naomi happily assisted Kelly in changing her traveler's checks into Euros. Kelly thanked Naomi when she complimented her outfit. Naomi, who knew Kelly had won her hotel stay in a competition, asked if she were a model in America. Kelly smiled and said she wasn't. As she made her way to the hotel doors, nearly every man turned to watch her walk by. It was something Kelly was used to in Savannah but somehow the attention felt more meaningful in Paris.

When she reached the exit of the hotel she recognized Henri behind his desk near the door. "Good morning, Madame," said Henri as he rose from his seat. "I have to say you look absolutely divine today," he bowed his head.

"Thank you," Kelly replied to the concierge's compliment.

"And where are you headed, this fine and wondrous Paris day?" asked Henri. "If I can be of any assistance, please let me know."

Kelly told Henri that she was going to take a stroll, look around Paris before maybe returning to the hotel to take dinner in the restaurant.

Henri raised his hand. "I shall reserve you a table. The best table, just in case you do decide to dine here. There is a big conference in the city over the weekend - high-powered businessmen and bankers. The hotel is fully booked and reservations for the restaurant are in great demand. I will make sure that no matter what, there is always a table available for you." Kelly thanked Henri and walked out into the Paris sunlight.

The Hotel Bonaparte was located in the center of Paris on the right bank of the Seine. Within minutes Kelly was strolling along the famous Champs-Élysées. She headed along the avenue, joining the thousands of office workers, visitors, shoppers, street sweepers, tree-fixers, Japanese businesspeople, school children, petty functionaries, *flics*, illegal parkers, aging movie stars, and pickpockets that were on hand to bask, gawk, snap photos of each other, window shop, dine or partake of coffee in one of the many cafés and bars that lined the well-known thoroughfare.

Kelly decided to head west, and walked alongside the river heading towards the Place de la Concorde. She had done some research on her destination before she had left Savannah and, accompanied by her guide books, she wanted to soak in as much of the Parisian atmosphere as she could, and see as many famous sites as she could possibly manage. The buildings, the people, the whole experience were just as she had imagined. Though still a little saddened by Tom's absence, she was now steadfastly determined to enjoy her brief stay in France.

She window-shopped and smiled and greeted passersby's. She was in heaven as she traversed the Place de la Concorde which separates the Tuileries Gardens from the beginning of the Champs-Élysées. Kelly arrived parched and in need of refreshment. She had already walked several miles, and it was fast approaching five o'clock. The Paris early evening was a pleasant one, and as she continued her walk westwards she passed bars and cafés full of couples, families, men and women of all shapes and sizes from all over the world. Kelly had noticed that the French men were not like the men back at home in Savannah. While Kelly at first had enjoyed the attention and wolf whistles she had received, it was now becoming boring and slightly annoying to her. Each time she passed a café with tables on the street, the waiters and male patrons would all stop and stare at her. Some would even whistle and shout at her in French, which of course she didn't understand. It was something that she was not used to and she wished Tom was with her. She was sure that those guys would have thought twice about ogling her and cat-calling her if she had been accompanied by her strapping husband.

Kelly had severely underestimated the time it would take for her to walk to her initial destination goal from the hotel. She had hoped to get back to the hotel for dinner. Suddenly thirsty, she decided that she would stop at the first bar or café that appealed to her. After just a few more yards she reached one that seemed fine.

Le Café Papillion was named after its owner, Jean Claude Papillion. It was a small place, tables covered with pristine white clothes both inside the café and outside along the famous Avenue. A red awning that provided welcome shade from the sun was pulled out over the outdoor dining area. In truth, the heat was not at all that bad, and the sun was actually beginning to set, the glow of the sky indicating that tomorrow was going to be another glorious day.

Kelly found an empty table outside and took a seat. It felt good to rest after her long walk. The setting sun had turned the sky orange and she delved into her purse and placed her sunglasses on her head. She relaxed. It had been a wonderful day, and she leaned back in her chair, soaking the atmosphere.

"Bonjour," said the waiter who appeared at her table dressed in black trousers, white shirt and black bow tie with a white apron covering his clothing. He had a white cloth draped over his arm and carried a small silver tray, just like in the movies, thought Kelly, smiling.

"Hello," she replied to the young waiter, who Kelly guessed was of Arabic origin. "Un Coca Cola, please," she said. "Diet?" she added, hoping her waiter would understand her.

"English?" asked the waiter. Kelly smiled and shook her head.

"American," she replied. The waiter nodded.

"Okay, Mademoiselle, one diet coke coming up," he said in perfect English. Kelly was relieved that her waiter spoke English and thanked him. Thirty seconds later he returned with her glass of coke. She thanked him once again as he placed the glass on her table. She looked up at him and noticed that he had not returned to her table alone.

Next to him, with his hands on his hips was a larger man, older; probably, Kelly thought, in his late fifties. He was dressed in a black pinstripe suit and had the biggest knot in his red tie that Kelly had ever seen. He had a large and bushy moustache, which seemed to cover half his face. His whiskers appeared to have been waxed, and it looked as if the rather odd-looking man had styled his facial hair to curl and weave around his lip. She had noticed him behind the bar when she arrived, catching a glimpse of him before she had taken her seat; he had been wiping glasses and generally tidying up the bar area. She had noticed him stare at her but had ignored him. He was only one among the many who had stared all day. It was still disconcerting, though, thought Kelly, having the man stand at her table, his hands still on his hips, just staring at her. Kelly felt embarrassed and a little uncomfortable.

"You are an American, yes?" asked the mustached man once the waiter had departed Kelly's table.

"Yes," answered Kelly, taking a closer look at the man towering above her, unsure who he was and what it was he wanted.

"You are model, I think. I see many pretty girls, but you are prettiest I have ever seen. You are model, no?" asked the man, in English, though not as flowing English as her waiter's but Kelly could still understand him. He smiled underneath his facial hair, displaying teeth that seemed to be all accounted for.

Kelly smiled; he was just being friendly. It was a nice compliment and his broken English was sweet.

"My name is Jean Claude Papillion," announced the man. "In English I am the 'butterfly'," he continued, "but look at me, I am no butterfly. I am a slug." He laughed at his joke and patted his large stomach and Kelly had to laugh. "This is my little bar. I am the owner of this fine establishment, and it is an honor for me that you have chosen my humble café to rest and take refreshment." Kelly took the man's outstretched hand and shook it. Once again she relaxed. He was friendly, and she liked the chubby, strange-looking café owner.

"So for you, because you are a famous model, the drinks here are free all night. Anything you want, on the home," announced Jean Claude. He raised his finger. "I mean on the house. Sorry for my English. I learn from a book."

Kelly thanked Jean Claude for his offer and tried to protest but he would not hear of it. He explained, in broken English, that just having her sitting at his café was payment enough, and he insisted she drink for free. It seemed that like her fellow passengers on the flight over to France, Jean Claude was convinced Kelly was a famous catwalk fashion model, and the mere fact that she was sitting outside his bar would mean trade would increase ten-fold.

Once again Kelly enjoyed the experience of being mistaken for a famous model, and she liked the fact that Jean Claude and her waiter, Thierry, fawned over her. She decided she would play along with them. What harm could it do? No one knew who she really was, and it seemed to her that people actually wanted her to be famous; she got the feeling it made them feel good. She sipped her Diet Coke and smiled. She even signed an autograph for Thierry when he returned with a refill. As she imagined what she might do the next day, she noticed a small, dirty looking boy walking along the avenue. He was handing out flyers and depositing them on the tables of the cafés that lined the pavement. When he reached Jean Claude's café and Kelly's table in particular, he smiled at her. She smiled back. The small boy placed a flyer on her table and continued his way eastwards, dispensing his literature as he went.

Kelly picked up the flyer, which was on an orange letter-sized sheet of paper. She read the text, which was printed in English, French and an Asian language—probably Japanese, she thought. She smiled as she read the pamphlet. Was it a joke?

Thierry joined her at the side of her table. "I think it is a joke," he said, peering at the flyer in Kelly's hand. "I think that students maybe send them out. Who knows?" he shrugged his shoulders and deposited bowls of fresh olives and nuts onto Kelly's table. "Monsieur Papillion offers you some snacks," he said indicating to the bowls. Kelly thanked Thierry, folded the flyer and placed it in her purse. She would show Tom when she returned home. It would make him laugh.

CHAPTER 10

Kelly felt different. Maybe it was because everyone thought that she was famous. She had a new air of confidence about her. She began to enjoy the nudges wives would give husbands and vice versa when they walked past her table. She began to enjoy the autographs she was giving out, which she simply signed "Kelly". She felt calm. If this is what it was like to be a famous model, then she liked it.

She had forgotten about her disappointment at being alone. It was hard to believe that Kelly was actually the same girl as the tear-drenched and forlorn woman who had flown into Paris first class the day before. She was having fun. Jean Claude ensured that Kelly had a full glass of Diet Coke and even sent over some hot food to accompany the snacks. Though Kelly didn't like the look or sound of escargot, she tried them anyway. She was simply having the most perfect time of her life. She forgot about Tom—not completely, but enough so that her stomach didn't knot when she thought about her husband stuck back in Savannah, probably bored to death.

She noticed the young man the moment he had arrived at the Café Papillion. He had taken the last empty table outside, further along the avenue from where Kelly sat. As it was a pleasant evening, it hadn't taken long for the café to fill. Throngs of tourists mingled with Parisians. The fact that a well-known model had been spotted along the Champs-Élysées that evening had attracted a larger than normal crowd to Jean Claude Papillion's small café. The young man that Kelly had seen arrive—behind her sunglasses so he wouldn't see her watching—was lucky to have gotten that last table, thought Kelly as he raised his hand to try and attract the attention of the now very busy Thierry.

The man was neither as handsome nor as athletic as Tom, but there was something attractive about him, thought Kelly as she covertly watched the new arrival. He seemed to know Thierry very well, as they had exchanged a handshake on his arrival and conversed for a few moments, laughing and joking with each other. The man was about medium height, clean-shaven and slimly built. He was dressed in a cream suit, which looked expensive, thought Kelly, over a plain white T-shirt and sunglasses that were perched on top of his head even though the sun had set hours before. Kelly remembered her own sunglasses and thought that maybe she should remove them; wearing them at night was not something she supposed even a supermodel would do. She perched them on her head in the same fashion as the new arrival.

She inspected the man further, now that her vision was not darkened by her sunglasses. She had a better view, although she maintained her discretion. He had a tousled mop of curly brown hair, cut short on his head, and he was well tanned. Kelly imagined he was Spanish or Italian, maybe even Greek. There was something about him, something mysterious, and something almost regal. He seemed to possess an air of authority, very impressive, especially for someone so young. Kelly guessed he must have been around her age or maybe a couple of years younger. She sensed something else about him: he looked wealthy. It just seemed as though he had money: the way he acted, the way he sat, and even the way he drank gave the impression that he was rich.

Thierry brought the newcomer a drink. Kelly saw that they exchanged a few words, and it seemed Thierry was very pleased with the tip he had just received. Thierry, upon leaving the man's table, proceeded towards Kelly's table, where he placed another drink in front of her.

"Count Enrico de Cristo wanted to buy you a drink, so I get you a Diet Coke, but I added a little brandy, I hope you don't mind," said Thierry, nodding in the direction of the man in the cream suit. Kelly smiled, the drinks were, of course, free, and she wondered how much Thierry would make out of her being there that evening. Not that she minded that the young waiter was profiting from her presence. She smiled at the man, sitting five tables down and he returned the smile. A count, like Dracula maybe, she thought? So she had been right, there was something regal about him. She watched him watch her as she sipped her brandy and coke. Thierry had mixed the drink well, as there was just a smidgen of alcohol in the drink, which suited Kelly.

She guessed that Count Enrico de Cristo was probably a regular patron of the Café Papillion. He seemed relaxed and blended in well with the Parisian evening. Kelly closed her eyes. She was sure it would only be a matter of time before he introduced himself.

"Buon giorno, Signorina," said the cream-suited man as he approached her table and bowed his head, clicking the heels of his expensive looking shoes as he did. Kelly had seen this sort of thing in the movies; she had never dreamt that people actually really acted this way. "My name is Count Enrico de Cristo. I hope you do not mind this intrusion." He held out his hand, and Kelly extended hers. Instead of shaking it he pulled her hand to his lips and kissed it gently before stroking her wrist tenderly. His touch was soft and gentle. She thought that maybe she should withdraw her hand, but she enjoyed his touch.

"My dear lady, I have traveled many places in the world, seen many beautiful things—the Pyramids of Cairo, the Trevi Fountain in my home city of Rome, the Mona Lisa here in Paris, the mystifying plains of Africa, the sun setting on a paradise Isle in the Caribbean. I have marveled at the beauty of the Taj Mahal and wandered through an English dale in springtime. But I have never before seen such beauty as I see before me now." He released her hand and Kelly was disappointed when he laid her hand down on the table.

His voice was heavily accented. Even though he spoke impeccable English it was obvious that he was European. His voice reminded Kelly of the old black and white movies her mother used to watch late at night, with exotic sounding men always eventually seducing their leading ladies.

"What, if I may be so bold, is such a beautiful lady like yourself doing alone in such a city of romance?" he asked, his Italian accent as smooth as it was full of passion. Kelly didn't know what to say. She couldn't admit to working in Macy's in the Oglethorpe Mall along Abercorn Street. Not after *that* introduction. Not after signing all those autographs and especially not after all the free drinks she had been receiving from Monsieur Papillion. She crossed her fingers before she spoke.

"I'm over here doing a photo shoot. I'm a model and I have been working all week. This is my first night off. I'm from Texas, in America," she lied. Why she had chosen Texas she didn't know. Texas? It had just come out of her mouth. And why had she felt the need to tell the Count that Texas was in America? Kelly guessed that not many people out of the States had heard of Savannah but was sure that they would have heard of Texas. Anyway, didn't Jerry Hall hail from Texas?

"And you?" Kelly asked the smiling count, hoping that he hadn't been offended by her assumption that the count might not realize that Texas was indeed part of the United States. The count's smile grew bigger. "First of all, may I say that I guessed you were either a model or an actress? You have what the French say, a certain *je ne sais quoi.*" Kelly could feel herself blushing; she had never received so many compliments at one time, not even from Tom.

"I am a mere count, of Veronese descent; you could say that I am an International businessman, I enjoy traveling, so I have many ventures around the world, and I am here in Paris only for the weekend, again for business, though I am lucky today for my business is over and I do not return to Rome until Sunday. I suppose that I have luck twice today," he added as their eyes met. His deep blue eyes seemed to pierce her skull; she felt butterflies in her stomach. What was wrong with her? This man, superficially at least, was not a patch on Tom. Tom was far better looking and built like a movie star. Maybe it was the Paris night or his wealth or accent or even just the fact that she was alone in a foreign country, but whatever it was she found herself drawn to him. She breathed in the smell of his cologne. She was enjoying this. She felt different, special, and it was as if Savannah had suddenly ceased to exist.

"My dear," said the Count, "I know not your name, please. You may call me Enrico, but what may I call you?" he asked, as Thierry brought over more drinks. Kelly thought for a moment. She didn't want to lie, but she needed to sound like a model. She looked around before replying.

"Jerri, my name is Jerri Gordonston," she said as she fondled the glass that contained her Coca-Cola and brandy. The count acted as if he recognized the name and Kelly was sure she could see him thinking hard before dismissing it. Maybe there was a real Jerry Gordonston; Kelly hoped not, and almost immediately she wished she had thought up a better alias.

They talked for hours. She explained how she had arrived earlier that week to pose for a famous French photographer. She made up another name, and Pepe Le Clic had been the first thing that popped into her head. The moment she said the ridiculous sounding name she regretted it. Luckily the Count just nodded. Either the name wasn't as stupid as she feared or maybe he just didn't hear. She had appeared in many magazines worldwide but was not in the supermodel category, at least not yet anyway. She was hoping to branch out into acting. She would be flying back to Texas, via New York, early Monday morning. Her agent had booked her into a catwalk show; otherwise she would have extended her stay in the Paris. It was her first time in Paris, and no, she didn't have a boyfriend or husband. She just wore the wedding ring to fend off men who gave her unwanted attention.

Kelly had no idea why she had said that. She had no reason to lie. She just thought that it was more plausible that a top model not be married. She regretted it the moment she said it. How could she have said she wasn't married? She loved Tom. She felt awful. Despite her regret about lying, she had plenty of opportunity to change her story, to get up and walk back to the hotel. But she didn't. Instead, she stayed where she was and listened to the count's story.

Count Enrico de Cristo was only twenty-six. He had inherited the title from his father who had died recently, leaving his businesses in the hands of his only son. He owned homes in Rome and Geneva. His businesses were mainly based around the manufacturing of clothes. He had factories in Rome and Milan that made suits and eveningwear to be distributed to the larger, better-known fashion houses, which branded them with their own labels. He also had an interest in several finance companies. His great passions were the casinos of Monaco and sailing. His yacht was at the moment undergoing a minor refit in Barcelona and he enjoyed nothing better than sailing to Monaco to play the tables at the famous casinos of Monte Carlo. Due to his traveling and business ventures he had had little time for girlfriends, though he had once briefly dated an Italian soap star and the Italian tabloids had followed and photographed the couple for months. Eventually, according to the count, the relationship ended due to the pressures of their celebrity. His great love was his mother and, like Kelly, he would love to stay longer in Paris but had promised the old lady he would fly back to Rome on Sunday to be at her side for evening mass.

It was just after ten o'clock when the count invited Kelly to dine with him. Neither of them was particularly hungry so he suggested something light, maybe a pizza. He knew of a great pizzeria, not far away, which did the most spectacular food.

Kelly considered the count's invitation. The evening had flown by all too quickly for Kelly and she really should be heading back to the hotel. Tom was expecting her to call. "I would love to dine with you," said Kelly as the count moved her chair from under the table to assist her rising. The count left a fifty-euro note on the table for Thierry. Both Thierry and Jean Claude Papillion bade them farewell. Jean Claude insisted that a photograph be taken of him and Kelly together before she left with the count.

They shared a pizza and continued their talking. Kelly didn't want the night to end; they ordered the house wine and chatted until two a.m., the pizza only half eaten. At one stage it seemed they were going to kiss, and after a lull in the conversation their eyes met once again, and she willed him to move his head towards her. But he was a gentleman. He offered to walk her back to her hotel but she said she was fine, so they arranged to meet early the next morning under the Eiffel Tower, where they would begin a day of sightseeing in Paris together. The count hailed a cab for Kelly. She just said "Hotel Bonaparte" to her driver and he nodded and sped away.

That night she could hardly sleep. She had never experienced anything like this before. An Italian count with a yacht and houses around the world was interested in her, although she was just a simple girl who worked behind the beauty counter at Macy's. She had begun to believe her own lies and had convinced herself that she was indeed a model. That night she dreamt of Enrico, of yachts, of show business parties, of diamonds, racehorses and champagne. It was only when she awoke did she realize she had forgotten one thing. Tom.

She grabbed the telephone at the side of her bed and dialed home. Tom answered immediately. "Tom," she said, hoping she didn't sound too guilty. Not that she had anything to be guilty about. She hadn't done anything wrong—just shared a pizza and a few drinks with a new friend.

"Huh?" said Tom, sounding as if he were half asleep.

"Tom it's me, Kelly. Are you in bed?" she asked, remembering that the telephone at her home was placed by the bed and for Tom to answer as quickly as he had, would mean he was lying in bed.

"Kelly? What time is it?" he asked, as if just rising.

"It's eight in the morning here, so I guess two in the afternoon there. Are you still in bed?" she asked, curious as to why her husband was still sleeping.

"No, silly. It's three in the morning. How is everything? Are you enjoying yourself?" Tom seemed to be regaining his senses from the initial shock of his abrupt awakening.

"Yes, it is wonderful here. I miss you, though," said Kelly

"I miss you, too," replied Tom. Kelly could hear the ruffling of sheets, and swore she could hear someone else breathing, and maybe a cough. It was as if Tom wasn't lying in bed alone.

"Is someone else there?" asked Kelly, not wanting to sound concerned. The truth was, she was very concerned and wanted to know what was going on in her absence.

Tom laughed at the other end of the line. "Only Shmitty. He jumped up next to me. He's on your side of the bed. I think he's missing you as much as I am. That's him you hear." Kelly felt awful. How could she suspect that her husband would be in bed with anyone else? What sort of woman was she? She felt bad, guilty and unworthy. It was she who had come close to kissing the count the previous evening. She suppressed her guilty feelings and carried on the conversation.

"Well, tell Shmitty I miss him too, will you." Tom promised he would, and before hanging up the line they each said 'I love you' five times.

After she hung up the telephone Kelly showered and dressed, finding the shortest skirt and the tightest top she had packed and made her way to reception. Henri, the concierge, greeted her as she entered the hotel lobby. "Good morning, Mademoiselle," he said. He tried hard to avert his gaze from Kelly's long and tanned legs, but somehow, as if he had no control over his own head, his eyes wandered back to them. Kelly smiled inwardly. If she were having this effect on old Henri, how would the count be able to resist her?

Henri hailed her taxi, which wasn't a difficult task as every cab made a beeline straight to the hotel once they saw Kelly exit the building. The ride didn't take long. and she arrived at the Eiffel Tower by nine. The count was waiting for her.

She knew that she looked good. She was wearing sunglasses and looked for all the world like a movie star. The count smiled as she approached. He was attired just as elegantly as the previous night. He wore a different suit, though the same style, this one dark blue. His sunglasses were over his eyes and he wore a black t-shirt under the single-breasted jacket. He kissed her on the cheek, just as he had done last night when they had parted and returned to their respective hotels.

"You look beautiful, like a Goddess. I am speechless. It is an honor for me to spend the day with such beauty. I thank you for brightening up my day." Maybe Kelly was getting used to the compliments or maybe she was just getting used to the count, but either way she didn't blush. She complimented him on his own outfit and thanked him again for such a wonderful evening the previous night.

Their first stop that day would be the tower that stood behind them. They would, however, take breakfast first. They ordered croissants, though while the count drank coffee, Kelly sipped fresh orange juice. They resumed their conversation of the previous evening. Kelly had been explaining how hard it was being a model and that though she had done a shoot for Vogue only a few months ago the traveling was difficult. The count was very interested in listening to all she said. The lies came easily for Kelly. Modeling had been her dream, and she had read all about the different locations and how photo shoots worked. After a while it didn't feel like she was lying; she actually believed that she was a model. And why shouldn't she be? she thought. If a man like the count could be interested in her then there must be something special about her.

After they ate breakfast they proceeded to the tower. She did not realize it at first. It was only when they got to the turnstile to pay that she noticed. They had been holding hands.

The Eiffel Tower was how Kelly had always dreamt it would be. It was a clear day, and she could see the whole of Paris. The count explained what spires belonged to which church and which building was what on the horizon spread before them.

The next place to visit on their list was the Church of the Sacré Coeur. They made their way through the back streets until they reached the old church. He explained its history, and they marveled at its architecture. The count suggested they visit Notre Dame next, and it was then that Kelly nearly blew it.

At first she thought she might have misheard him. Why would they want to see a football game, especially at that time in the morning? She said nothing at first, but when he mentioned it again she had asked, "Who are they playing?"

He looked at her, a puzzled expression on his face. Then he laughed. "You are not only such a gorgeous creature but you are also very funny. Come my dear, let's take the Metro." He grabbed her hand and off they rushed. When they arrived at the old church she could have died. What a fool! She hadn't realized that Notre Dame was actually a real place and not just a football team. The count pronounced the words in an unusual way, but she kept her trap shut; he couldn't help being foreign. Anyway, the count was convinced she had only been joking with him earlier, and she had bluffed it off. It had been a close call.

They lunched at a curbside café not unlike the Café Papillion, and decided their next place to see must be the Louvre. Kelly was mesmerized by the paintings and sculptures, and when they reached the Mona Lisa she let out a squeal of familiarity. Of course she had seen the painting on TV many a time, but here she was, face to face with the enigmatic features of Da Vinci's most well known model. She turned to the count; he too was spellbound by the paining.

"It is beautiful," she said.

"Like you," he replied.

The kiss had been expected. She fell into his arms and their tongues entwined. Kelly knew what she was doing was wrong but didn't care. The count suggested that they abandon their tour and return to his hotel. She suggested hers, and the count agreed with her that it would be better as it were nearer.

Henri greeted Kelly and the count as she entered the hotel lobby. He looked the count up and down and smiled politely. Luckily, room service had already cleaned Kelly's room and the count was mightily impressed with the room and the view.

It was an afternoon of pure passion. She had never felt this way with Tom. The sex had just been a small part of it. The tenderness he showed, his accent, his whole persona had made her tremble. After they had made love they lay in each other's arms and slept. When they awoke they made love again. They forgot about dinner and instead made love for a fifth, sixth and seventh time. She was in ecstasy. They slept through until the following morning, holding each other tightly as they slept.

The sunlight seeped through the center gap of the curtains and the sun's rays flooded the palatial room. Kelly awoke and looked at her watch. She thought about calling Tom but decided against it. How could she call him with another man in her bed? She looked over at the count as he lay sleeping. She kissed him on the cheek and fell back to sleep. Kelly slept well for another hour. When she awoke this time it was the count that was watching her sleep. He smiled at the woman next to him.

"I have to go," he whispered and kissed her on the lips. "I must return to Rome today, to be with my mother. I have chartered a jet I cannot cancel, and though it pains me, my dear, I have to leave you." Kelly nodded. They both knew their romance was over. Brief and passionate, not quick and sordid, was how she would remember it. She watched as the count dressed. She would miss him, but she had a life at home, and it was impossible to carry on the lie so she didn't offer him any way of finding her. She kissed him once more and mouthed "goodbye" before eventually closing the door of the room and returning to bed.

She slept for a few more hours and when she awoke again, bathed and took a shower. Somehow she felt the need to cleanse herself. She tried to forget him, but the smell of his fragrance lingered in the air. She knew she should really call Tom but couldn't bring herself to do it. She was already missing the count and wished he could have stayed the rest of the day.

Kelly spent the rest of the day sightseeing the monuments and churches still not scratched off her list. She felt lonely traveling around Paris without the count at her side; everywhere she turned she thought she had seen him. As hard as she tried, she couldn't get the count out of her mind. She returned to the hotel exhausted. Henri recommended that she eat in the hotel restaurant, as it was her last night, and she did.

Kelly ate well. She tried an assortment of dishes. Frogs legs, veal and dishes she had never heard of. She had ordered a bottle of red wine and drank it all. By the time she returned to her room she felt queasy. By midnight she felt rotten. She must have thrown up at least seven times during the night. The alcohol, coupled with her upset stomach, had brought about a dramatic change in the way she felt. This was punishment, she was sure, punishment for her unfaithfulness. It was punishment for sleeping with a complete stranger, despite his being a count. She felt disgusted with herself. She toyed with the idea of calling Tom and confessing, but luckily she was too drunk to remember her home phone number. She eventually fell asleep in the bathroom.

She awoke at six thirty and felt awful. She rubbed her head and saw that she had vomited all over the bathroom floor. She was a wreck. She looked in the mirror. She looked like anything but a model now. She felt guilty to the pit of stomach, wretched and remorseful. Poor Tom. How could she have done what she had?

She called home but Tom didn't answer. Maybe he was walking Shmitty or even at the Gym. No matter, she would be home soon. Her flight was at seven that evening, which gave Kelly plenty of time to pack and do some last minute shopping for gifts and postcards. She showered and cleaned as much of her vomit up from the bathroom floor as possible. She threw her clothes into her suitcase, along with anything else that looked like it needed packing. She glanced at the orange piece of paper on the floor and tried to remember what it was. She couldn't, so she threw it in the case anyway, should it turn out to be something important after all. She took breakfast on the terrace and left what she thought was a big tip for François. She really was tired of Paris and couldn't wait to get out of the place. It was funny how her whole perspective on things had changed. Yesterday it was the most wondrous place on earth, but now she would quite readily swap it all for an afternoon in Gordonston Park.

The day dragged, and by the time she arrived back at the hotel after her afternoon of shopping for gifts and postcards it was three o'clock. Henri informed her that the hotel had organized a car for her and that it would pick her up from the lobby at four. That would give her plenty of time to get to the airport to catch her flight. She repacked her suitcase, jamming into her luggage the gifts and postcards she had just purchased and called reception to send up a bellboy to take her case to the car.

She took one last look at her room before turning out the lights and closing the door. In the hotel lobby, she bade farewell to Naomi and Henri, thanked them both for their kindness, and wished them all the best for the future. The same driver who had collected her from the airport on her arrival was waiting to take her back.

Henri watched as the Mercedes disappeared into the Paris traffic. He shrugged and shook his head before returning into the hotel. He saw Naomi alone at reception and walked over to where the young woman stood. They both nodded and raised their eyes skywards.

"What a slut," said Naomi.

"Indeed. Typical American woman. Or so I am led to believe. They are all the same. So they tell me." Agreed Henri.

"You know, she is married?" said Naomi.

"Yes, I did. She was the competition girl. Left her poor husband at home. Poor man."

"You know she threw up in the bathroom," complained Naomi. "And she left a cheap tip for François," she added indignantly.

"Filthy American," commented Henri.

"They all are, I hear," confirmed Naomi.

"Cheap," said Henri.

"Nasty," added Naomi.

"No morals," proclaimed Henri.

"Pretty, though," said Naomi.

"Good legs," agreed Henri.

"As good as mine?" joked Naomi.

"Never," said her father.

How could she have done it? How could she have been so unfaithful? What had possessed her? Tom, oh poor Tom, waiting for her, walking Shmitty, keeping fit, such a good man. How could she have been so rotten? What had she done? The more she thought about it the more sordid and dirty she felt. And now, as her thoughts turned to Tom, she realized that it was the count's accent and money that had attracted her, not his looks; in fact, take away the tan and the clothes and he was really nothing special; she wouldn't have looked twice at him at home. Her stomach felt hollow, and she was unable to drink her coffee. As they announced her flight she vowed never to be unfaithful again and put the whole week out of her mind. It would be her secret. She would tell nobody. She would spend the rest of her life as a devoted wife. She would cook for Tom, clean for Tom, do anything for Tom. There was no way she was ever going to jeopardize her marriage again.

As far as she was concerned it never happened. Only she and a couple of random people in Paris knew what had happened, and Tom would never be any the wiser. She was already beginning to feel better. Her mind was made up. It would be a fresh start, and Tom wouldn't know what hit him when she got home. She would make sure that the sex with her husband was better than it was with the count. It had never been bad anyway, but this would be the turning point in their relationship. She smiled; things were going to be okay. She took one last look at France before boarding the plane that would take her home to Savannah.

Four hours later Billy Malphrus, Cindy's nephew, arrived at the Charles de Gaulle airport from his cheap hotel in the center of Paris. He checked in what little luggage he had and, with the few Euros he had left in his pocket, bought himself a coffee. He checked his watch and yawned. It had been a great week. They would never believe it back home; he'd bedded a model. He had never heard of her, but still she was gorgeous, and he would make a point of buying next month's edition of Vogue to see if she was in it. It had cost him, though, all the money he was saving to visit Vienna was spent. He had paid for everything, and to keep up the pretence, he had even slipped the waiter at that bar an extra fifty Euros to pretend he was a regular and to call him "Count." He was glad he had made up the story about having to leave on Sunday. He had simply run out of money, and there was no way, he thought, that a count would not be able to pay for a cab or even a cup of coffee.

Then again, would she have noticed? She hadn't been the sharpest knife in the tool shed, that was for sure. She may have been rich and beautiful, but she was stupid. Billy had no doubts about that. How had she fallen for his lies? He had slipped up a few times, but she had not noticed. And what was that whole Notre Dame thing? It was worth putting up with her stupidity, though, thought Billy as he took a sip of coffee, just to have slept with her. Billy shook his head and smiled. She was just like all the others, really, totally gullible and just looking for romance. He wondered how far he could have actually pushed it before she would have gotten suspicious.

He finished his coffee and tilted the sunglasses perched on his head over his eyes. He checked his reflection in the full-length mirror next to the bar, brushed off some dust from his second-hand navy blue suit, and smiled. Looking good, he thought. He made his way to the security check and handed over his American passport for inspection.

The downside, he supposed, was that pretending to be Count Enrico de Cristo had been an expensive business, and he would have to scrape together more money before his next adventure. Luckily, his Aunt Cindy had said he could stay with her for a few months. Apparently there was a chance she could maybe help him find him some odd jobs to do. There were always part-time jobs during the summer in Savannah. He had a plan, anyway, and was sure he would be back in the money sooner or later.

He was really looking forward to putting faces to the names he had heard so much about in his aunt's regular emails, the Gordonston Dog Walkers, Elliott, Heidi, and his aunt's new nemesis, Carla. But especially, he was looking forward to meeting Tom, the fireman who lived next door to his aunt, and his wife Kelly, who worked at the beauty counter in Macy's.

CHAPTER 11

The email had been brief and to the point. Doug really hadn't expected anything more from his former employers. Quite simply, there was nothing currently available in his area, since the company didn't have much interest in that part of the United States, but should anything turn up that suited his skills and qualifications, then they would contact him. The email advised him to periodically check that his company email account remained active, just in case something suitable did materialize. According to their records, the company no longer had a contact telephone number for him.

Doug sighed and closed down his laptop. He supposed it was something, though he suspected that the email had been a standard pre-drafted reply that the company probably sent out to many of its former employees looking for work in their own areas. Now that his old employer knew he was available for local work maybe they would consider him for a position elsewhere within the United States; he didn't mind traveling inside the country.

Katie was playing with Bern in the den, and he could hear her screams of delight echoing through the house. He peered inside the den, and his daughter waved. Bern was busy licking her face. As the dog's tongue tickled her, the friendly German shepherd tilted his head forward, and Katie screamed excitedly. Bern was a good dog and had reacted well when Doug and Veronica had brought Katie home from the hospital. A few days before, Katie had climbed up on Bern's back as if he were a pony, and Doug had to laugh at the poor dog's look of fear. Doug guessed that Bern also enjoyed the fact that Katie would drop food from her high chair into his mouth—at least he was getting fed more often.

Life wasn't that bad, Doug thought. At least he had a family, and Katie was happy. He just hoped that she would be as happy in five years and then in twenty years. He patted Bern on his head gently, and Katie imitated him, slapping poor Bern around the face. Doug lifted his daughter into his arms and kissed her on the cheek.

"Be gentle with Bern," he whispered and his daughter looked at him as if he were mad. She grunted something in baby language and then laughed out loud.

Doug hoped that she would get the best education and aspire to be anything that made her happy, but most importantly that she would have the opportunity to do whatever she wanted in life. He wanted the best for her, and though he knew he had already done a lot, he felt he could do more. Money had never been an issue before. He had always been successful and had traveled and seen the world, but this was different. This was a long-term commitment, and he was filled with self-doubt.

Veronica had called earlier to say that she would be working late that night at the hospital, so he would need to prepare dinner, first for Katie and then for him and his wife and have it ready for when she returned home. This meant a trip to the grocery store. Doug loaded up a diaper bag for Katie and filled it with water, milk, snacks, spare diapers, and baby wipes. He was becoming an expert at looking after his baby. It was getting easier all the time.

Doug lifted Katie up to his chest. "Come on, Monkey Girl," he said, Katie giggled and pointed to her chest.

"Yeah, that's right," Doug said. You are the monkey girl." He kissed her on the forehead and carried her outside to the car. Bern followed them to the door, then slumped down on the porch, disappointed that he would not be joining them on their outing. "Don't worry, Bern," Doug called to the dejected looking dog, "when we get back we'll all go to the park, I promise."

Doug wanted to prepare a special meal for Veronica, something easy to cook but tasty and healthy, too. Disappointed that she still hadn't shed the excess pounds caused by her pregnancy, his wife had been complaining about her weight recently, and Doug didn't want to compound his wife's notion that she was getting bigger by presenting her with a frozen pizza. He settled on fish—Mahi Mahi—which he decided he would grill and serve with a salad.

"She sure is a real beauty." Doug looked up from the fish counter to see who was complimenting his daughter, thinking he vaguely recognized the voice. "She is such a good girl. Are you shopping with Daddy? Are you going to have some fish tonight, sweet pea?" Doug smiled at the old man he saw often in the park.

"Hi," he said. The old man pulled himself up from Katie, looked at Doug and smiled.

"Hi there. You not working today?" he asked. "Got a day off to look after this pretty little thing?" The old man rubbed Katie's chin, which made her squeal with delight and kick her legs as she sat in the shopping cart seat.

"Every day is a day off for me," Doug joked as the fish counter clerk handed over his pound of fresh Mahi-Mahi. "I think this is the first time I have ever seen you without your dog," he said as he placed the fish into his shopping cart.

"Old Chalky?" said the old man. "He's in the car, waiting for his lunch. I ran out, and he's very particular." The old man laughed. "Well, enjoy your fish," he said, pointing to Doug's recent purchase, then set off towards the pet food aisle. "Bye, Katie," he said turning and waving. Katie raised her hand and flopped it around at the friendly old man, a smile across her face.

Elliott had not been to the Piggly Wiggly since Thelma's death. Usually, his wife would accompany him on his grocery shopping trips— before she became bedridden at least—and it felt strange being there without her. He had decided that to avoid the many looks and glances he guessed he would receive, he would wear his old Georgia Bulldogs baseball cap. It wasn't an attempt at a disguise, more that he felt he needed a little privacy. Since his announcement that he was running for mayor, he had become something of a local celebrity, and that, coupled with the recent death of his wife, caused the good people of Savannah, polite as they were, to take every opportunity to offer their condolences. There was also the chance that potential voters would take the opportunity of seeing their mayoral candidate in the store to pass on their views of how the city should be run, and Elliott wasn't ready for that just yet.

Tom Hudd hated grocery shopping. He was out of milk, bread, coffee, sugar, and cheese, and Kelly wasn't due back for two more days. He had never used this store before, but it was close by and he had heard Kelly say that it was reasonably priced and far more convenient than the Publix store out on Wilmington Island.

Tom had spotted the sugar aisle at last "Excuse me," he said as he barged passed the old man, who seemed to be waving at a small baby. In the process, he bumped into the old man, who had not been watching where he was going. The old man wobbled a bit on his feet as Tom brushed passed him, but he luckily kept his balance and carried on to the pet food aisle, shaking his head.

As Doug waited in line to pay for his fish at the checkout, plus a few other supplies he had purchased to assist in his dinner preparation, he noticed a familiar face. It was one of the ladies he saw every afternoon in the park. She was in line in the checkout lane adjacent to his. It looked like she was planning quite a day's work. Her shopping cart contained an abundance of cleaning supplies and products. There was something different about her, though, and Doug couldn't quite put his finger on what it was. She reached her cashier before Doug reached his, and the Englishman watched as she reloaded her cart with her newly purchased bleaches, soaps and assorted cloths and disposable mops. As she bent forward, loading her cart with the bagged goods, Doug smiled. Now he realized what was different about her. It had obviously done the trick, if the trick was attracting a man's attention. Doug also noticed who accompanied the older, still very attractive woman at the checkout and made a mental note to remember to tell Veronica what he had seen.

Elliott was relieved that no one had recognized him at the store. He had loaded his cart with everything he needed and next time, he thought, he would shop in the evening, when it was quieter and there would be less chance of being seen.

Carla Zipp didn't feel any guilt. So what? Why shouldn't she have some fun? They weren't children, and she was sure he had enjoyed it as much as she had. They were consenting adults, and it wasn't like they were breaking the law. It was obvious, though, he was missing his wife and she had been hesitant at first. Maybe it was too soon? Maybe he wasn't even interested in her. She had always liked him, from the moment she had first set on eyes on him, but he had a wife and well, what would people say? Now his wife was gone and she had taken a chance and thrown caution to the wind and made the first move.

It had proven lucky for her. She didn't usually venture into the park before noon, but Walter had needed to stretch his legs and was in an unusually feisty mood. She had entered the park a few minutes before he arrived. As their dogs played they chatted and passed small talk and pleasantries, about the weather and so forth. She hadn't deliberately set out to do what she had done, but she could tell he was lonely, and she had grasped the opportunity. Cooped up in that house by himself, he had needs, she knew that. When he suggested she come back to his home for maybe a "drink or something" she didn't need to be asked twice.

The sex had not been fantastic. She hadn't slept with another man since her husband had passed away. She enjoyed it, though, and even afterwards she had no regrets. It had been inevitable. It was going to happen sooner or later, and why wait? Her operation had paid off more quickly than she could have hoped, and she considered it money well spent.

Afterwards, she let him sleep, and collected her things and crept out of the house before he awoke. God forbid Cindy see her sneaking out. Cindy, her friend, was the only regret she had. What would Cindy say if she ever found out? She would be furious, Carla knew that, and it would no doubt end their friendship and by proxy her friendship with Heidi. It would mean she would have to leave the Dog Walking Club and Walter would just hate that. These possible consequences of what she had just done, though, were not worth thinking about.

Where they would go from here, Carla didn't know. It would be complicated, and the neighborhood tongues would wag. Maybe she should do nothing and leave the ball in his court.

Cindy was beyond herself. She was frantic. She had always secretly held a torch for him, even before Thelma had died. She admired not only his looks but also his demeanor and style. He was a true southern gentleman, and she worshipped the very ground he walked on. Some might not have called him good looking but she found him attractive. Secretly she had dreamed of one day being there for him, ever since the day Thelma discovered cancer was eating away at her. Thelma had once told Cindy that if Elliott were to marry again, after her death, she hoped he would find someone like Cindy—someone kind, somebody who knew how to look after a man, a good Savannah woman.

The news that Elliott was going to run for Mayor just compounded Cindy's stress. He was hot stuff. Every divorcée and widow in Savannah would be after him now. He had a good chance of getting elected, which meant whoever snared him would be propelled into the high profile role of mayor's consort and wife.

She should have known that Carla Zipp would have her claws out for him. She had seen the way she looked at Elliott, all smiles and fluttering eyelashes, as if she really cared about him. The woman hardly knew him and Cindy knew that her so-called friend was after just one thing.

The way Carla dressed was ridiculous, Cindy thought, as she adjusted the new tight denim jeans she had just purchased. She had initially struggled with the zipper. Eventually though, after lying down on the bed and sucking in her stomach, she fastened the button and let out a deep breath. Cindy thought of the awful trouser suit Carla had worn at the funeral. It seemed as if it had been painted on around her waist; it was that tight. Carla's buttocks had looked simply frightful, thought Cindy—a woman of her age dressed like a tramp. And the new tops she was sporting, designed to show off her fake tits, were vile, thought Cindy. Cindy inspected the cropped leather jacket that she had bought to compliment her new jeans. It was one size too small, but that was the idea—the tighter the better she had heard and besides, Kelly wore hers that way.

What angered Cindy most was the boob job. What was she thinking? Did she really think that Elliott would be interested in a woman's chest? He was far too refined and intelligent to be swayed by the sight of a woman's ample décolletage. So what if she looked good? Had she forgotten her age? Exactly how old was she anyway? It was undignified for a woman of her years to be parading around like she was. She was making a fool of herself, or so Cindy hoped.

Cindy wondered about Carla, remembering she had been a dancer in Las Vegas. Well, Cindy knew about "dancers" and "Vegas." It wouldn't have surprised her if Carla had been a whore. She was certainly acting like one now. Cindy had read about how, during the sixties, the mafia ran the town and how all the misfits and losers and two-bit hustlers from all over the country congregated there. Cindy pushed the thought from her mind. No. Carla wasn't a whore. She was manipulative, she was man hungry, and she was after Elliott. She wasn't a whore, but she was a threat.

Cindy stood up and looked out into Kentucky Avenue. She wouldn't be surprised if right now Carla was planning some way of getting into Elliott's bed. Carla had already started walking Walter in the mornings in the hope of "accidentally" bumping into Elliott. Elliott walked Biscuit and Grits in the morning, and it was obvious to Cindy what Carla was trying to do.

Cindy loved Elliott, though he didn't know it yet. She was sure that it was what Thelma would have wanted. Elliott would love her back, she was sure of it. They were ideally suited, the perfect couple. But Carla Zipp, the evil bitch, was ruining everything, coming between Elliott and Cindy with her little tricks, flashing her false eyelashes and her fake tits, practically throwing herself at the man that she, Cindy, was destined to be with.

Cindy was practically ill with rage. She wasn't thinking straight; it was as if she were consumed. She could cook, but she couldn't eat. She spent sleepless nights worrying that maybe Carla had already found her way into Elliott's bed. Why was Carla here anyway? Why couldn't she just go back to Florida where she had come from? She didn't belong in Savannah, especially not in Gordonston. Cindy clenched her fists so tightly that her knuckles turned white. That woman, that so called friend of hers, why couldn't she just disappear, just vanish, just . . . die.

By now Cindy's resentment had turned to hate. She picked up a vase that had sat for years in her living room and threw it hard against the wall. That bitch! That whore! She was going to steal Elliott from her, marry him, move into the big white house and become the mayor's wife! She knew it. She knew what her deceitful so-called "friend" was planning. How could she?

Cindy calmed down long enough to log onto her computer. She saw that she had an unread email from Billy, so she opened it. It seemed he was still in India but planned to return to the States so he could make some urgently needed money. He had found a small charitable mission just outside Mumbai and had volunteered to help. Unfortunately, though, they were running out of funds, and he had promised he would return to America and begin collecting for them so they could purchase the medicines they so desperately needed. He asked his aunt if he could possibly come and stay with her in Savannah while he attempted to raise money for the charity. He would then fly back to India where he was needed. Maybe she could help him find a part-time job, maybe with some of Uncle Ronnie's old friends at the car lots, or maybe there would be a chance he could clean cars—anything to help the poor sick children of India.

Cindy smiled. At least there was *some* goodness on this earth. She emailed Billy and told him that of course he could stay with her. She also said she herself would donate a thousand dollars to assist the poor Indian children. She would make enquiries to help him find a part-time job and suggested that there could even be jobs around the neighborhood; she knew many elderly neighbors who would jump at the chance at having a young man help out. Cindy wrote that she was very excited he was coming to stay. She even said that she would ask Tom Hudd next door to pick him up from the airport, though she wasn't sure if he would be able to. Kelly was going to be arriving earlier the same day and maybe two trips to the airport in one day would be too much to ask of the poor man.

Carla decided that she needed a drink. She twisted open a bottle of beer and poured it into a glass. She tucked her face into her chin and looked down at her cleavage. He had certainly enjoyed them, she thought, recalling their afternoon of passion. All men were the same, she thought as she grinned and took a swig of the cold beer. Why had she ever thought that he would be any different?

Luckily, the groceries fitted into one plastic carrier bag. It meant Doug could carry Katie and bring the groceries into the house at the same time. He placed the bag on the kitchen table and carried Katie into the den, where Bern had waited patiently. The dog lifted his head from his slumber and wagged his tail. Doug was sure Bern had been pouting the whole afternoon, disappointed that his afternoon walk had not yet materialized.

"Okay, I'll grab your leash," said Doug to the forlorn looking animal as he looked at his watch. It was approaching four, and as Katie had slept in the car she was now ready for her afternoon stroll.

Katie was eager, just as Bern was, for her afternoon jaunt to the park. Doug unpacked the groceries and quickly chopped some lettuce and cucumber for the salad. He threw the fish into the refrigerator. He grabbed his daughter, her stroller, and Bern's leash, and all three left the house.

The park was unusually quiet that afternoon. In fact, Doug, Katie and Bern were the only ones there, which was odd. Usually the ladies would be sitting at the picnic table while their dogs ran amok. Doug began his circumnavigation of the park and released Bern from his leash. The dog made his way into the wooded area as Doug and Katie began their walk. It was good being alone in the park. Though he didn't mind the old ladies, Doug always felt they were watching him, as if they policed the park. He also suspected that they were gossiping about someone or other, probably him. There was something about the oldest woman that Doug didn't like; she looked sinister, kind of stern. Veronica had once told him she was German or "something" which didn't surprise him. She had that look, the look of superiority, and he guessed her two younger friends followed her lead. He imagined them agreeing with whatever she said.

From his bedroom window, Elliott had watched Doug enter the park, accompanied by Bern and Katie in her stroller. Elliott liked the young Englishman; he always said hello and the whole family, Veronica especially, kept to themselves and minded their own business. Bern was a good dog; he always came when he was called. Elliott liked the fact the park was being used by a variety of Gordonston residents, and not just the members of the Dog Walking Club, who, though his wife had been a member, had somehow come to view the park as their own personal domain. Elliott thought about his own dogs and how they probably needed to get some exercise. Biscuit and Grits used to enjoy their afternoons in the park, yet Elliott had been taking them out in the mornings; maybe the afternoons would be better. He looked back toward his bed, at the ruffled sheets and empty wine and beer glasses on each of the bedside tables. He suddenly felt very alone. He felt the urge to shower, and maybe he would just brush his teeth again to help eradicate the taste of stale alcohol.

Elliott hadn't always imbibed during the day, but since Thelma had become bedridden he had gotten into the habit, and it was beginning to take its toll. He was tired and felt a bit disheveled. This was no way for a future mayor to behave. He had to clean up his act. The people of Savannah wouldn't want a slob running the city. They would want an upright man, a man of standing, a man of respect, a family man, a married man. They wouldn't want a mayor who spent afternoons drinking and lying in his bed. Thelma would never have allowed him to sleep in the afternoon like that. She would have woken him and ordered him to shower and shave. Elliott Miller realized that he missed his wife more than ever and felt ashamed of himself.

Cindy had sent the email to Billy and was already preparing for his visit. She would need extra groceries and she would need to make up a bed for him. She had much to do. She would host a little welcoming party for Billy, she thought. She would invite Tom and Kelly and maybe Veronica and her husband around for drinks, and maybe she would ask Betty Jenkins to make some fried chicken. They were all about the same age, give or take a few years, and Billy could do with meeting some of the younger people in the neighborhood. So what if Veronica's husband was a little strange—they all were, those English, and maybe Kelly could put whatever it was he said to her behind them. She considered inviting Heidi but that would mean inviting Carla also. She didn't want Carla coming—she hated the woman—and in fact she wondered if she could even face her old friend anymore. It wasn't fair. She had been the one who had started the Dog Walking Club and if she stopped talking to Carla it would mean the Club would die.

Cindy's mind was racing. Carla was a threat to her very existence. She had become a thorn in her side and that thorn had to be removed before it did any more damage. With Carla around, then the Dog Walking Club could still feasibly exist without Cindy. Heidi and Carla would just find new members. Heidi was very influential and could recruit new members easily; she had a persuasive nature. The last thing Cindy wanted was Carla gossiping about her in her absence, and God forbid she ever found herself on the wrong side of Heidi.

The Dog Walking Club, though, was the least of Cindy's problems; it was the Elliott situation that worried her more. Carla was a threat to her future plans. With Carla in the picture, Elliott's attention was divided between them. Carla was competition for his affections and dangerous competition at that. With Carla gone and no longer an option for Elliott, then Cindy was the natural candidate for his affections, once he was ready, when he realized he needed a wife.

Cindy was still logged on to her computer and online. She typed "Google" into her explorer page and the search engine's web page appeared on her screen. She thought for a moment, as if deciding what words would be best to assist her in her search. She typed quickly and pressed enter. She opened her eyes in surprise. There were quite a few sites that dealt with that sort of thing, but one in particular caught her eye. She clicked onto the description and found herself being redirected to the advertised website.

She read the warning emblazoned across her screen before entering the website and made sure that computer met all the criteria required and possessed the necessary components to view the site. She clicked to acknowledge that she understood the disclaimer and that she was entering the site at her own risk.

For a moment Cindy had thought she had lost her connection to the Internet. Her screen went blank and then jumbled images and words reappeared. It was as if she were visiting a thousand different sites per minute, and she wondered if she had clicked onto the wrong site. Maybe she had downloaded a virus. She had never encountered a problem like this before, and she considered switching off her computer. Just as she was about to shut it down her screen settled. It looked like she had finally reached the site.

These people seemed very well organized, thought Cindy, as she read about how she was to proceed. There was some terminology she didn't really understand such as "encrypted" and "untraceable ISP address," but she persevered. There was an online form, similar to an application form, that instructed her to insert details regarding the type of service she required, including the names of all involved, as well as her own name and proof of funds. Initially she was hesitant before filling out the form, but she decided that she had no choice, and that really, there was no other way to do this. Besides, Carla had brought it all on herself.

After completing the form and pressing the submit button she was redirected to another page, a price list. The service was expensive. In fact, it would virtually wipe out her life savings. Nevertheless, she thought, in the end it would be worth it, especially if it meant she would marry Elliott.

The instructions were simple. Her actual "job"—the one she asked them to do—was not guaranteed, and payment would be required only if the "organization" decided to accept the "contract," as not all contracts were practical nor deemed viable. Cindy took a deep breath and clicked that she understood all that she had read. Once she had completed the online form and committed herself to the "organization," as they called themselves, she exited the website. She then followed the detailed instructions she had received with regard to deleting her internet history and removing any trace that she had visited the site.

Cindy realized that she was shaking. She had done it, and now there was no turning back. The website had informed her it was now up to the "Director," whoever he was, whether her contract would be taken on or not. She would be advised once proof of funds and her ability to pay for the service had been verified.

A chill ran down her spine. She had just done something that she had only read about or seen in movies. She had crossed the line between what was regarded as normal and acceptable behavior and what was not. She had just contracted a murder. But more importantly, or in her mind at least, she had begun the process of ensuring that she regained control her life. The fact that she had earmarked her friend Carla for death didn't bother Cindy one bit. She was too great a threat to Cindy's plans and future ambition. Elliott was hers, and there was no way she was going to let Carla stand between her and the man she loved. She had to go; it was that simple. Anyway, Cindy now had more pressing matters to deal with—worry about organizing a dinner party for one thing, and preparing for the visit of her nephew, Billy Malphrus.

CHAPTER 12

By the time Doug had returned from the park, prepared dinner, bathed and put Katie to bed, fed the dog and cats, tidied up Katie's toys and folded and hung up some laundry, Veronica had arrived home.

"I got us some fresh fish," he announced as his wife threw her keys onto the dining room table and purse onto an adjacent chair.

"Great, I'm starving. Is she in bed?" she asked, referring to Katie. "Yeah. She went down about an hour ago," answered Doug as he served up a plate of Mahi-Mahi and rice for his hungry wife.

"How was your day?" he asked, as Veronica tasted the food.

"This is good. Well done. Tastes great," she said through mouthfuls of food. "Sorry, what did you say?" she asked, looking up at her husband. Doug had just remembered the salad he had prepared and was busy retrieving it from the refrigerator.

"I asked if you had a good day?" smiled Doug. His wife tilted her head as if trying to recall whether she had had a good day or not.

"Not bad," she replied. "How about you? Did anything interesting happen?" Doug thought for a minute. Yes. There was something he had wanted to tell his wife, something he felt could be classified as "interesting."

"Well, we went grocery shopping, for the fish." Veronica was busy eating and while listening was not looking at her husband but reading one of her magazines that she had collected from the mailbox on her way into the house. "And I saw something pretty odd. Well, not odd, more interesting really." Veronica carried on, devouring the seafood on her plate.

"Oh yeah, what was that then?" she asked. Doug wasn't sure if she was really listening to him but told her anyway.

"I saw one of those old ladies, the ones that hang out in the park with their dogs." Veronica looked up.

"You mean Cindy?" she asked.

"No. The other one. Not the older one, the younger looking one."

"You mean Carla," confirmed his wife with her mouth full.

"Well, you know she's had a boob job, don't you?" said Doug.

"Oh, yeah, I'd heard that. She looks good, I hear," confirmed Veronica.

"Well, that's not it. There was something else," said Doug. "She was at the checkout, buying loads of cleaning supplies and stuff, I wasn't sure what it all was but there was a lot of it."

"So what? She can buy whatever she likes. There is no law against cleaning your house," joked Veronica.

"No," said Doug. "That wasn't it, silly. It was something else, something I bet you didn't even know."

Doug then proceeded to tell Veronica what he had seen earlier that day at the Piggly Wiggly when he had spotted Carla paying for her groceries in the adjacent aisle. When he finished relaying what he had seen to his wife he lifted a fork full of Mahi to his mouth.

"Are you sure?" asked Veronica, sounding dubious and lifting her head from the magazine she was reading.

"I am positive," replied Doug, as he chewed on his fish.

"Well, don't say anything, especially to anybody around here. That's how rumors start in Savannah," smiled his wife, "and there is probably a perfectly innocent explanation for it. She was probably just trying to help out."

"Don't worry. Who am I going to tell anyway?" answered Doug, "I don't know anybody."

Veronica laughed and then changed the subject. "Do you think Katie has a small head?"

"No," replied Doug, "and neither do you, before you ask again."

After they finished their meal Veronica collected the dirty plates and cleared off the dining room table. Doug opened his laptop as his wife cleared the kitchen. He thought it wouldn't hurt to check if anything had come up on the work front yet. Veronica had told him not to be silly, that he really shouldn't expect anything. The chance of them needing a representative in Savannah or the bank opening a branch, even in Atlanta, was highly unlikely.

Despite his wife's pessimism, Doug logged into his email account. Nothing. His inbox was empty. He sighed. Maybe he was clutching at straws, and maybe Veronica was right. However, he thought, it wouldn't hurt to check his email account every now and then. He would hate to miss an opportunity.

"Why don't you just get them to call you?" asked Veronica, noticing the dejected look on her husband's face.

"I don't know," he replied. "The time difference, for one thing." He shrugged. "Also I don't want them ringing in the middle of night or early morning and waking Katie. Chances are, I would be out in the park anyway if they called. At least if they send an email I know I would read it, eventually." Veronica conceded that Doug had a point. She could see, though, that her husband was upset, and was worried that he could quite easily be slipping into a mild depression. She placed her hand on his arm.

"Well, just relax, honey. It isn't that big a deal. We can pay the bills, and that's what matters." Doug smiled at his wife. She was right of course, but that didn't really make him feel any better, he just hoped he could find some work and make some extra money, and soon.

She had not left her home in two days, which was unheard of for Heidi, as it was usually guaranteed someone would see her tending her garden or walking Fuchsl in the park. She had called both Carla and Cindy and told them that she felt unwell, but it wasn't anything serious. Both her friends had offered to come around and bring food as well as provide a little company. Heidi had thanked each of them, refused their kind offers, and told them not to worry about her. It was nothing major, and she preferred to be alone and anyway, she said, she would be fine in a few days, but appreciated their concern. She told them that Betty Jenkins had promised to exercise Fuchsl by letting him wander in the large rear garden of the house, so there was no need to worry about him, either. She could, she said, open and shut the back door, and that she wasn't bedridden. She was probably contagious, though, so it would probably be best all around if they just stayed away for a few days.

Betty Jenkins had prepared several meals that she had bagged, labeled and stored for her employer, filling her refrigerator and her freezer. Heidi had told her not to come in for a few days, as she wouldn't need her. Betty had jumped at the chance of a few days off and thanked the old woman, as Heidi had promised she would pay her for her time anyway. Heidi had informed her housekeeper she would call her in a few days and let her know when she should come in again.

The truth was that Heidi Launer felt perfectly fine. In fact, she had never felt better, and her little lie to her friends had been designed to keep them away from her house. As for Betty Jenkins, if for one minute her loyal housekeeper had thought Heidi had been ill she would have called Doctor Victor immediately and prepared the spare bedroom so she could be Heidi's on-call, twenty-four hour nurse. Betty would have insisted on staying the night and waiting hand and foot on the elderly lady, which was the last thing Heidi would have wanted. No. Feign sickness for the Gordonston Ladies Dog Walking Club and give Betty some free days off, that was the only way to ensure she would not be disturbed and guarantee her privacy.

Heidi Launer spent the day alone with her memories. It was the only company she desired or required that day. She hunted and found several old photograph albums and spread them out on the side table she had positioned in front of her chair. She smiled as she scanned through the photographs and portraits the albums had contained, photographs of her husband Oliver, her son, Stephen, as a baby, as a child, as a youth and as a young man. She flicked through the pages and smiled at the images of Stephen's wedding and her grandchildren's christening photos. She even found some old newspaper clippings that included a picture of Stephen with one of the Mafia bosses he had successfully defended.

She dug further into drawers and closets and found even older albums containing faded black and white photographs of her parents—her father, standing proudly outside his butchers shop, clad in his white apron, her mother at his side, proud of her husband and his achievement. There were pictures, too, of Heidi as a child, standing outside her father's shop with her school friends. In some of these she was dressed in her school uniform. She had attended an all-girl's day school and once again she smiled at the faces of friends whose names were now long forgotten. She gently traced her finger along an image of herself with her mother and father—a family portrait —and smiled. They were good people, honest and hard working, but above all they were loyal.

As she turned the pages of the old photo album from front to back and traveled the years back she found a photograph of herself, taken on the day her family had arrived in America. She had been fourteen. As she sat in her parlor room, with the old album on her lap, she recalled the voyage across the North Atlantic as if it had been yesterday. The family had arrived in Southampton from Hamburg aboard the SS Bremen on the last voyage between Germany and Great Britain before the outbreak of war. Heidi recalled that there was a feeling of despair among the crew at the thought that soon they could be fighting the friends they had made in England. Her father had told her not to listen the chatter among the crew, that whatever happened it would all be for the best.

The family boarded the Queen Mary in Southampton after an overnight stay in a plush hotel not far from the port. The voyage to New York had taken sixteen days, and Heidi had enjoyed every minute of the journey. The family had traveled first class. The crew had been made up of the friendliest and most polite people she had ever encountered, and she and her family were treated like royalty. Heidi had marveled at the finery of the dining room and its silver cutlery and plush furniture. The food had been spectacular, and her mother and father had smiled throughout the whole voyage. She recalled the games and fun she and her family joined in with on deck. It had been a good time, and it was as if all the troubles that loomed on the horizon were a million miles away. Heidi gazed into the distance as she remembered the governess who traveled with them; her main role was to teach Heidi English, which she had, and very well. Heidi fondly recalled the days sat in her cabin with Helga as she taught her the language of her new home.

Helga had been English on her mother's side and she spoke the language perfectly. She had been hired especially, not only to teach Heidi English, but her parents also. It had been difficult at first. There were so many distractions and things she wanted to do on the large ship. Eventually though, she had settled down to study, so that by the time she and her parents had arrived in New York she spoke enough English to get by, and her mother and father were competent enough in the language to build their new lives.

Heidi stared into the distance and wondered whatever had become of Helga. She wondered if she had returned to Austria, for when the boat had docked in New York, Heidi and her parents were whisked away in motorcars, and she never saw Helga again. Had she, wondered Heidi, returned to her mother's homeland or had she returned to the Fatherland? No matter what, Heidi guessed that somehow Helga would have been caught up in the war that engulfed Europe. Heidi just hoped that she had survived.

Heidi returned to the memory of her family's arrival in New York. She thought of the photographer who had taken her portrait. He had been brought to the port to await the family's arrival with the cars and the important looking men in suits and top hats and a man in uniform who was the attaché and was a very important man, she had been told. She remembered her parents being treated like royalty, her father signing papers and shaking hands; her mother laughing and smiling and speaking in German to the men who had collected the family's luggage. Heidi recalled a man who never spoke and who wore the dark suit. He seemed worried, scared even. He had nodded to her politely before ushering them all into a waiting car.

The family had been driven to a grand looking building where everyone spoke her native language. It was a busy place with people rushing round with papers and briefcases. She had run to a window and marveled at the scene outside. She had never seen such tall buildings, and the man who never smiled told her that one day every city in the world would look like this. She laughed and told him not to be silly, that there were too many beautiful buildings in the world for them all to be knocked down. He had looked somber and he told her that what men had made, men could destroy. She had gotten the feeling that the stern looking man didn't like her, and she turned back and watched the city scene below her. She had never seen so many cars and people, moving around like so many ants.

The family left the German Embassy later that day, after her father was handed a briefcase that he held tightly to his chest. They were driven the long distance to Savannah by a chauffeur who spoke both German and English and told them about the towns and cities they passed through. They had driven through the night and Heidi had slept most of the way. They stopped twice, and spent the night in small hotels. Their chauffeur paid for everything—rooms, food, and even Heidi's first taste of Coca Cola. It was as if he knew how important the people that he was driving were. When they eventually arrived on the Georgia coast it was daybreak, and Heidi marveled at the scenery and the houses as they approached the small coastal city. When the car pulled up to a big house, set on a square in the center of the town she squealed with delight when her father told her it was to be the family's new home. She ran from the car onto the porch and jumped for joy, only to stop dead in her tracks when she saw the three servants.

Heidi had never seen negroes in the flesh. She didn't know what to think when she saw the family's new housekeeper, gardener and butler, all standing waiting for the arrival of their new employers. She ran straight into her father's arms, more frightened than she had ever been in her life. Her father assured her that the colorful people were indeed just people and not to be afraid. He reminded her of the time she had gone to Berlin and watched the Olympic Games from the special box a few years earlier. "Do you remember Jesse Owens," her father asked Heidi, "and the way he ran so well?"

Heidi said she did, she had cheered and clapped along with everyone else, despite what everyone said later, when he was presented with his medal. Her father explained that he was the same as the people who would now be sharing their home. That they were people, just like them, and to forget anything that she may have heard to the contrary. Heidi had not believed this. She always thought that there was no one else like her, her family and her countrymen. They were superior in every way. Her father certainly had some strange ideas, and she felt like reminding him that he should not say such things.

Heidi took a deep breath. She had been at the Berlin Olympics in 1936, and despite what she read years later, and even to this day she remembered the cheers and the ovations all the medal winners received, irrelevant of race or nationality. Propaganda, thought the old lady, was something that her own country was not alone in using during those dark times. Heidi remembered sadly that there were no photographs of her life prior to her arrival in Savannah. There was none of her homeland nor any of her before she had arrived in Savannah. It didn't matter, though, she thought as she sat back in her easy chair in her parlor, she still remembered. She didn't need photographs to remind her. Her memories were enough, and you couldn't change the truth.

Heidi remembered what she had looked like and felt tears beginning to well up in her eyes. Heidi remembered everything; she remembered the truth. Maybe it was because the man she had called her father, that the whole world called her father that had said the black people were the same as them, wasn't her real father. Her real mother would never have said or allowed such a thing, and if she had ever known her real father she was sure he would not have either. She knew for certain her uncle would have been horrified to think that she had been told such nonsense.

Heidi sighed, as memories of her childhood before her arrival in Savannah flooded back, memories of her real mother and her real family. Though the couple she called her parents were not actually even related to her, they were good people, and she couldn't have wished for more loving guardians. The truth, though, was that they were not her flesh and blood. They were friends of the family, and she had known them for many years. She was told to call them mother and father, but that was not who they really were.

She had never known her real father; he had died a week before she was born. Her mother had been devastated. They were not married, but the wedding had been planned, and despite the scandal of her being pregnant at the altar it hadn't caused too many raised eyebrows. There were hard times back then, and the family had been poor, and if it hadn't been for her mother's brother, Heidi's uncle, she doubted that she would have made it through the depression that had engulfed Austria and Germany after the First World War.

With the help of her brother, Heidi's mother had managed to bring up an intelligent, bright and attractive young woman. Heidi closed her eyes, remembering the fun times with her mother—her real mother—and her uncle, the uncle she had loved so dearly. They spent so much time together that he had become more like a father to her, praising her, encouraging her interest in arts and music, listening to what she had to say, encouraging her to become a person of courage and honor and to be proud of what he taught her to call her "Aryan roots." She longed for his visits, and though he was a busy and important man, he always seemed to have time for his niece.

Heidi stood up from her chair and slowly made her way up the stairs to the second floor of her home. The old woman paused as she passed the normally locked room. She had unlocked the door earlier that day, after Betty Jenkins left, knowing that she would be entering it sometime later during the day. She felt the door handle and closed her eyes. The room contained many secrets, many memories, and it would devastate her if anything untoward occurred—a fire, maybe—that would damage her precious memories. She let go of the door handle and entered the room where she housed her collection of books.

Ten-foot high shelves lined every wall. There were thousands of books, all lined up like a library, categorized by genre and writer.

Heidi ran a finger along a section of books. She breathed in the smell of them, the smell of old paper, musty even, and once again fleetingly closed her eyes. This was her other sanctuary, the place where she could come and sit and gaze at her vast collection. It was her special place. Though not a secret like the room next door, this one she allowed visitors to enter and Betty Jenkins to clean. Fuchsl stood at the door and tilted his head as he watched his owner wander around the room, pausing at different shelves to inspect this book or that, lifting it from its allotted space then returning it to its home.

Heidi finally stopped still at the section she had come to inspect that evening. Her hand reached up to the shelf and she selected a book, then another, and then a third. She carried the three books to the reading table and chair that sat in the center of the room. She placed the three books on the table, drew out the chair, and took her seat. She opened the pages of the first book and briefly read a few paragraphs. She did the same with the second and the third. She flipped each book over individually, as if inspecting it, front cover and back. She was pleased to see that they were still in mint condition. They had been well cared for and were still like new, despite the fact she had read each of them many times.

She placed the books face up on the table and read the title of each aloud. Fuchsl stared at her, not sure if his mistress was calling him or not to join her. He decided she wasn't and once more sat down on his hind legs at the entrance to the room.

"The Bavarian Forest of Magic," she said aloud. "The Wizards and the Boy, Fairies in the Forest and Other Tales."

Heidi's expression had changed; she was no longer smiling, her mouth contorted into a sneer. How dare he, she thought. How *dare* he! The man was an imposter, a liar of the highest magnitude, a fraud and a cheat, he was vermin. She clenched her fists, and the wrinkles on her hands seemed to fold like layers of old pink leather. Her eyes clouded with hate, and her lips trembled. She stared at the three books on the table, not at the titles, nor at the illustrated covers. No, she stared at the name of the author, the author of all three books. The name stared back at her, and it seemed to the old lady that the name mocked her. She despised the name, had done for years now, and soon she would take her revenge on the man who bore the name for the wrongs he had done. Emblazoned across the bottom of each cover, printed in bold, black capital letters was the name.... Elliott Miller.

Heidi stood up from the reading table, steadying herself on the chair as she did so, and carried the three books with her as she exited her private library. She proceeded, slowly and with Fuchsl trailing behind her, along the second floor landing towards the "special" room that she held the only key for, the room that no other soul had ever entered, the room that her late husband had tried many times, always unsuccessfully, to enter. This room contained secrets within its walls and its contents were for her eyes only. She slowly opened the door, Fuchsl following loyally behind her, and she entered the sunlit room.

She carried the three books with her as she made her way towards the glass-doored bookcase that was central to the room. She placed Elliott's books on the floor and opened the glass display case and removed the object she so had lovingly caressed and cradled a few days earlier.

The Lugar was in excellent condition. She had no doubt that it would still function, and she raised it above her head so the sunlight that entered the room from the draped windows reflected on its black shiny surface. The Lugar was the favored German handgun in World War Two for the officers of the Reich, though it was developed prior to the First World War. Her uncle had referred to the weapon as his"Pistolen-08." It had been adopted by the German Army in 1908. For Heidi, this gun was far more than just a weapon. It had been *his* Lugar.

As she gently stroked the barrel she recalled the day her uncle had presented it to her. It was one of the last things he had ever given her, and she treasured it. It had been at a dinner party, held in her honor, just before she had departed for America. Seated around the table were her mother and her soon-to-be new "parents" plus faces she recognized from the newspapers and the movie reels. She remembered the gleaming medals and the highly pressed uniforms, the spit-polished boots, and the way the men seated at the table applauded everything her beloved uncle had said. Every utterance that left his mouth had been met with agreement; the whole table was in complete awe of him, but to Heidi he was just her uncle, a man she loved more dearly than anyone else, even her own mother. He had handed her the weapon, cleaned and polished, after the servants had cleared their plates.

He told her how it had been presented to him in the trenches of France, and how it had saved his life on more than one occasion. He told her that in the future, should anything happen to him, she should use it to extract her revenge. The whole table had laughed loud and long, including her uncle, at his own joke. Maybe it hadn't been a joke; maybe it had been a veiled warning to those seated around the table that should anything ever happen to him he had a successor prepared to take his place, who would avenge him from beyond the Atlantic. Heidi often wondered what her uncle had meant by his comment and she had, on more than one occasion, filled the pistol with bullets and aimed it through the window that let the sunlight into room—the window that overlooked the garden next door, the garden of Elliott Miller.

The gun wasn't the only reminder Heidi had of her uncle. Adorning the walls of the room were portraits of him, photographs and paintings. There were drawings and art he had produced himself, which he had secretly sent her after she had arrived in Savannah, as well as other memorabilia, such as medals, newspaper clippings and copies of his famous speeches. The old lady made her way to the projector that sat just off the center of the room and switched it on. She pulled the drapes of the windows closed, blocking out the fading sunlight of dusk. The countdown numbers that told her the film was about to commence flashed on the screen that took up the entire west wall of the room. She had painted the wall white so she could watch the old movie reels she had acquired years before. The old eight-millimeter film wheeled its way through the projector, and black and white images appeared on the wall.

There was no sound on the film but the images sufficed. They were images replayed the world over, footage of Heidi's uncle being driven in the back of an open top Mercedes, images of her uncle addressing a large crowd, being cheered wildly by his countrymen. Heidi marveled at the images, as she always did. She moved slowly over to the window, gently adjusted the drapes and gazed out at the large white house, the house that seemed to taunt her, Elliot Miller's house.

This was the reason why she had wanted her own house in the first place. Why she had insisted that Oliver purchase not just a house in Gordonston, but this house in particular. She had wanted to be within reach, to be able to watch him, to be able to see what *he* was like. The thief, the fraud, the liar. She turned her attention back to the three books on the table. The anger inside her welled up again. It hadn't taken long to find him. A few inquiries here and there, a private detective and a little money went a long way in America. She had contacts, friends of her uncle, in high places, who were all gone now, though there had been a time when men of influence had been of the same mind. When she found out where Elliott lived her heart could have stopped. He was so close and always had been. Who could have known?

She hated him. There was no other way of describing the way Heidi felt about Elliott Miller, for along with the Lugar, portraits, films and medals; she had one other memory of her uncle. The most special memory of all. The stories he used to tell her, the stories he made up, especially for her, of wizards, magical forests, unicorns and little boys lost in woods. When she had read the new author's books for the first time, all those years ago, she had nearly collapsed. They were the same stories her uncle had written for her, and some fraud named Elliott Miller had passed them off as his own. He was a thief. Not only had he stolen the stories, he had prevented the world from knowing what a truly remarkable man her uncle actually was. Not only was he a great leader; he was a great writer, a writer of stories for children. Over the years, Heidi had read many things about her beloved uncle that she just knew were simply lies and propaganda perpetrated by the shameless Zionists. He was a hero to millions, and he had come close to achieving his goals. She was certain that if the world had known about these wonderful tales and the mind that created them, history would not have been so cruel to his memory. The world would know that the man who had produced these fantasies couldn't have been responsible for the things they claimed he did. And what if they were true, anyway? She despised those people. They were parasites, just like he had taught her. They were locusts and the scourge of the earth.

The stories, though, would have cast doubt, she was sure, on the reports of a so-called holocaust. Elliott Miller had ruined that. How he had gotten hold of the stories, Heidi didn't know. All she knew was that Elliott Miller had profited from her uncle's work and prevented the world from knowing the true writer of the works. Some critics had called them the greatest stories for children ever told. She gripped the Lugar tightly. Those stories had been especially written for her, and somehow the Zionists had profited from them. Elliott Miller—she despised the man and had waited for this day for what seemed an eternity.

Her call to Stephen the previous day had come as a surprise to her son. When she told him what she wanted he had at first thought she was joking. Nevertheless, her voice on the phone sounded angry, almost frenzied, and he knew he had no choice. It wasn't that he was afraid of his mother. She just had a way of getting her point across, something that, as she often told him, ran in the family.

Stephen made the calls and organized everything. With his contacts it wasn't difficult. There was a whole network out there. Of course he had been curious as to why his mother would want to have somebody killed. She told him that it was personal and that the less he knew about his family history the better it would be for him. Stephen accepted this; he was used to that sort of talk in his business, especially with the clients he dealt with. The less you knew the better. So he had done his mother's bidding.

Heidi screwed up her face as she took the three books in her hand and carried them over to the corner of the room. She had prepared the small metal trashcan earlier that morning and had doused the inside with sufficient fluid. She dropped the books into the trashcan and lit a match. It didn't take long for the fuel she had placed in the can to burn the old books. Flames shot up, and after a time, began to die out. A red glow reflected in the darkened room, as the images continued to play on the white wall. Heidi reached into her pocket and produced an armband, she kissed the insignia that ornamented it and placed it on her arm.

So, Elliott Miller was running for mayor. Over her dead body! She had liked Thelma and was sure that she had had no part in the theft of her uncle's work. She had deliberately waited until after her friend's death to execute her plan. The pain Elliott was feeling at his wife's passing was a bonus for Heidi. She was happy to watch him suffer, and his misery was her delight. Maybe it was part of Elliott's penance, watching his wife die. Now, though, she was gone, and he was going to be mayor, and as far as Heidi was concerned that was her sign, her signal to put into place what she had been planning for years. The murder of Elliott Miller.

She turned to face the flag that hung on the north wall and she walked once again to the center of the room. It took up the whole wall. Its red background stood in stark contrast to the whiteness of the walls while the white circle in the center of the flag seemed to compliment it, as if the cloth and surface formed a mosaic of black on red and white. However, it was the image in the center, black and proud, that made the hairs on the back of Heidi's neck stand on end, as it did every time she saw it. It was the same image she wore on her armband, the same image that had adorned her uncle's homes and castles, the same image that she worshipped, the same image she and the rest of the world knew so very well, the same image that had struck fear into the hearts of millions: the swastika of the Nazis.

Heidi stared at the flag and brought her old frail body to attention, as if suddenly the years had been rubbed away and she was once again a brown-clad schoolgirl, leading her troop, carrying the flag and proud to be a member of her uncle's Youth Movement. She had been the first one ordained into the movement, and she was proud that she remembered the marches, the speeches in Berlin, Nuremburg and Munich. As the flames flickered, the remnants of Elliott's book turning to ash in the old metal bin in the corner, and the projected images still playing on the wall, Heidi raised her right hand into the air, angled in front of her face at forty-five degrees. Her voice was crisp, sharp and harsh, her Austrian accent suddenly to the fore. "Sieg Heil!" she cried, her voice echoing not just in the room but throughout the whole house, "Sieg Heil!" she cried again, as if in a frenzied trance. Fuchsl crouched down in fear; he had never known that his mistress possessed such a voice. Heidi was now moving her right hand back and forth, in the rigid wave and angled movement that had struck fear into those who had first witnessed the styled salute. "Sieg Heil!" she cried again, her voice now reaching a pitched crescendo, her voice filling the whole house, its echo amplifying the old woman's almost hysterical cry. "Sieg Heil, Sieg Heil, Sieg Heil!"

CHAPTER 13

"What time does his flight arrive?" asked Kelly, smiling broadly as she hugged her husband's bare torso.

"In a couple of hours, apparently, according to Cindy, anyway. He had a six hour layover in Atlanta." Tom smiled as his wife gently rubbed his chest, her left hand playfully caressing his right nipple.

"Well," she said as she leant over in their bed, the bed she hadn't slept in for five nights, "I think that was a really nice thing for you to volunteer to pick him up."

Tom shrugged. "It was the least I could do. The poor guy's been working his ass off over in India. He is only coming back so he can make enough money to buy medicine and supplies for the kids he's helping take care of."

Kelly hugged her husband hard. "Still, two airport trips in one day, I have to say that a lot of people would have made up some lame excuse. You're great. I am so lucky to have you." She kissed her husband's chest and thanked God that she was indeed lucky enough to have found and married Tom.

Kelly had literally run into Tom's outstretched arms several hours earlier, when her connecting flight from New York touched down in Savannah. Anyone witnessing her arrival would have thought she had been away for five years, not five days, the way she hugged and kissed her husband. After they loaded her luggage into Tom's SUV and drove the short distance to Gordonston, Tom finally asked her how her trip had been. Kelly smiled and told him that while she had had a good time in Paris, it was overshadowed by the fact that she was missing him. Though she had seen all the sites she wanted to see, eaten delicious food, and soaked in the Parisian atmosphere, she still regretted that Tom had not been with her to enjoy it.

Tom asked Kelly if she had met anyone interesting on her trip or managed to maybe tag along with anybody for company. Kelly shook her head; she had spent the whole trip on her own, the only people she had really spoken to were Henri the concierge and Naomi the pretty receptionist, who, she had suspected, were probably lovers. She told Tom that while the hotel was fantastic and the amenities excellent, it had meant nothing without her husband by her side to share it all. She vowed never to leave him at home again.

Kelly was relieved that Tom hadn't quizzed her further. She had already put her experiences in Paris well and truly behind her and was determined to spend the rest of her life making her husband as happy as she could. What happened in Paris had been a mistake, and as far as she was concerned there was no need for her to dwell on it. It was done, finished, over and forgotten. As Tom lifted the sheets off the bed, making his way to the bathroom so he could shower and prepare for his next airport pick up, Kelly thanked her lucky stars for such a wonderful husband. Not only was he good looking, with the body of an athlete, he was also kind and considerate. As well as volunteering to drive back out to the airport to pick up Billy Malphrus, Tom had spent the previous day preparing the house for Kelly's arrival back to Gordonston.

The house was spotless when Kelly walked through the door. Tom had cleaned not only the house but the dog, too. Shmitty smelled like summer roses when he jumped up at Kelly as she walked through the door. The Labrador's tail wagged so hard that Kelly thought it was going to fly off his body. There was even a casserole simmering in the oven. Kelly lay on the bed and relaxed. What had happened was in the past. Tom suspected nothing and he would never find out. Kelly truly believed she was the luckiest woman in the world.

The office was filled with high tech gadgetry and equipment. Photocopier, printer, fax machine, and several telephones connected to separate lines were placed around the room. However, the main feature of the office, as in all high-powered and important men's offices, was the desk and the chair behind it. It was a big desk; made of old mahogany and so highly polished that the occupant could see his own face reflected whenever he took his position behind the impressive workstation. The chair was leather, plush and designed for comfort. There was no doubt that this was the office of a very important and influential man.

The view from the only window was stunning; the occupant of the office could see for at least half a mile, the location being the tallest building in the area and his office was on the top floor.

The "Director" switched on his computer, which sat on the center of the mahogany desk. The level of technology was so high in the office that the computer immediately came to life, and within seconds he received the information he had been informed would be headed his way.

The Director read the contents of the two files that appeared on his screen. Interesting, he thought, very interesting. He rubbed his chin. A remarkable coincidence: two contracts in the same town, but even more remarkable, the very same neighborhood. He wondered (as always out of habit) why anybody would resort to murder to settle their differences, what their reasons were and why they felt that contacting the "Organization" was the only way to resolve their problems. He dismissed the thoughts as quickly as they entered his head. He was, after all, a businessman, and this was a business. He didn't have time to dwell on the reasons or motives of his clients. He had a job to do.

They called it the "Organization," but it had been known by many different names over the years—Murder Incorporated, The Gun Club, Guns for Hire, and The Assassination Squad were just a few that had been bandied about from time to time by the press and the television media. Most people thought the Organization was a myth, that it was just a figment of the media's vivid imagination. How on earth could there be a global network of highly skilled assassins linked together via encoded communications, secret bank transfers, and clandestine contracts?

But there was. And the director was at the center of it. He wasn't in charge—he was merely a cog in a large machine. His role was to vet the potential contracts that were propositioned from every corner of the planet. He would make the final analysis of whether or not the contract would be profitable—or even viable—for the Organization, and he would make his recommendations to the "board," whoever and wherever they were. Once they agreed or disagreed with his recommendations they would ask him to select a contractor from his vast list of resources to complete the job. They, the board, would deal with the financial side of the contract, ensuring payment was received from the client and that contractors were paid.

Once a price had been negotiated and the contract agreed to, the contractor would be paid, but only after the Director had confirmation that the contract had been fulfilled. Obviously, the contractor received the largest percentage of the contract price. The Organization was a business, though, and they had overheads plus the need to turn a decent profit. They took their generous brokerage commission, which included the Director's comfortable salary.

The Director dealt with many potential contracts each day; he himself was a former contractor, and he knew how hard it was to find decent people to work these days. He re-read the files. Savannah was an obscure little town. He doubted he had anyone locally who could do the job, or jobs, for him. He wasn't going to select both contracts for approval at the same time, in any case. He would keep the other on file, in reserve, dependant on how the one he selected went. The golden rule was only one contract at a time. They certainly didn't want to attract undue attention to the Organization—one murder was enough, especially in such a small area. He reached over from his desk and took a file from the filing cabinet behind him. It was his list of available contractors, and he began to thumb through it, searching for a suitable man or woman who, he felt, could complete either of the recently proposed contracts.

Elliott looked around the house. It was spotless. She had done a fantastic job. Since Thelma's death he hadn't had the time to clean and vacuum or do all the things she had done. In fact, since Thelma became bedridden a few months earlier, the house had begun to fall into slight disarray. When she had offered to clean for him he was delighted—he had been meaning to get some help for months but had just not had the time. She had definitely outdone herself.

Elliott sat at the recently cleaned table in his spotless kitchen. He had made himself a sandwich, and was enjoying being able to eat in such a clean environment for the first time in weeks. He had been doing a lot of thinking recently, and as he took a bite of his cheese sandwich he reflected again on his most pressing tasks at hand. First of all there was the problem of the books. He often wondered why he had never come clean in the first place, why he had passed the stories off as his own. He had told friends, and of course Thelma, about the old man and who he actually was, or who Elliott had later suspected he was, but no one had ever believed him. They just assumed Elliott had purchased the copy of *Mein Kampf* at some auction or other and made up the whole "kind old man story" as an interesting after dinner anecdote.

He supposed it didn't really matter now, anyhow. The books were long out of print and the royalty checks had stopped years ago. If some snoopy reporter ever dug up that Elliott had once been a best-selling author, he was sure he could use it to his advantage. Maybe his books could even be reissued. They could become bestsellers again, and then the royalty checks would start coming in. But then again, so might the letters.

Elliott shuddered as he recalled the two anonymously written letters that had arrived in his mailbox twenty years before. They were brief and to the point. The writer accused Elliott of plagiarism and fraud; the writer of the letter claimed that they knew the true identity of the real author of the books that Elliott was passing off as his own, and that sooner or later he would be made to pay for what he had done. The letter said that "they" knew where he lived, "they" were watching him, and that "they" wielded considerable power and influence. Elliott had been frightened—if the old man was indeed who Elliott suspected him to be, then Elliott would be involved with people who were at the least extremist nuts or worse, part of the organization responsible for the most absolutely evil deeds in history.

Elliott never told Thelma about the letters. As abruptly and as suddenly as he had received them they stopped. The two were all he ever got. They had been posted locally, though. Elliott recalled retrieving the envelopes from the trash to check the postmarks and the fear he felt when he realized that the threats were postmarked "Savannah." He thought "they" must have done this to drive home the point that their people were watching him close by. The handwriting had been neat and the grammar had been well punctuated, too, as if written by a person who meant business and not some crackpot.

As the years passed and nothing bad happened, Elliott gradually forgot about the threatening mail he had received. But what if his books were re-released? What if the nut was still out there? What if there was indeed an active network of the man's followers, still waiting and watching? Elliott pushed the thought from his mind. He was being ridiculous. It was history, and the chances of the books being reprinted, without his authority, were slim. He had maintained all rights to them. He had nothing to worry about, he assured himself.

What was more pressing for Elliott was his current status—not as a politician but as a man. He was a widower; everyone knew that. Thelma had been very popular, and her passing was well publicized. But how would the voters feel about electing a single man as mayor? He hoped it wouldn't matter, but the more he thought about it, the more he was coming to one conclusion. He needed at least a respectable consort, a woman whom he could be seen with. It was too soon, though, to go and marry someone new. He knew that. That would be as counter-productive as being single, and he needed to be careful how he conducted himself, especially with regard to his personal affairs.

Elliott knew several divorced and widowed women, but not all were suitable. Firstly, he needed someone who was presentable, articulate, and willing to work the long hours that being the mayor's wife would entail. He had already whittled down the number of women who met his criteria to just two. The fact that they had both been friends with his dead wife was a bonus. It meant that people would understand that he had already known his new consort innocently; that nothing inappropriate had gone on while his wife was still living. Elliott knew that people in Savannah loved a scandal, and he knew the press did too. There was no way he was going to fall into that trap.

Cindy Mopper he had always liked. She had been a good friend to Thelma and a good neighbor. She had run the neighborhood association ably and efficiently for years, and she was well respected in the community. She was presentable and well informed. She was definitely a candidate.

His second and only other candidate was obvious. Carla had been a rock. She was always on hand, it seemed, to offer assistance and cook meals for Elliott. She had also been a good friend of Thelma's, and though not as close as Cindy she had still been regarded as part of Thelma's inner circle of close friends. She was intelligent and was also wealthy. Not that money mattered, but it was always a point to consider. He sipped on a glass of sweet tea as he considered the pros and cons of both Carla and Cindy. Of course Carla was a stunner. There was that. He found her very attractive—even sexy, and, of course, she knew it. She knew that every man over forty in the neighborhood lusted after her, especially now after her recent surgery. Carla always reminded Elliott of Raquel Welch; looking so much younger than her years, sexily dressed and always groomed to perfection. It excited him to run into her in the park, early in the morning when they were alone and there was no one to gossip about their meeting, despite it being nothing more than two friends walking their dogs.

Biscuit and Grits interrupted Elliott's thoughts of Carla. Their feet pit-patted along the tiled kitchen floor towards where Elliott sat, his sandwich finished and the last drop of tea drunk. "Okay you little guys," he said, "time for another run in the park."

The casserole had been delicious. Tom had surpassed himself, thought his wife. Kelly took one last forkful before flinging herself back in her chair. "That," she said pointing at her empty plate, "was delicious."

Tom smiled. "Well, I'm glad you enjoyed it. You know I had to go grocery shopping on my own—first time ever. I was going to get cheese, milk and bread, but I suddenly thought, why not make Kelly a welcome home dinner?"

Kelly leant across the table and kissed her husband on the cheek. "Thank you," she said. "I really don't deserve you."

Tom smiled again. "It was weird, though." He took his plate to sink to rinse it before placing it inside the dishwasher. "I saw Elliott at the grocery store."

Kelly looked up from the table. "How is he, how is he bearing up?" she asked.

"That's just it. I didn't speak to him. It was as if he were trying to disguise himself. He had a big coat on, despite the heat, and he was wearing sunglasses and a baseball cap. He looked really odd."

"Did he see you?" asked Kelly, intrigued by her husband's encounter at the Piggly Wiggly.

"No, he didn't." confirmed Tom. "Weird, though."

Kelly agreed that it was strange behavior, but well, this was Savannah.

"Listen—I got to go and collect this Billy kid," said Tom, checking the time on his watch. Before Kelly could say anything the doorbell rang. It was Cindy.

"Welcome back!" Cindy cried as she hugged Kelly. "How was it?" she asked, scrutinizing Kelly as if she hadn't seen her for months. Kelly explained that she had had a fantastic time, but despite everything she was glad to be home with Tom. Cindy smiled and told her that she was indeed lucky to have such a good man to come home to. Tom had helped unblock her sink a few days earlier and had offered to take her garbage out for the Wednesday pick up.

"You know, I think he secretly missed you," whispered Cindy as Tom disappeared to search for his car keys. "I think he was pining for you. I think he spent most of the day in bed."

Kelly nodded. "Well, I won't be going away again. Not for a long while, anyway, and certainly not without him," said Kelly. "I missed him so much. You know, being away from here made me realize how much I actually have and how much I have to lose."

Cindy agreed with her young neighbor but was slightly confused by her last comment. How could she possibly lose Tom? Cindy let the comment pass. She had far too much on her mind as it was.

"Well, you must be very excited," said Kelly as she handed Cindy a glass of sweet tea.

"I am. I haven't seen Billy for a few years. I can't believe he is actually coming. You know I am so proud of him. Can you believe those poor little Indian kids?"

Kelly nodded her head and told Cindy that Tom had already explained the good works her nephew was doing. Kelly said that he must be an exceptional young man and that Cindy was right to be proud of him.

"Well, you must meet him," said Cindy. "Not tonight. I expect that he will be exhausted. It is a long flight from India, and I imagine you need to unpack anyway," Cindy motioned towards Kelly's suitcase sitting next to the front door.

The fact that she already had been home ten hours mustn't have gone unnoticed by Cindy, Kelly thought. She wondered if she suspected that Tom and she had been in bed for six of those hours.

"I bet you had some catching up to do," commented Cindy with a wink and a nod. Kelly flashed a smile at her intuitive neighbor.

Kelly was about to relay Tom's story of how he had seen a disguised Elliott at the grocery store to Cindy, but thought better of it. She would leave it for later. Cindy was far too excited for gossip.

"Ok, I'm leaving. Don't want to keep him waiting at the airport all night." said Tom as he peered back into the den, dangling his car keys.

"Change of plan," announced Cindy, "Do you mind if I come with you to the airport?"

Tom replied that there was room in the SUV and since he didn't know what Billy looked like, it would definitely be a help. Cindy and Tom said goodbye to Kelly, who said she would clean up after Tom's delicious home-cooked meal. Tom kissed his wife on the cheek and promised that he would drive carefully.

Kelly considered unpacking her suitcase but decided it could wait. She wasn't in the mood and anyway, the kitchen was a mess. Though Tom had cleaned and tidied the house, there were still the plates to clear and cutlery to wash from their dinner. Kelly began her chores, and as she did she threw some leftovers into a bowl for Shmitty, who wagged his tail at the prospect of food.

Kelly rubbed her eyes. She must have fallen asleep, the jet lag finally catching up with her. She was in the den on the sofa and remembered that she had cleaned up the kitchen and fed Shmitty before stretching out to watch TV. She checked the time on the wristwatch Tom had bought for her birthday three years before: it was midnight. She vaguely remembered waking up when Tom had called earlier from the airport. Billy's flight had been delayed and Tom and Cindy were still waiting for him, so they would be much longer than they had thought.

Kelly could hear voices outside in the driveway—the slamming of a car door and the sound of a suitcase being dragged along the ground on its wheels. It must be Tom, Cindy and Billy, thought the still half-asleep and groggy Kelly. She considered going outside and greeting Billy but decided against it. She looked a mess after snoozing, and she didn't want her new temporary neighbor's first impression of her to be a poor one. She had an image to uphold. Instead, she decided to peek around the curtain and watch as Cindy led her nephew into his new home. She shifted the curtain and peered into the darkness. She could see that Tom was talking, laughing and smiling with Cindy and her nephew, who had his back to the window so Kelly couldn't get a good look at him. She could hear Tom's laugh as it echoed in the night, and she saw him shake Billy's outstretched hand. Cindy then leant over and kissed Tom on the cheek. That was sweet, thought Kelly as she strained for a better view of her neighbor's nephew, whom she had heard so much about. As Tom waved Cindy and Billy good night, the trio shifted position and Kelly got her first clear look at Billy Malphrus.

Kelly's eyes widened and her whole body stiffened. She suddenly felt herself go cold, as if her blood had just stopped and frozen solid in her veins. She blinked several times, not believing what she was seeing. She rubbed her eyes and blinked some more. Suddenly the coldness she had felt was replaced with heat, a hot flush erupted from her stomach, seeming to engulf her whole body. Nausea gripped her. She felt as if she had been punched and the wind knocked out of her. She panted for breath and slowly her breathing returned to normal. She was trembling as Tom inserted his key into the front door of their home, unaware that his wife was watching his every move. She was still trembling when Cindy and Billy disappeared through their door. "Oh my God," she whispered, "Oh My God!"

CHAPTER 14

"Are you sure you don't want me to call a doctor?" asked Tom, concerned as he stood outside the bathroom door. Kelly, who had been locked in the bathroom for well over an hour, didn't answer. Tom heard the sound of her throwing up for the third time and then the toilet flushing. It was well past two o'clock in the morning, and Tom had resigned himself to the fact that tonight he would get little, if any, sleep.

"Listen, honey, are you okay? Look, I am going to call Doctor Victor," said Tom, his head pressed against the bathroom door.

"No!" screamed Kelly. "I'll be fine, it's probably nothing. You just try and get some sleep."

Tom was worried. Maybe the casserole had done this to her, she was fine before he left her to go to the airport.

Kelly vomited again, and Tom winced at the sounds coming from the bathroom. "Do you think it was the casserole?" he asked, his voice fraught with worry.

"What?" said Kelly, sounding confused.

"The casserole, you know the one tonight?" clarified Tom.

"No. Maybe. I don't know. Look, it could be anything, something I picked up in France probably." The irony of Kelly's last statement wasn't lost on her and she groaned as soon as the words left her mouth.

"What was that?" said Tom, alarmed at the grunt of pain she had just uttered.

"Nothing just missed the bowl that's all," lied Kelly. "Look, you just go to bed, I'll be fine."

Tom scratched his head. He had eaten the casserole too, but he felt fine. It must be something she put in her mouth when she was in Paris, the fire fighter decided. His watch at the firehouse started early in the morning. He couldn't take an extra day off, not after having the last six days at home. "Well, if you are sure," he said to the bathroom door, "then I am going to try and get some sleep."

"I'm sure!" yelled back Kelly. "Just go to bed, I'll be fine."

"Okay, well, goodnight then," replied Tom. "Call me if you need me; is there anything I can get for you before I turn in?"

"No! Look, just to go to bed, Tom, there's nothing you can do. I just need to get it all out. I'll be in bed in a few minutes." Kelly was glad of her husband's concern but she really needed him to go to bed.

"I love you!" shouted Tom, as he headed towards the bedroom.

"Me too!" shouted Kelly, not sure her husband had even heard her declaration of love.

Kelly listened as her husband closed the bedroom door and then she promptly threw up once more. She had begun vomiting just seconds after she had seen Count Enrico de Cristo enter Cindy's house. She'd made it into the bathroom just as Tom walked through the door. That had been two hours ago. Tom had tried to persuade Kelly to let him enter the bathroom so he could check that she was not in too much discomfort, but she refused steadfastly, telling him there was nothing he could do and that she needed to just ride it out.

Kelly was frantic. Her nerves were shot and her poor stomach just couldn't take it. She had needed the time in the bathroom alone - not just to throw up, but to figure out what exactly was happening. Initially she had wondered what the Count was doing in Savannah. At first she thought that maybe he had traced her here. She had imagined that maybe he had returned to Rome, lovesick and enchanted by the famous model he met, and had contacted the hotel Bonaparte in Paris and discovered her true identity. It was possible that the hotel could also have passed on her address in Savannah and then he had chartered a jet immediately, because he couldn't bear being apart from her. Kelly dismissed that theory as just as quickly as it formed in her head, though. It was a highly unlikely scenario - for a start she was sure a ritzy establishment such as the Hotel Bonaparte didn't give out their guest's personal details and secondly, how did Cindy Mopper fit into the whole thing?

Her second theory was far more plausible and indeed was exactly what had occurred. Kelly had been duped. And by some tragic and horrific twist of fate she had actually slept with Billy, Cindy's nephew from just outside of Atlanta, and not an Italian count with business interests in Naples and Rome as well as a yacht he sailed to and from Monaco. She had almost dismissed that theory as well, remembering that Cindy's nephew was supposed to have been in India, looking after starving kids and performing charitable work. Kelly, however, quickly realized that if she had believed that the young man she had seen shaking Tom's hand and entering Cindy's home had been an Italian count, then there was no reason why Cindy wouldn't be fooled that her nephew had just flown in from India.

Kelly wasn't bright, but even she could see what had occurred. She had been taken in by the far-fetched story of some horny redneck. The fact, however, that she had also tricked him didn't once enter Kelly's mind as she sat with her head draped over the toilet bowl. It never once occurred to her that she had also lied and misled and had done so deliberately, without a care for any of the consequences. She didn't consider herself just as bad as Billy. No. The only thing that was going through Kelly Hudd's mind was that her perfect and contented life had just been invaded, and all that she had was now under threat.

Kelly wondered what Tom would do if he ever found out that his wife had been unfaithful—and not with just anyone, but with Cindy's nephew? Tom would leave her; she had no doubt about that, and then what? Without him she was nothing; she needed him. It wouldn't take long for Tom to find somebody else. Kelly couldn't bear to think of Tom in the arms of another woman; she couldn't bear to think of living without him. However having Tom discover her infidelity wasn't her only immediate concern. How could she face Billy? The moment he saw her he would realize immediately who she was—and then what? The consequences were just too disastrous for her to imagine. Not only would Tom leave her, but she would be the laughing stock of the neighborhood by the time Cindy spread the story around.

Kelly knew that Billy, too, had something to hide. He had told everyone, including his aunt, that he had been in India performing all sorts of charitable work. Cindy had even told Kelly she was going to donate funds to Billy's medicine fund, destined for the poor children of India. It was all a lie and Kelly knew it, and once Billy saw her he would realize that she would know his whole India story had been a fabrication.

But what if he didn't care about that? What if Billy suddenly started telling the truth? What if he told Cindy he had really been in Paris, and had slept with Kelly in a fancy hotel, and that she'd pretended to be a top model? Would anyone believe him? She could just deny it, but she was sure her nerves wouldn't be able to take it, not if her continual vomiting was anything to go by. No. This was a drastic situation and it called for drastic and immediate action.

Kelly had to think fast, something she rarely did. There was no way she was going to risk losing Tom—especially because of some lying, two-faced, double crossing kid from Atlanta. She flushed the toilet one last time, cleaned up the bathroom floor, then crept quietly out of the bathroom and slipped through the open bedroom door. Kelly saw that Tom was sleeping soundly; he had to be exhausted, she thought. Shmitty watched inquisitively as Kelly gently closed the bedroom door and then tiptoed along the hallway to where her unpacked suitcase still sat. She opened up the case and winced when the noise made by the click of the latches seemed audible throughout the whole house. Satisfied she had not awakened Tom, she delved into her suitcase, rummaging among her clothing, searching for the one thing that might be the solution to her problem.

Eventually, after emptying half the contents of the suitcase onto the hallway floor, she found what she was searching for. She grabbed the neatly folded sheet of orange paper and opened it. She read it, and then to make sure she had not made a mistake, she read it again. She recalled what Thierry, the waiter, had said to her in the café, that it maybe was a student prank. Well, maybe it was, thought Kelly, but she had nothing to lose. She was desperate, and desperate times called for desperate measures. Kelly took the orange-colored flyer into the kitchen and lifted the telephone handset on the wall. She took a deep breath and then replaced the receiver. She crept back down the hallway and opened the bedroom door, Tom was still sleeping soundly.

She returned to the kitchen, all the while with Shmitty watching her, confused as to his mistress's unusual nocturnal activity. Kelly lifted the telephone handset for a second time and then dialed the number that was emblazoned across the bottom of the orange flyer that she clutched in her hand.

Kelly tapped her finger on the kitchen cabinet impatiently—the call seemed to take forever to connect. She relaxed slightly when at last she heard the familiar sound of a ring tone.

"Bonjour," said the voice at the end of the line.

Kelly paused. "Do…you…speak…English?" she asked slowly, her voice a hushed whisper.

"Good morning, yes I do, Madame. How may I be of assistance?" inquired the accented voice. Kelly guessed that it was probably around seven in the morning in France.

"Well, the thing is, I picked up one of your flyers while I was in Paris, and I was wondering . . . ."

Doug had not slept well. He woke at three and spent the rest of the night sitting in the den, flicking through television channels. He had turned the sound low, though, so as not to disturb the sleeping Veronica and Katie. He was getting used to the sleepless nights. The money situation was worsening. After returning home that evening, Veronica had announced that her car had broken down on the Truman Parkway as she headed to work. She had managed to get a lift from a passing colleague, but her car still sat abandoned on the shoulder of the two-lane expressway that linked the downtown Savannah area with its southern suburbs.

It was going to cost a fortune to replace his wife's car, and Doug had no idea where he was going to find the money. He had assets—plenty of them, including property in England—but they were impossible to liquidate quickly, and his family needed money now. He switched on his laptop, which he had brought with him into the den, and checked his emails. His in-box was empty. Maybe he was wasting his time, he thought. Maybe he should figure out another way of making money. He had considered another yard sale. He and Veronica could sell the household items they no longer needed. They had done one before, in less desperate times, just for fun and to clear the house of junk. They had made a few hundred dollars. He needed more than that, though. He needed thousands. They needed a new car, and he wanted to at least be able to treat his wife and child every now and then. He also needed some reserve funds, just until he could sell some property—it would be a buffer, and keep him from worrying.

Doug wasn't sure he could get through another yard sale. He smiled as he recalled the previous one. He had risen early and laid out sheets in the front yard, to display the items he and Veronica intended to sell that Saturday morning. He then strategically hung announcements throughout the neighborhood, which he had prepared on his laptop and printed the night before, directing potential customers to his yard. The signs were pretty specific: 'YARD SALE, 401 KINZIE

AVENUE, 8AM SATURDAY'. He also placed a giant "Yard Sale" sign on the gate that opened onto his home's garden.

Later, Veronica had told him he should not have been so rude, but Doug had not been able to help himself. He'd never taken much notice of the old adage about dumb blondes—but *that* girl, wow, he recalled, she was plain stupid! She came to the gate and peered into the yard, her golden Labrador by her side on his leash. Bern was frantic, trying to get out of the yard to play with Shmitty, so Doug had had to banish Bern into the house, before he damaged anything. Doug had seen the girl (*Kelly*, that was right) before in the park, sometimes walking Shmitty but usually just waiting at the entrance while her dog ran wild with all the others.

"Are you having a yard sale?" she had asked. Doug had looked at the then-pregnant Veronica, who was sitting on the front porch swing, and screwed up his face in disbelief at Kelly's question. It was obvious that they were having a yard sale. Their belongings were strewn all over the garden on sheets, all marked with prices, and the big sign was placed directly where the girl stood. She had read it moments before opening her mouth.

"No," Doug answered, "actually we are not." The girl had looked confused, which Doug thought was a look she probably wore often. "What we are doing is moving outside to live. We don't like it anymore, you know, inside. I'm going to relocate the shower out here and then the kitchen and everything. It's the way forward, I reckon. We will definitely save on heating bills and electricity. Actually, I'm going to knock a hole in the living room wall later," Doug pointed to the side of the house, "So I can drive my car into the den. I think it would be better, you know, the car in the house rather than on the street and us sleeping outside." Kelly had just nodded, her face a blank. "So later on, I'm bringing the beds out here, so we can sleep out here tonight. I'm going to dig a little hole, so we can use it as a bathroom." As he laid out his "plans" to her, Doug pointed to the areas in the garden where the beds and toilet would be put. Kelly had simply nodded, then smiled and walked her dog away without responding to Doug's words.

"That was so rude of you." Veronica said, chastising Doug for his remarks.

"What?" he protested, laughing. "It was a dumb question. Anyway, I doubt she has any idea what I was saying."

"Well, it's not the way for you to get to know our neighbors. You know she'll tell Thelma, and then it will get around that you're an asshole. You don't know it yet, but everyone gossips incessantly around here." Veronica smiled. It *had* been a stupid question, but still, Doug should not have taken it so far.

"Oh well," said Doug as he shrugged.

"It was funny, though, what you said," laughed Veronica.

Doug checked his watch. He had scratched it the day before—more expenses, he thought. It was a Swiss Rolex, and the warranty was expired. He had scratched the crystal face while unblocking the garbage disposal the day after the warranty had expired. Just his luck. It seemed everything was breaking down at the same time. It was four in the morning, which meant it would be ten in Europe. He logged into his email account again, not really expecting to see any messages in his inbox. He wondered why he was even bothering to check. He was surprised to find one new email requiring his immediate attention.

Kelly crept into bed without waking Tom and slept soundly until ten that morning. Tom showered, dressed, breakfasted, released Shmitty into the yard and left for work, all without disturbing his wife. He even called her supervisor at Macy's and advised him that his wife would not be in to work that morning, that she was suffering from food poisoning contracted in Paris. Kelly read Tom's note, explaining what he had done, and she clutched it to her chest. There was no way she was going to lose this sweet man.

As Kelly lay in bed, she went through the events of the previous night in her head. She had called the number advised on the orange flyer and spoken to a charming sounding man with a French accent who had taken her details. He had quoted her a tentative price, which would totally wipe out her recent winnings, and then told her that her proposed contract would be forwarded immediately to the next stage: consideration. If they accepted it, she should expect to pay the full amount immediately and without delay.

Kelly had no regrets about it. As she saw things, she had no choice. She had been forced into a corner, and it was either sink or swim as far she was concerned—and there was no way she was going to sink. She had followed the Frenchman's instructions precisely and had logged onto the website address he had given her. As advised, once she had completed the online forms, she deleted her recent internet history, took the flyer into the garden, and burnt it. It was five a.m. when she quietly crept into bed next to the snoring Tom.

The Director couldn't believe it; in all his time with the Organization he'd never known anything like it. Yesterday he had received two files containing proposed contracts; both not just in the same small American city, but also in the same neighborhood. Now, today he had received two more, separate and different contracts, again, in not only the same small southeastern American city, Savannah, but it appeared they were yet again in the same Gordonston neighborhood. It was unprecedented. What in blazes was going on? He stood up, walked towards his window, and stared out at the view. This needed some serious thought. He would select one contract and hold the other three on file for the time being, following his organization's policy. Of course, there was the money aspect to consider; each contract was of varying value with no fixed price, but each had a minimum value. It would be up to the contractor, ultimately, to agree to carry out the contract for the agreed price.

The director returned to his desk and hit a button on his computer keyboard. The printer to his left whirred into action. Once the printer had finished, he collected four sheets of paper and brought them back to his desk. This would require some serious thought. He spread the four proposals out and leaned back in his chair. It was going to be a long day.

When Doug Partridge read the email he received earlier that day, he felt a shiver run down the back of his spine. It was unexpected. He wondered what the implications of the email were. He considered his options and decided that the best thing to do, at this stage, was nothing. His main concern was to protect his family from anything that could jeopardize their quiet and peaceful existence. He suddenly felt the urge to see his daughter. He crept into the nursery where she slept peacefully in her crib. He lovingly stroked Katie's hair and adjusted the blanket that covered her small and fragile body. He leant over and kissed his child on the cheek. No matter what, Katie and Veronica were his priority, and he would make provisions for them, should anything ever happen to him.

Billy Malphrus enjoyed the breakfast his Aunt Cindy prepared for him. He hadn't eaten like that for months. European breakfasts were so different from the American variety. He had yearned for eggs, bacon, grits, sausage, biscuit, and pancakes for months. He'd hated the French version of breakfast, apart from the coffee. It was as boring as the place itself, after a while. Apart from the women, of course. He had been very successful with his conquests in France, and not just with the French girls, either. He'd slept with women from all over the world. Not bad for a country boy from Georgia, he thought.

As Cindy collected Billy's egg-stained plate from the kitchen table he wondered what breakfasts the Indians ate. Curry, probably, he thought as he raised his coffee cup to his lips. That was something he needed to research, should the question come up, which could quite easily happen. Billy watched as his Aunt Cindy cleaned and fussed around him. Staying here in Savannah with his aunt had been a great idea. For a start, it was free; she wouldn't charge him board and lodging. In addition, the food was great, Cindy was a fantastic cook and he knew he was in for a culinary treat. All his favorites: fried chicken, dumplings, Brunswick stew—not to mention the famous Savannah shrimp.

His Aunt Cindy had told him he was welcome to stay as long as he wanted, and that she had already put the word out around the neighborhood that should anyone have any odd jobs that they needed doing, Billy could help and maybe make a little extra money—anything that would help him raise funds to help those poor Indian children.

Billy offered to take Paddy for a walk while his aunt cleaned up the kitchen. Cindy fetched Paddy's leash and issued Billy directions on how to reach the park. Kelly watched from behind the draped window of her living room as Billy left her neighbor's house, Paddy in tow. As she observed his movements, her face obscured by the curtains, she felt nothing but contempt for him. It was definitely him—there was no doubt about it, but now he looked like a skinny, spotty and scruffy country boy. That's how Kelly saw him. Trailer trash, nasty little hick, she thought, as the slightly-built youth disappeared towards the park. Your time will come, she thought. Oh yes, your time will come, you lying, cheating bastard.

Heidi watched as he took a full bag of trash from inside his house and deposited it next to the larger trash can near his garage. From her window, the window in her secret room, she could see every move that Elliott made. Look at him, she thought, totally oblivious to what was going to happen to him. She felt nothing but hatred, and her old frail hand began to shake as Elliott went back into his home. Thief, she thought. Nothing but a common thief.

As Cindy stood at her kitchen sink, dishes soaking in the hot suds, she suddenly felt a surge of anger overcome her. Billy was a good boy; he always had been, and she was pleased he was here, spending time with her. Of course she would give him five thousand dollars for those poor kids; she was pleased that she could aid him in his charitable deeds. Her anger had nothing to do with Billy. It was all directed at her so-called friend, Carla Zipp. She was nothing but a tramp, a common whore who was not going to steal Elliott from her, no way, not as long as Cindy had breath in her body.

Cindy was abruptly jolted from her thoughts. Her hands were bleeding. She had crushed the fragile glass she'd been wiping. She fished the glass shards from the sink. It was the same glass that Billy had drunk his orange juice from. If only everyone were like him, she thought—honest, hard working, caring and thinking of others. She stared as a droplet of blood fell into the soapy suds. She shrugged, and dabbed at her mild lacerations with the dishtowel before placing band-aids over her wounds.

Billy found the park easily and released Paddy from his leash. He reached into his pocket and pulled out the packet of cigarettes that he had been yearning for since he had arrived in Savannah the night before. His aunt didn't know he was a smoker, and he was afraid that the sight of him sucking away on a cigarette could in some way detract from the image he was trying to create. As he lifted the cigarette to his mouth, he realized he was not alone in the park. A grey-haired man, slightly overweight, was approaching, two poodles closely following behind.

"Good morning," said Elliott as he passed Billy. Billy nodded, the unlit cigarette dangling from his mouth.

Billy returned the greeting as Elliott marched past him. Billy watched as Elliott, Biscuit and Grits left the park, only to be replaced by an old black man and a little dog. Billy watched as the old man started on the trail that circumnavigated the park, the small white dog following obediently.

This damn park is busy, thought Billy, as he fumbled in the pockets of his jeans for his Zippo lighter. He flicked the flint, and the flame appeared as if magically summoned. He sucked hard on his cigarette, the menthol flavor filling his mouth. He released the smoke into the warm Savannah air.

CHAPTER 15

The Gordonston Ladies Dog Walking Club reconvened after a hiatus of over a week. The three women resumed their usual positions around the picnic table outside the Scout Hut in the center of the park. Each woman had before her the familiar plastic cup containing her favorite cocktail. Paddy, Fuchsl and Walter—all delighted to have been at last reunited—chased one another and played their usual games, as their owners sat and did what they liked to do best, gossip about their neighbors and happenings in their neighborhood.

The big news in Gordonston was the arrival of Billy Malphrus. Cindy extolled the virtues of her kind-hearted young nephew to her two friends, who were most impressed by Billy's recent selfless and charitable work in India. Both Carla and Heidi had chores that young Billy could do, and they would be delighted to spread the word to their other friends and neighbors that a fit young man was willing to carry out any job, however nasty or dirty, and not only was reliable, but one hundred percent trustworthy.

The other big story in Gordonston was the unfortunate news that Kelly Hudd had contracted a highly contagious infection of some unidentified virus and was bedridden and quarantined within her house. It was a shame, because Cindy had planned a little get-together to welcome Billy to the neighborhood. The ladies all supposed that Kelly had contracted her sudden and rather unusual virus while in France. Unusual, because though highly contagious, it seemed that Tom was immune to it, as he seemed perfectly fine to Cindy when she had seen him that morning. He wasn't sure what the name of the virus that Kelly had contracted was, but thought it was caused by food poisoning.

"Has anyone seen Elliott lately?" asked Carla, gazing towards the big white house that overshadowed the east end of the park. Heidi and Cindy both shook their heads. Cindy eyed her friend suspiciously. It seemed that Elliott was always at the forefront of her buxom friend's thoughts.

"I was wondering if we should extend him the invitation we discussed, to allow him to join us in the afternoons?" continued Carla, whose attention, Cindy noticed, was still focused on Elliott's home. Carla, however, was actually focused even more precisely—on Elliott's bedroom window. She had seen that the drapes were still shut and was wondering why.

"Well," began Heidi, "I am not sure how interested Elliott would actually be in joining us." She took a swallow of her cocktail, prepared with more vodka that usual, before continuing. "What with his mayoral campaign I would think he would be far too busy to join us now." Carla and Cindy were disappointed to hear this, but neither revealed how she felt.

"That's probably right." agreed Cindy. "But maybe we should just offer, in any case I took the liberty of drafting a letter already, for you both to read." Cindy removed the draft letter from her purse and handed it to her companions. Heidi read it first and then passed it over to Carla. Both women nodded, agreed that it was a well-worded letter and gave their approval that Cindy should proceed.

"Good," said Cindy as Carla passed the letter back to her. "I'll send an original signed letter this afternoon."

"What about our friend, "Mr. No Pooper Scooper," said Carla.

Heidi smiled and said, "Well, as you know, I had my Betty Jenkins do some investigating on our behalf," said Heidi triumphantly. "It turns out his name is Jackson, Ignatius Jackson." Heidi took another gulp of her cocktail. "He lives over there, in that big house with the turret-shaped things. An ugly house, I have always thought." She pointed to the northwest corner of the park, towards the green-colored house that overlooked that corner of the park. "His dog is called Chalky; apparently he goes to the same church as Betty Jenkins."

The other two women took simultaneous sips of their drinks and looked over to where Heidi had pointed. "So I have his address, and I have drafted the following," she said. Heidi removed from her purse the neatly handwritten note she had drafted earlier that morning. She handed it first to Carla, who, once she had read it, passed it on to Cindy.

Dear Mr. Jackson,

It has come to our attention, we being the Gordonston Ladies Dog Walking Club, that on several occasions, while walking your Cairn terrier, Chalky, within the boundaries of the Gordonston Park, you have failed to sufficiently clean up after your animal has performed his natural functions.

We, as residents of Gordonston and as responsible dog owners, feel that your failure to assume responsibility for your dog's mess is an affront to not only us, but to other users of the Park, your fellow neighbors. It would be much appreciated if in future you would "scoop up" after your dog and collect his business, thus ensuring that the Park, which belongs to us all, is maintained in a way that will permit us all to enjoy its amenities.

For your information, the Gordonston Resident's Association has provided a "poopa scoopa" for the use of dog owners. It is located adjacent to the Scout Hut, and we implore you to seek out this user-friendly appliance and in future use it accordingly.

Yours Faithfully,
Heidi Launer

Cindy returned the handwritten note to Heidi. "Well, I think that's great. It'll get the message across," she announced.

Carla agreed with her friend. "Absolutely!" she cried.

Heidi smiled. "Well, let's hope so," she said as she folded the note and placed it back in her purse.

The ladies' attention was diverted from the note the moment Heidi had returned it to her purse. The squeaking of the east gate caused each woman to turn her head to see who had just entered the park. It was Doug, with Bern and Katie in her stroller. As he always did, he released Bern from his leash, and the dog promptly bounded straight over to the other three already at play. Doug then began his slow walk around the park.

"You know, I am still not sure about him," said Heidi, while fixing the Englishman with a scowl. The other two ladies turned to face their friend.

"In what way?" asked Cindy, unsure why Heidi would say such a thing.

"Well, for a start, he doesn't work. He sends his poor wife off each morning. I find that odd."

Carla and Cindy didn't disagree or agree, they just listened as the old woman spoke. "I mean, what type of man wants to spend all day with a baby? There is something decidedly un-American about it. That may well be the way they do things in England, but here, well, the man works and the woman brings up baby. That's the way God intended it, and that's the way it should be."

Cindy and Carla found themselves agreeing with their older companion.

"It's a good point. I know my Ronnie worked every day of his life, and even though we had no young ones at home he would have been horrified if I were out working. My job, a woman's job, was home-making," said Cindy.

Carla nodded, "I suppose you're right. Maybe the man is just lazy—or useless. Accountant? Banker? Well, *I* was married to a banker for thirty years, and that man worked hard for his money. Maybe he just doesn't want to work." The three women glared at Doug as he pushed the stroller around the park.

"I don't like him," announced Heidi.

"Nor me," agreed Carla.

Cindy watched as Doug disappeared from view. "He's certainly a strange one," she added.

Doug, who had no idea he had earned the universal disapproval of the Gordonston Ladies Dog Walking Club, continued his regular route through the park. He was in a buoyant mood; he had finally secured some work. It was temporary, but it was a start. The head office had come through and had decided that they might need a branch or at least a representative in this part of the world after all. It meant that maybe Veronica could start working part-time hours and spend more time with Katie. He hadn't yet told Veronica the good news—instead he spent the morning cleaning the house from top to the bottom and catching up on the family's laundry. He had also found the time to water the plants and cut the grass on both the front and back lawns. He was exhausted, but didn't want to deprive Bern or Katie of their regular afternoon jaunt. He had skipped his lunch to ensure that their usual routine would not be broken.

After completing a full circuit of the park, he called Bern to join him and Katie. He waved at the three ladies sitting around the picnic table. They smiled and waved back in unison.

"Lazy man," said Heidi under breath and behind her toothy grin.

"Idle, if you ask me" said Cindy behind her false smile.

"His poor wife, having to support her whole family, while he just lazes about," contributed Carla.

Doug re-attached Bern's leash and led the dog with one hand while he pushed the stroller with the other back towards Kinzie Avenue. He smiled as he saw the old man with the white dog walking slowly towards him. "Beautiful day again," Doug announced as Katie began rocking with excitement in her chair, delighted to have encountered the old man and his dog.

"Well, looky here," said Ignatius Jackson as he bent down and put his face close to Katie's. "The pretty girl been in the park again?" he said softly. Katie opened her arms and pushed herself forward in her seat.

"I think she wants you to pick her up," announced Doug. The old man laughed, "Well maybe old Ignatius might just lift you." He looked at Doug, who indicated it was fine for the old man to pick up his daughter.

Katie laughed and giggled in his arms. "You know, you make my day," said the old man as Katie pointed at him and made gurgling noises. After a moment he put her back in the stroller again. "Well, I got to make sure old Chalky here gets his exercise," he said.

"Have a good day," Doug said, as Ignatius Jackson proceeded towards the park.

"Your little girl just made my day," smiled the old man as he patted Doug on the back. "She's precious," he added. "You cherish this time. It only comes once." Doug smiled at the old man and headed home. He was happy with life, pushing his baby girl with the exhausted Bern walking slowly behind them.

"Oh no," said Cindy as the old man entered the park. Heidi and Carla once again turned their heads to the direction of the gate. "It's him, Mr. 'No Poop a Scoop.'"

"Just ignore him," instructed Heidi. The old man waved at the three women but didn't even raise his head to see if they had waved back. The women hadn't acknowledged him, in any case. He proceeded slowly around the perimeter track, Chalky faithfully at his feet.

"So, what is young Billy up to today?" asked Heidi, her question directed at Cindy.

"Relaxing. I think he may be working on the computer, actually, looking for sponsors, you know, to help the poor Indian kids. I think his main priority is fundraising."

"You must be very proud," said Carla as she patted Cindy on the back. Cindy looked at Carla and smiled. The woman was so false, thought Cindy. She had one thing on her mind, one thing only, and it wasn't Billy. Despite the fact that they all sat together, secretly Cindy felt nothing but hate for the woman to her right. She ignored Carla's comment and took a drink of neat bourbon from her cup. It didn't matter anyway. Soon Carla would no longer figure in any aspect of her life, she thought, her eyes fixed on Carla's ample, artificial chest.

Billy spent the best part of the afternoon, as Cindy had suggested, using his aunt's computer to search the Internet. He had not been looking for sponsors for the imaginary Indian children from the equally imaginary village but surfing his favorite pornography sites. He had also been searching for information pertaining to the elusive Jerry Gordonston, the model he had screwed in Paris. He was trying to find pictures of her, or maybe even a biography. He realized that Texas was only a day's drive away, and while he was in the US, if he could scrape together enough money, he might be able to visit his one-time lover and reprise his role as the Count. Unfortunately, despite his expertise with computers and the workings of the Internet, he was unable to find any trace of her. Eventually he gave up.

Billy Malphrus had never graduated from High School, despite the certificates and diplomas that hung on the wall of his parents' home in Atlanta. He had flunked every subject and dropped out long before graduation. The fake diplomas and certificates were purchased using money stolen from a friend's school locker. He had pompously presented them to his parents the morning after the ceremony. They had felt guilty about missing his graduation. He became a thief at the early age of fifteen. He had at one time or another broken into every vehicle parked in the staff parking lot at his high school, while skipping class. His criminal career had progressed since then, and though he had never graduated from any accredited college, he held a master's degree in the art of the confidence game.

Billy had never been able to hold down a proper job for longer than a month. During those brief periods of employment he would con, steal from, and generally attempt to part his co-workers and employers from as much of their money as possible. It was quite remarkable that he had never spent any time in jail. What was even more remarkable was that he had never been caught once or charged with any crime. Billy was good at his chosen career, and he could fool most people. This was how he made his living, and he had managed to travel around Europe on his ill-gotten gains. Even in Europe he had managed to continue his mini crime wave, stealing a wallet here, a purse there, and working a con game every now and then.

Sometimes the money he stole or swindled would last for a little while and he would indulge himself in clothes and accessories—expensive sunglasses and shoes, for instance—which he would use as props in his next con. Other times he would have to find temporary or part-time work as a bus boy or a janitor so that he could eat but as soon as possible he would continue his grifting. Billy always had an angle. Where there were people, there was money. That was Billy's philosophy.

His current plan was—he often congratulated himself on it—ingenious. He planned to remain in Savannah for a month, no longer than that. In that time he would accumulate as much cash as he could. He would gain the trust of his aunt's friends and neighbors doing boring and even obnoxious tasks and chores for little or no payment. Of course, people would insist that the hard working boy take some payment, but he would steadfastly refuse. He would then ask if his new admirers needed other tasks done, maybe even inside the house while they were working or out of town. He was sure that at least one of his aunt's wealthy neighbors would require some sort of assistance or other of this kind. When this happened, he would search out their valuables and maybe even cash hidden away under mattresses or floorboards. Billy knew what these old birds were like; they were old fashioned, and he was sure at least one of his aunt's cronies would have something hidden away just waiting for him.

Billy had heard that the people of Savannah were an odd bunch, and he guessed that a lot of these old houses and the people who lived in them had many a secret treasure hidden or on display but no idea of its value. Once he had discovered such a cache—which he was sure he would—he would plan a day of thievery. He would have already planned his departure from the city. Everyone would be aware he would be leaving for India, of course, to continue his charitable work. They wouldn't be suspicious that he had left town. He imagined the suckers would even throw him a farewell party! He made a mental note to himself to plant that idea in his crazy old aunt's head. The very next day, after he had supposedly left for India, he would return to the neighborhood and either force his entry or use the keys he would have copied, to relieve the trusting residents of their property.

He also had another plan—his backup plan—should he not find hidden valuables in his aunt's friends' homes. He would try to obtain as many donations as he could for the poor children of the Indian Village he was set to return to with medical supplies and other items to aid the poor unfortunates. He was sure the wealthy widows of Savannah would jump at the chance at being able to donate a little towards his charitable venture. After all, hadn't he been good enough to mow the lawn, clear the drains, and clean up the yard?

The first setback in his plan, however, had been the postponing of his aunt Cindy's proposed "welcome to the neighborhood" gathering in his honor. The quicker he could meet people and gain their trust, the better. Tom Hudd, who had picked him up at the airport, seemed an easy mark. Big and stupid, that's how Billy had viewed the kindly fireman, and his wife sounded no brighter. Anyone who spent their days putting out fires or selling makeup to fat women in a mall deserved to be relieved of their best china, he thought. As for the English guy and the woman who worked at the hospital, he was sure they would have some good stuff—newlyweds always did. Maybe rings or watches. It was a shame that the stupid bitch next door had gotten food poisoning or the virus or whatever it was she had.

Billy didn't dwell on his initial lack of success for too long. His aunt had already promised him a contribution to his charity project and that was a good start. There were plenty of potential targets. The old lady, the German one, had a big house, and he just knew that a woman like that would have a stash of goodies hidden away. She would be his first target. He couldn't wait to get his hands on her heirlooms and trinkets.

Next would be the big house, the white one that belonged to the guy with the poodles. His wife had just died, so Billy reckoned there would be plenty of her old jewelry just lying around. Billy rubbed his hands and walked to the front window of his aunt's house and peered out into the street. Yes, there were some rich pickings to be had in this neighborhood, and soon his fun would start.

As Billy Malphrus was peering from his aunt's front window facing the street, Kelly Hudd was also peering out hers. She wondered how long she could keep up the pretence of her "highly contagious disease." Tom had bought it. She'd told him that the doctor had told her to stay indoors and that on no account was she to accept visitors. As Tom hadn't yet caught the strain of the virus she had contracted, the doctor told her it was unlikely that he now would. Tom had been relieved. He was already receiving a ribbing from his fellow firefighters for his wasted vacation time, and to take even more time off would have been impossible.

Thanks to the amount of makeup that Kelly possessed, she was easily able to fake a sallow and pale complexion, as well as create a spectacular rash she told Tom was a symptom of her disease. As long as Tom didn't get too close, which he hadn't, she was able to paint on lipstick mixed with blusher without his actually realizing that the blotchy areas of skin seemed to shift around from one day to another. She got Tom to spread the word around the neighborhood that visitors should stay away from the Hudd household, and her plan seemed to be working for now, at least. Shmitty though, was a problem. He needed his exercise, and Tom couldn't just come home at his leisure to walk the poor dog. It meant she had to release Shmitty into the back yard and call him back, disguising her voice should her next-door neighbor's house guest recognize it. Another problem was work. She couldn't expect to stay off work indefinitely without a doctor's note. Sooner or later her supervisor would want to see some sort of documentation as to why she had not shown herself at the beauty counter for days now.

Kelly frowned. How long would she have to wait? When would the decision be made, whether or not her contract had been accepted? When could she rid herself of the thorn in her side who was just yards from where she stood? She had been told she would have to wait and that when the time was ready she would be notified. Well, she was becoming impatient. He had to go.

Heidi had enjoyed her first afternoon in a week with her fellow lady dog walkers. She missed the bitchiness of their afternoons, whether aimed at their fellow residents or each other. Heidi knew that all was not well between Carla and Cindy, and enjoyed being a spectator to their verbal sparring. It made her smile. It was futile, though, she thought, bickering and fighting over Elliott Miller. He would never become Mayor, not if she had any say in things. She wondered how long Elliott actually had left, and when the contract would be accepted. Stephen had warned her that things could take a while, and that there was no guarantee, despite his connections, that the contract would be taken straightaway, if it all.

Heidi was unconcerned, though. She had marked him, and sooner or later his time would come, she was sure. She brushed aside thoughts of Elliott for the time being and concentrated on the new matter at hand. Cindy had persuaded her to find some task her young nephew Billy could perform. There were several things that needed doing about the house and in the garden, and she would spend the rest of the afternoon compiling a list of jobs for the boy.

Cindy had returned home from the park with Paddy following, exhausted and out of breath behind her. Billy was vacuuming. The boy never ceased to amaze her. He was truly an angel. He explained that it was his intention to spend the whole afternoon tidying up his aunt's home, but he had become distracted by the task of scouring the Internet looking for pharmaceutical companies with whom he could hopefully convince to arrange a free contribution of drugs and medicines for those poor sick Indian children.

Cindy demanded that Billy put the vacuum cleaner down and put his feet up. She would make him a sandwich, and he really shouldn't overdo it, she told him. If poor Kelly next door could catch a rare strain of some sort of food poising virus while in France, heaven only knows what he could have gotten in India. Billy's ears had pricked up the moment his aunt had mentioned France.

"Oh really?" he said, trying to sound unconcerned. "Where in France was she?" suddenly worried that maybe he, too, had contracted some awful disease and that unbeknownst to him it was spreading inside of him that very moment.

"Paris," replied Cindy. "She stayed in a fantastic hotel, too. Five Stars she said, near the center, Hotel Bonaparte, very famous place she said, or something like that." Billy froze. That was the same hotel where he had spent that one night with Jerry Gordonston, the famous model. What if there was an epidemic and the source had been that hotel? He would need immediate medical treatment. But how could he explain it, if he had caught the exact same rare disease? Billy wasn't listening as his aunt continued to talk.

"Well, I have managed to find you your first work," she said as she entered the den with a ham and cheese sandwich. Billy dragged himself from his thoughts.

"What . . . . Oh, sorry, I was miles away," he said. Cindy patted her nephew on the head.

"You have a lot on your mind, those poor kids and everything. I was saying that I have found you your first job. With my friend Heidi, you know the one I told you about?"

Billy nodded.

"Well," Cindy continued, "she is making a list of jobs she needs doing and, well, I said you could start tomorrow."

Billy nodded once more; however, he was more concerned with getting himself to a doctor and even more worried about the symptoms and effects of the illness he was now convinced he was carrying. Cindy noticed that Billy hadn't touched his sandwich; he usually devoured his food the moment it was placed in front of him.

"Have you lost your appetite?" she asked, pointing to the untouched sandwich. Billy smiled weakly at his aunty.

"No. I was just thinking," he began, "about that poor girl next door. You don't by any chance know her symptoms, do you? And how bad she is?"

Cindy smiled. That was so typical of Billy, more concerned about others than himself. He didn't even know Kelly, had never even met her, and here he was, worried sick for her.

"I am not really sure. Tom, her husband, the one who picked you up at the airport, told me she has an awful rash and is very blotchy." Cindy sighed. "It's such a shame because she is such a pretty girl," Cindy stood up. "Hold on, I think that I have a picture of her somewhere, I'm sure Tom took a snapshot of us last month when we were out in the yard together. You sit there while I go and find it." Billy didn't move. His mind was racing. He couldn't afford to be quarantined. It would mean his whole plan would be ruined. He hoped that the virus was not air-based, that it couldn't be contracted by touch; if that was the case then he'd be fine, he was sure. He hadn't eaten anything at the hotel, he was positive, all he had done was lie in the bed screwing (a few times, granted), but he was positive he had eaten nothing during his brief stay at the Hotel Bonaparte, and anyway, what were the chances of Jerry Gordonston contracting the virus? She had seemed fine to him.

Cindy returned clutching a photograph. She gazed at it while she held it in her hand. "She is so pretty, you know she really *should* think of modeling, I know she wants to, but I think she'll probably just end up stuck in Macy's until she has kids." Cindy handed the photo of herself and Kelly, arm in arm, to her nephew.

Carla was annoyed that he had not so much as called her since their time together. She was more than annoyed, she was furious. Of course she knew he was busy, but the fact that she hadn't even seen him in the park, which she had hoped that she would, had just increased her frustration. Was he avoiding her? Was he having second thoughts? Surely he hadn't just used her for sex. He didn't seem that type. She glanced at Walter, who was sleeping on his favorite cushion. She couldn't take Walter back to the park, in the hope of just casually bumping in to him; the poor dog was exhausted. No, she had to sit it out. There was no way she was going to call him. She would give it a few more hours.

Elliott picked up the receiver and began dialing. Before he pressed all the numbers needed to complete his call, though, he replaced the telephone receiver. What would he say? How could he call her out of the blue and ask her to come over? He didn't want to appear too eager. He gritted his teeth. He missed her since he had last seen her, and he needed her there. He decided he would wait. Maybe a day or two more. The last thing he wanted to do was upset anyone, especially not any of his neighbors.

Veronica was delighted that Doug had done so much work in the house that day. She could see that he was exhausted and let him sleep on the sofa. She collected Katie in her arms and carried her into the dining room. Doug's laptop sat on the dining room table. Veronica noticed that he was still logged in, and for no other reason than curiosity she bent down to read the open page that lit up his computer screen.

Veronica took a deep breath. Doug had kept this quiet. She had no idea that he was in so much trouble. She suddenly realized that maybe things *were* as bad as Doug had said. Doug had been keeping a journal in secret. Usually he was very good about closing down his computer, and he was highly sensitive about her even touching it. He must have been so tired, thought Veronica, that he had just fallen asleep and not had the chance to log off from his diary. Veronica scanned the page again; she could hear Doug stirring in the den so she read as quickly as she could.

. . .I realize now it was a stupid thing to do. Taking so much money from them had been a mistake. Of course they

would come looking for me, and God knows what these people would do. It wasn't the amount I had stolen, even though it was a substantial sum. It was the mere fact that I had broken their trust. I knew the consequences, yet I had still done it. I am sure that it is only a matter of time before they come looking for me. And I know they will find me. My first priority has to be my family; whomever they send mustn't harm them. These people are serious people, they wouldn't think twice about having me killed. It had been easy, though, transferring money into my offshore accounts, filtering small amounts from the accounts I was administering; how was I to know that one of the companies had been a front? How was I to know that? They had tricked me, finding out where I lived; through my own greed, asking for work, I should have known they would be reading my emails, and now they know where to find me…'

"What the Hell do you think you are doing?" Veronica turned quickly and in the process almost dropped Katie who she was holding. Doug's face was like thunder.

"Nothing," she lied, "I was just wiping the table." Doug eyed his wife suspiciously before closing his laptop.

He smiled. "I see," he said, ignoring the fact she had no cloth in her hand. Doug lifted the computer from the table and put his arm around his wife. "And how was your day?" he asked, kissing Veronica on the forehead and stroking Katie on the cheek.

Cindy was being as quiet as she could be. Billy had not looked at all well. As soon as she had handed him the photograph of Kelly he had begun to shake. He had also gone deathly pale, despite his tan. She had ushered him off to bed without any argument. The poor boy. It must be the stress of it all, trying to organize so much for those unfortunate Indian villagers. Never mind, she thought, as she collected his plate and untouched sandwich and carried it back into the kitchen. Paddy raised his head and Cindy threw the sandwich in his direction. The Irish terrier caught it in his mouth and swallowed it whole.

From the kitchen window Cindy could just see into her neighbor's yard. Tom was out in the garden, cutting his lawn and tending to Kelly's flowers. They were a good couple, she thought. He was such a saint. She wondered what sort of husband Elliott would make.

Would he and Cindy have the same sort of honest and trusting relationship as her young neighbors? Soon she would know, once Carla was gone and out of the picture. Cindy wondered how long it would be before she got news. As far as she was concerned, the sooner the better.

Elliott decided that he would not call her. He would put what happened behind him. She wasn't suitable. He really needed to find someone a little less pushy, maybe even a little younger.

Carla knew that he wasn't going to call. If he were going to, he would have called by now. Once again she had been used by a man and discarded. Well, it was the last time. She picked up her telephone receiver and began to dial. She had guessed this might happen and had already made tentative arrangements. Now was the time to finalize things.

Billy lay still in the spare bedroom of his aunt's home. The bed was comfortable, and he pulled the sheets tightly around his body. There was no doubt about it—it had been her, Jerry Gordonston. He had been duped, tricked, fooled, and now he was carrying some sort of disease. That whore, how could she? He'd have to avoid her at all costs. The last thing he needed was her wrecking his plan. He'd just have to lie low. Hopefully he hadn't caught her messed-up virus, and hopefully she would remain quarantined for the duration of his visit. He wondered what else she might have given him. No matter what, he was going to avoid her like the plague.

Tom finished pruning his wife's roses and stood up. It had been a tough day at work, and he had hoped that she would be feeling better. The fact that her condition had worsened was terrible news. It meant that he would have to get up earlier than normal the next day and walk Shmitty, as well as prepare dinner and collect some groceries. Tom sighed, and as he did he saw Cindy staring blankly through her kitchen window. He waved, but she didn't notice. Oh well, thought Tom, as he entered his home, she must be daydreaming.

Ignatius Jackson was dying. He knew it and had known it long before the doctors had told him the cancer inside him was slowly eating away at his body. It had been the Agent Orange in Vietnam, he knew. The very fact that he'd survived so long was a miracle in itself. The old man lifted himself from his easy chair and made his way over to the collection of medals which hung on the wall of his living room. Purple Heart, Vietnam Service Medal, Snipers Medal, Silver Star, Distinguished Service Cross and Gallantry Medal—all proudly framed and presented. He was a hero, and in all fairness they had treated him like a hero; they found him a job at the Pentagon, and he had been promoted up the ladder, higher than he had ever expected.

Ignatius sighed. At least May hadn't lived to watch him die. In a way, it had been a blessing that she died first, and not by some illness that slowly and painfully ate away at her insides. Her death on the interstate had been sudden and quick, and the doctors said she died instantly. Ignatius closed his eyes and recalled the day he had received the news of his wife's death.. She was on her way back from a nearby town after visiting her sister. The other driver had been drunk, he was told, and claimed he hadn't even seen her car before he ploughed head on into it.

Chalky looked up at his elderly master, and Ignatius smiled. The dog was one his few pleasures in life. Walking him in the park around the wood chipped path was an important part of his day. There was the baby, Katie, whom he enjoyed seeing. Her smile brightened his day, and he liked the young man who spent so much time with his child. It was an odd neighborhood. He smiled. He'd heard that Betty Jenkins had been asking questions about him, trying to find out his name. His minister had told him on Sunday that she had been making inquiries about the church's biggest donor. Ignatius had just smiled and nodded.

The old man also smiled to himself when he recalled his recent trip to the supermarket. It was amazing what went on in this place, he thought. The secrets that people had, the lies they told, and the ghosts from the past that always seemed to come back to haunt you when you least expected it.

CHAPTER 16

The Director read his most recent communiqué again. Not that it affected his decision; it really just confirmed what he already knew. Since his decision had already been made he lent no credence to it. He spent many hours reviewing each contract. Each one had its pros and cons. Price was not a factor in his final decision; it was practicality and what was best for the Organization.

He leaned back in his plush leather chair and raised a pen to his mouth, tapping it against his lower teeth. It would happen tomorrow. He had already set the wheels in motion, and there was no turning back. The contractor would be receiving his instructions any minute now, and that would be that. The director wondered if the three people who had been reprieved, albeit only temporarily, would ever have any idea how close they had come to being killed. Of course, now that he had their details and the details of the person who had organized their contracts, there was no guarantee that they would continue to live. Their details would remain on file and, dependant on how the contractor felt about operating in the same location again, the Director would choose a second contract for processing at the right time.

The Director stood up from his chair, went to his window, and looked out onto the world beyond. Tonight was someone's last night on earth. Usually the contracts didn't affect him; usually it was just business. But there was something different about this one. Maybe it was the fact that when he made his final decision there had been a choice. Maybe it was the fact that they were all so closely linked. He didn't know, it just felt . . . odd. He sighed as he surveyed the view from his office window and wondered if they knew that tomorrow they would be dead. He wondered how the target would spend their last night on earth. He sighed again. May God have mercy on their soul.

He took a long draw on his cigarette and tasted the menthol tobacco. He really needed to cut back, he thought as he stubbed the cigarette out with his foot. It was an expensive habit he meant to quit. He had received his final instructions earlier that day and had done what he always had, irrespective of location or target; familiarized himself with the area and identified his victim. He had already checked his equipment and begun the advance preparations, as the dirt-stained spade in the trunk of his car confirmed. He was focused and professional. He had done this many times before and had no doubt of his own ability.

He had driven around the neighborhood several times. It was late, though he had seen some movement: an old man walking his little white dog. The old man had waved to him and out of politeness, he waved back. He watched though, as the old timer approached the park gates. The last thing he needed was for the half-dug hole he had just finished to be discovered. Luckily, the old man had not entered the park; it seemed as if his old dog had just needed a late night toilet trip.

The contractor shifted his car into gear and took one final look at the park; he had the padlocks, so he could dictate which entrance would have to be used, and he was ready. As he slowly edged away from the curbside he marveled at how peaceful the neighborhood was. He shrugged before disappearing into the night.

CHAPTER 17

Billy yawned and stretched. He checked the alarm clock and closed his eyes. It was too early for this. Why had he even suggested it? He knew though, if he were to hide in the house all day, avoiding Kelly, the only chance he would get to smoke a cigarette would be in the morning. His suggestion that he take Paddy on an early morning walk had been one of desperation. Billy dressed quickly, and checked that his cigarettes were in his jeans pocket and that he had his Zippo to light his menthol-flavored smokes.

Elliott had already been awake for thirty minutes. He had already showered and dressed and was on his second cup of coffee. He had a big meeting that morning with some potential backers of his mayoral campaign. The last thing he wanted to do was keep these men waiting. Maybe before he went off for the day a quick run in the park for Biscuit and Grits would do them good, he thought. They could use the exercise, especially as he didn't know when he would be home that evening. It seemed the most logical thing to do; at least they could relieve themselves.

Doug had had another night with little sleep. Even though the sun was up, it was still really early. Bern, he thought, would love an early run on a day like this. He rubbed his eyes and yawned.

Carla had guessed that he would probably be walking early that morning. Call it a hunch, call it intuition. When she had seen him walking by her window she had quickly grabbed Walter's leash, put on her coat and followed him along the sidewalk.

CHAPTER 18

He took one final draw on his cigarette before flicking the wet butt into the hole he had just dug. It was still dark; the sun not due to rise for another thirty minutes. He checked his watch and confirmed the time. He was still on schedule. He turned suddenly to his left, surprised by the rustling noise he had heard in the undergrowth. A grey squirrel peered out from the bushes before rapidly disappearing into the wooded area to the right. Overhead, a woodpecker began to tap against a nearby oak tree. The 'rat-a-tat', like a hammer, echoed through the densely forested landscape.

Satisfied that he was still alone, he re-inspected the freshly dug hole. Ideally, it should have been six feet deep, but four, he thought, would do. It was not the first time he had dug a hole like this, but he wondered though if this one would be the last. He had begun digging the night before and hoped that no one would discover his half-dug hole and half-empty bag of lime salts, which it now appeared, they had not. Usually he would have poured more lime salts into the bottom, to cover the unpleasant smells that would rise from the ground later, but he had decided that the extra bags would be too much to hide. He crouched and leaned over the hole, stretching his arm to full length to pick up his discarded cigarette butt. Unprofessional, he thought. He really knew better than that. He slipped the butt into the packet it had come from, alongside the other nineteen yet unsmoked menthols.

From his vantage point he could see anyone entering or leaving the park. There were three gates, but he had taken the precaution of locking the north and south gates with padlocks, which he would remove and discard once his task was complete. Now the only way to enter the park would be via the east gate, which was the main entrance anyway, and the one he knew would be used that morning.

The recently prepared hole was ensconced just off the well-trodden path that encircled the park; he couldn't have asked for a better spot to perform his task. If only they were all this easy. He picked up his shovel and placed it out of sight in the undergrowth. He would need it later to fill the hole back in. Though he had dug holes like this before, they were usually not necessary. But the instructions he had received were very specific, that there should be no trace of his work for at least one week. He hoped that four feet was deep enough. He considered his surroundings and decided it was.

The park was located in the center of a middle class neighborhood of approximately 300 homes. It was protected by a wrought iron fence and three gates—perfect for his purposes. Signs proclaimed that this was private property, designated solely for the use of those who lived there. At least half the families in the area owned a dog and regularly used the park to exercise them. Not everyone walked his dog in the park. He estimated that only fifty or so people ever ventured where he now stood.

The Girl Scout Hut, an old log cabin-style building that stood in the center of the park, was available for hire for private functions and neighborhood gatherings as well as for residential association meetings. An extensive wooded area, home to an abundance of wildlife, dominated the interior of park. Trees and shrubbery surrounded the perimeter railings, hiding the interior of the park from anyone traversing nearby streets. A children's playground in the northeast corner of the park offered wooden swings and forts. These, along with sliding boards and monkey bars delighted the children of those privileged to play there.

Dog walkers took advantage of the wood-chipped track that circled the park. The path wove around the trees and crossed ditches and natural moats. The occasional jogger who ventured into the park would sometimes make use of the track but would have to watch for fallen trees and avoid the sprawling roots that sprouted from the earth. He pulled another menthol from its packet and lit it. He sucked in the mint-flavored smoke and exhaled it into the early morning air. It was hard to hold the cigarette in his gloved hand, so he removed the leather pair that he wore. He wore the gloves not due to any coldness but as necessary to his task.

The sky was no longer black but a dark blue, the sun now on the verge of rising. The first birds of the morning began their song and the temperature was slowly beginning to rise. The unnatural sound of a car engine straining into life could be heard in the distance. Its owner was probably an early morning worker, beginning his day while most were still enjoying their last few minutes of sleep.

It was going to be another warm day, and air conditioning systems would be on high throughout the city. He considered removing the dark coat that he wore but didn't. It, along with the gloves, was his standard attire when working: an unofficial uniform of his trade. More rustling, this time from the north, made him twist his body and alerted his senses. As before, another squirrel disappeared into the dense wood as the streetlights that illuminated the avenues and streets that ran alongside the park switched off in unison, announcing that daybreak was approaching. Soon bedroom lights would turn on as early risers prepared themselves for the day ahead.

He was conscious of the four homes that backed onto the park on the west side where he waited. He had considered the possibility of being discovered by a dog, released into the morning to relieve himself and to stretch his four legs, but had decided that the chances of any animal being able to navigate both a garden fence and the iron railings and still see him through the dense trees were minimal. He was a professional, and he had taken no chances. He never did. The previous morning he had stood in the exact same spot where he was now, at the exact same time, and was confident that neither dog nor man would discover him.

He placed his gloveless hand into the front lower pocket of his jacket and felt the cold stainless steel held snugly there. One final check was required, one final inspection. The last thing he needed was some equipment malfunction.

He removed the Beretta M9/92F 9mm semi-automatic pistol from his pocket and ran his hand along the smooth barrel. It was his weapon of choice for up-close hits, and it had never let him down. For jobs such as this, it was ideal. He checked the safety catch and the clip that contained six bullets. He hoped he would only need one, two at the most. He delved into his other pocket, produced his M9-SD silencer, and caressed the long, sleek black cylinder before attaching it to the barrel of the Beretta. Once again, it was a tool of the trade that had never let him down.

He had always considered silenced, close-up hits to have a personal touch, and strived for perfection whenever tasked with such a kill. It was important to hit the selected vital organ. The quicker a target fell, the quicker one could leave. The heart or the middle of the forehead were his preferred targets, though a well-placed single shot in the center of a chest or the stomach could also result in instantaneous death without the need of a second shot. He considered more than two shots poor form. What separated the best from the rest, he thought, was the swiftness and accuracy of hits. It was easy to kill, but not so easy to kill smoothly, efficiently and quickly, leaving behind no clues or trace as to the identity of the killer. The less blood the better, especially in a situation like this, where instructions demanded the disposal of a body and no immediate trace of a crime.

The sun was rising now and the sky was turning from dark to light. It was going to be another beautiful day in Gordonston, an older but stylish neighborhood where he stood, two miles to the east of downtown Savannah, Georgia, and the Historic District, a five-minute drive at most from the center of the city. He yawned and stubbed out the cigarette before placing into its pack with the other eighteen and the one smoked butt. He put on his gloves and slipped the Beretta with the silencer screwed into the barrel into his pocket.

He could hear voices close by and the barking of excited dogs. Two voices bade farewell to a third voice and the iron gate creaked, opening and then closing as the owner of the one voice entered the park. From where he crouched near to the ground, he could see a dog having its leash removed, then running into the woods. He drew his weapon. His heartbeat didn't quicken, and his breathing didn't rise. He fixed his gaze on his intended target and waited as the darkness gave way to daylight.

A beautiful day indeed in Juliette Low Park, but for one individual, that day would not last long.

Billy managed to crawl out of bed and find Paddy's leash. Taking care not to wake his sleeping aunt, he had made his way, with Paddy following, to the front door of the small cottage-type house. He fixed the leash to Paddy's collar and led him into the street.

Biscuit and Grits were delighted with the early morning exercise. It was not often that they got the chance for a run this early, and with no traffic on the streets Elliott was happy to let them loose into the road while he struggled to put his shoes on.

Carla managed to fix Walter onto his leash just as she saw Elliott walk past her window. She was now heading in the direction of the park; maybe they could speak and discuss things before it was too late.

Billy reached the corner where Edgewood and Kentucky Avenues crossed. Biscuit and Grits ran to greet their friend Paddy just before Elliott arrived.

"Good Morning," said Elliott to the younger man. "You must be Billy, Cindy's nephew." Billy looked surprised. Elliott pointed to Paddy. "Paddy, I know him." Billy understood how the man with grey hair had guessed his identity and nodded.

"Hi, and you must be Elliott?" Elliott nodded and went to shake the young man's hand. Billy cursed under his breath. This was all he needed. He hoped that the alderman hadn't noticed the cigarette he had hurriedly discarded.

Carla reached the corner of Edgewood and Kentucky Avenues at precisely the same time Elliott did, though she had not expected a crowd, especially at this time in the morning. There was no way she would be able to confront him now. She would have to wait until they were alone. She just hoped that it wasn't too late. She decided to join the throng on the corner of the street just yards from the gate of the park and act as normal as she could.

Doug wasn't used to being up this early, and he was surprised at how many of his neighbors were actually walking their dogs that morning. Tom was also surprised to find Elliot and Billy chatting on the corner by the park as he appeared with Shmitty on his leash. It was quite the party. As Kelly was still housebound, he'd decided to take Shmitty for an early run in the park. After all, it wasn't Shmitty's fault that Kelly had gotten sick.

He watched as the dog ran into the dense wood and the dog's walker started the walk along the path in a counterclockwise direction. He raised his collar, checked that his weapon was loaded and then proceeded along the path in a clockwise direction.

"Good Morning."

"Good Morning."

"I think it's going to be another nice day."

"Let's hope so."

"Walking the dog?"

"Sure am, how about you?"

"Well, I was, but he has kind of eluded me," said Doug as he placed a cigarette in his mouth and lit it. The menthol-flavored smoke filled his mouth and lungs; he paused and then released it into the morning air.

"Can I help you find him?" offered Tom as the two men walked together in a counterclockwise direction along the track.

"That's very kind of you," said Doug. "You live around here? You look familiar," asked Doug, taking another draw on his cigarette.

"I live along Kentucky, but it's very rare that I come here. My wife usually walks the dog, but she's ill, covered in a rash. How about you, I've seen your face before."

Doug blew out of a puff of smoke. "I live along Kinzie. I have the baby and the German Shepherd dog, Bern." Tom nodded. Of course, Veronica's husband. He should have guessed by the accent.

"It's amazing how many people are actually up and around this time of the morning," said Tom to his new acquaintance.

"Yeah, I saw Elliott with his dogs. I think he just went home, though," replied Doug.

"There was a crowd earlier on the corner. You know Cindy? She's our neighbor. Her nephew was there but was headed back, I think he was a having a sneaky smoke," laughed Tom.

"Same here," said Doug, indicating to his cigarette. "My wife has no idea. I am going to stop though." Both men smiled.

"Oh, and Carla was there, too, do you know her?" asked Tom.

Doug shook his head. "Not really. Seen her around, though."

"Well, she thought Walter—that's her dog—needed to go, but it was a false alarm." Tom smiled, as did Doug.

As the two men walked along the pathway, winding in and out of the trees, Doug recalled a conversation he'd had with his wife a few days earlier.

"Well, we went grocery shopping." Veronica was busy eating and while listening was not looking at her husband. "And I saw something pretty odd. Well not odd, more interesting really. I saw one of those old ladies, the ones that hang out in the park with their dogs."

Veronica looked up. "You mean Cindy?" she asked.

"No. The other one. Not the older one, the young-looking one."

"You mean Carla," confirmed his wife with her mouth full.

"Well, you know she's had a boob job, don't you?" said Doug.

"Oh, yeah, I'd heard that. She looks good I hear," confirmed Veronica.

"Well, that's not it. There was something else," said Doug. "She was at the checkout, buying cleaning products and stuff. I wasn't sure exactly what but that's not important."

"So? She can buy cleaning products. She's over twenty-one," joked Veronica.

"No," said Doug, "that wasn't it. It was something else, something I bet you didn't know."

"Which was?"

"She has a toy-boy," said Doug. "The fire-fighter. I saw them together, in the store. They were holding hands. Very odd."

Veronica frowned. "Rubbish. Tom Hudd? No way."

Doug shook his head. "I know what I saw. They didn't see me, but I swear it. He was all over her." Veronica looked shocked as she forced another forkful of fish into her mouth.

"Well, that's strange. He has a beautiful young wife. I just don't get it. Are you sure?" asked Veronica.

"I'm positive," replied Doug.

"Well, don't say anything. That's how rumors start in Savannah," smiled his wife.

"Don't worry. Who am I going to tell anyway?" answered Doug.

Veronica agreed and then changed the subject. "Do you think Katie has a small head?"

"No," replied Doug, "and neither do you, before you ask again."

"When did you last see him? Your dog?" asked Tom as they turned the corner and both he and Doug headed along the west side of the park.

Doug shrugged. "About ten minutes ago. He just bolted." Both men called for Bern but he didn't return. Doug looked around, raising his gloved hand to shield his eyes from the glare of the morning sun. "I'll check over there," he pointed towards the Scout Hut. "Could you look over there?" Doug was pointing towards the far southwest corner of the park, where he had spent the last two nights digging.

"Sure," replied Tom.

Tom headed towards where the Englishman had pointed as Doug headed towards the Scout Hut. After walking a few yards Doug stopped, turned and followed behind Tom. Tom was standing just where Doug had wanted him. He slowly approached the bigger man. Tom turned quickly, shocked by Doug's sudden reappearance.

"I think you're out of luck . . ." began Tom.

"That makes two of us then," said Doug as he raised his silenced Berretta and put one bullet straight between Tom's eyes. Tom was dead before his body crumpled into the already prepared grave. The bullet had passed through his skin and skull and was imbedded deep inside his brain. Doug wasted no time. It had all gone exactly according to plan. He retrieved his hidden spade and began filling in the four-foot deep hole.

He knew that sooner or later Tom Hudd's grave would be discovered, but there was no way the death could be linked to him. He was a professional. It took Doug only six minutes to fill the hole. He grabbed the bag of fallen leaves he had collected earlier and covered the mound of earth. Very few people ventured into this area of the park, and if they did they never left the track. Not that it mattered. He could have left the body lying there unburied, but his instructions had been specific. Dispose of the body so it wouldn't be found for at least a week. Those types of instructions usually meant only one thing: there were more contracts to be filled.

Doug, now satisfied that the hole was sufficiently filled and hidden, made his way to the two gates he had padlocked shut earlier. He undid the locks and placed them in his coat pocket. He exited through the north gate and made his way along Gordon Avenue until he reached Virginia Avenue. He turned left and reached his home in less than two minutes. No one had seen him enter or leave the park. He inserted his key into the door of his house and entered. Bern raised his head from where he lay, then lowered it, satisfied that it was no intruder, just his master. Doug removed his shoes, gloves and coat and stuffed them into the laundry room adjacent to his home's entrance hall. Silently he tiptoed into his and Veronica's bedroom, she was still sleeping. He climbed in bed beside her and closed his eyes.

Doug Partridge was not—never had been and never would be—an accountant. He had first come up with the cover story four years previously, during his first visit to Savannah. He had used the ruse of being an investment account manager for a Swiss bank to gain entry into a financial gathering held at the Savannah Conference center, located across the Savannah River. He had been selected by the Organization to carry out a very lucrative and high profile contract.

Vladimir Derepaska had many enemies, and one of them had paid a lot of money to have him killed during the banking conference. It had been a successful hit—the police had assumed the Russian banker had been mugged while exploring the city, inadvertently wandering into a less desirable part of town.

The trip to Savannah had been doubly rewarding for Doug. He had met Veronica, and for the first couple of years he had tried to juggle his work and a relationship. After the birth of Katie he made the decision to remain in Savannah and retire. However, his finances and investments had failed, and he had contacted the Organization and offered his services for any work locally available. He hadn't been too hopeful of a response. It wasn't usual for a contractor to work in his hometown, but he had done some good work over the years for the Organization. Though he had never met the Director, or any other member of the Organization, he knew that he was a well-respected operative.

The email he had received informed him that there was indeed work for him. In fact, the organization was considering operating far more extensively in the area, since there had been a sudden surge of potential contracts, all of varying value. Doug's main priority, though, had to be the security of his family, and he had considered the implications of being caught in the act. Satisfied he had every angle covered, it came as a shock to him when he discovered the intended victim's identity. He wondered who would want his Gordonston neighbor dead, but he knew that it was not his prerogative to ask questions. So he didn't.

Doug had worked for the Organization for six years, recruited from the British Secret Service, where he had carried out a similar type of work for considerably less money. His ambition spread further than being an assassin, though. He dreamed of one day writing a novel, based on the exploits of a fictional hit man and an intended victim. It was a secret. He didn't want Veronica getting her hopes up. He knew she couldn't help but tell her friends at the hospital that her husband was writing a book. What if it never got published? It would be embarrassing. He had been horrified when he had caught her reading a page of his draft manuscript after he left his laptop open and logged on, in full view on the dining room table. Luckily, she hadn't seen too much. She had no idea what she *had* seen, and he had told her, to allay her fears, that it was some sort of journal entry. He eventually had told her that he was writing a book and his wife promised not to mention to anyone he was writing a novel and promised not to snoop around his computer ever again.

As Doug slowly drifted into slumber he considered his future options. At least now they could retrieve Veronica's car and even buy a new one. He would get his watch repaired and would set a sum aside for Katie's college fund. What he would do with the remaining money was the fifty thousand dollar question. It wasn't enough for Veronica to either retire or cut down her hours. He would have to stash it until more local work materialized, which he was sure it would. In the meantime, he would focus his energy on trying to stop smoking. He was tiring of the menthol smokes anyway, and was sure it would only be a matter of time before Veronica smelt smoke on his breath or clothes, and his secret would be out.

CHAPTER 19

Carla had seen Tom talking with Elliott and Billy and decided against joining the men. Despite her desire to speak with Tom, it was just too risky—the last thing she wanted was for the gossiping to start. She waved, shouted "false alarm" and led Walter back indoors.

Anyway, it was too late now. The caller had been brief and to the point. "It's done," is all the voice on the phone said before hanging up. The call came from Las Vegas, and she realized that it meant that Tom was dead. What did he expect anyway, she asked herself, staring at her reflection in the mirror on her dresser. As she brushed her dark hair she went through the events of the last week in her head.

She had bumped into Tom—purely by chance—in the park the day after his wife had flown to Paris. They were both walking their dogs and struck up a conversation. She found him, like all the women in the neighborhood, handsome and charming, and he in turn found it hard to keep his eyes off her chest. One thing led to another, and he invited her back to his home. Carla hadn't slept with a man in years, and she would challenge any woman not to be flattered by the advances Tom Hudd made.

Tom was charming, and he had seduced the older woman. Despite their age difference Tom told Carla he found her very sexy. Considering that she looked half her age, it wasn't hard to imagine that the younger man would find her appealing. Carla had felt guilty about sleeping with a married man, but when Tom explained that his wife had practically abandoned him she felt sorry for him and her guilt passed.

She should have realized that Tom's story of abandonment didn't ring true after Kelly called while the two of them were in bed. She had coughed, and Tom told his wife that it was his dog lying next to him. That angered Carla, but she let it go. What had made her *really* mad was the fact she helped him clean and prepare the house for his wife's return and even prepared a casserole for her homecoming. It had been risky, together at the grocery store, but they were sure they hadn't been seen. They had seen Elliott, looking ridiculous in his disguise, but luckily he didn't see them.

She had not been sure what to expect once Kelly had returned from Paris, but when she learned from Cindy that the reason Kelly had traveled solo was due to Tom's lack of a passport and not because she had wanted to travel alone, as Tom had suggested, she became enraged. When he didn't call her, well, that just made her angrier.

Tom was just like her late husband. He was philanderer, a user of women, a man who just wanted sex and didn't care how he got it. He had lied to her, misled her, and totally tricked her into thinking that maybe there was the potential for a long-term, albeit clandestine relationship. She felt used and stupid. How the hell could she continue life as normal with him just around the corner? How could she be expected to pretend that nothing had happened? Her lust had turned to hate, and there was no way that bastard was going to get away with it.

She had called Gino, the one man who had always respected her. Gino knew people who knew people who could get rid of problems. She explained to her wealthy Mafia-connected admirer what had happened. He listened and did not judge her and suggested a permanent solution to her problem. The conversation with Gino took her back thirty years, recalling the day she discovered her husband was sleeping with his secretary. It was Gino who had provided the coronary producing drugs, but it had been Carla who had slowly administered them to her husband in his breakfast food. Ian Zipp had no idea that the eggs he ate each morning were slowly eating away at his heart; it had only been a matter of time before his heart stopped. It was ironic that it happened while he was in the arms of that little tramp.

Carla continued brushing her hair. Tom deserved what had happened to him, and thanks to her association with Gino and his Las Vegas connections, it had not cost her a penny. He took care of it all on her behalf; he knew of a certain organization that did jobs for some of his associates. It wouldn't be a problem. Carla was sure Kelly would get over the loss of her husband. Now that she was a widow, and met all the other criteria, she could become the fourth and newest member of the Gordonston Ladies Dog Walking Club. Carla reconsidered her last thought. Actually, if Elliott took up his invitation to join the club they could rename it. She felt The Gordonston Widowed Dog Walking Club had a certain noble ring to it.

Betty Jenkins had waited for Elliott's call, but it never came. Maybe he was looking for someone younger to be his housekeeper. She was disappointed; she had enjoyed cleaning the big white house and thought that she had done a good job. She expected that Elliott didn't want to upset his neighbor, Heidi Launer.

It happened during the impromptu day off that Heidi had given Betty that Elliott had found her strolling around the park. He offered her one hundred dollars to clean his home: she accepted and got straight to work. Afterwards she offered her services on a more permanent basis, but Elliott did not want to commit to anything without first talking it over with Heidi. No doubt he had reconsidered and decided it wasn't worth aggravating his neighbor by poaching her home help.

Betty thought it probably was for the best anyway. She had seen the book that Elliott tried to hide, hidden under the bed in the spare bedroom. She might not speak German but she recognized the title and the author. There was no way she was ever going to work for a Nazi sympathizer like Elliott Miller. No, she was far better off working for Heidi, a nice genteel old lady, who wouldn't harm a fly.

CHAPTER 20

From where he had stood watching, the Director had seen everything. He was very impressed with the methods Doug had used—not only in killing Tom, but also in disposing of the body. He was especially impressed with the one shot to the temple. He was indeed one of the best killers the Organization had ever contracted. Maybe this would bring him out of retirement. There were three more hits currently pending, and if it was local work he wanted then the director was sure he could accommodate the highly skilled assassin. The Director understood his reasons for no longer wanting to travel, and he hoped that the Organization could accommodate him in the future. The pay would be less than he was used to, but anything would be better than nothing. A good professional like Doug was hard to find. It would be good to get him back aboard. The Organization needed killers like him, and the Director was sure that the hundred thousand dollars he had just transferred into Doug's offshore account would be well received.

The Director lowered his binoculars and returned to his seat behind the mahogany desk. He had paperwork to catch up on and needed to contact the Las Vegas office to let them know the contract had been fulfilled so they could inform whoever had paid. He switched on his computer and sent the relevant information across cyberspace. He had a busy day ahead of him. Another Russian executive needed to rid himself of a rival and a third world dictator needed to eliminate a political foe. Once the money was received he would send in two of his men. These were big money contracts, not like the one he had just witnessed, and would ensure a big payday for all concerned.

Before he commenced with planning the organization's weekly schedule of murder and assassination, he wondered at the remarkable coincidences of the past few weeks. To have four proposed contracts land on his desk at virtually the same time, all in the same small city, let alone the same neighborhood was unprecedented. The majority of the contracts he administered usually took place in more traditional locations such as the South of France—especially popular among holidaying businessmen aboard their private yachts—or major European cities or South American back waters.

It was amazing, he thought, how many people actually knew how to contact the Organization. The Mafia connection was not hard to work out. He had heard of the mob lawyer who had contacted the Organization's office in New York on behalf of his mother, and anyone who knew how to use the internet would not be long in discovering the Organization's untraceable and encrypted website. As for the marketing ploy in Paris, well, that had been ingenious. The Paris office had surpassed itself by using children to hand out flyers as if they were advertising a shoe sale, to café-goers along the Champs-Élysées. The Director had initially dismissed the advertising gimmick as highly likely to fail, despite the fact that a major business conference was taking place in the city, involving executives from some of the biggest oil companies in the world. Even if one of the visiting executives had needed to take out a business rival it was dubious whether or not he or anyone else, for that matter, would have contacted the number on the flyer or logged onto the website address advertised. Printing them in English had proven a very fortuitous decision indeed.

The Las Vegas connection was also easy to understand, the organization had done a lot of work for the west coast Mafia, even if this job was by proxy, an old friend doing an unrequited love a favor.

The Director stretched in his chair and yawned. It had been an early morning for him and maybe he didn't need to plan the weekly schedule just yet. The Organization had many cells and he was merely the one who decided which contractors to use and which contracts to accept. Time was not really an issue, and he relaxed.

He considered the latest victim of the Organization, now lying in the unmarked, shallow grave. The Director had no doubt that Tom's body would be discovered sooner rather than later, but the police would have absolutely no leads or any way of tracing the killing back to Doug. He wondered if the others had known just how close they had come to dying that morning. He had not based his decision to have Tom killed on money (even though it was the highest paying contract of the four) but on the fact that it was plain good business sense. Why have Carla killed before her own contract had been paid and honored? Now that the money had been received and her request fulfilled, she was fair game. It would be interesting, he thought, deciding who would be next.

The Director was hungry. Maybe he would make some coffee or even grab some breakfast. He rose from his seat. The first thing he needed to do, though, was to attend to the scratching outside his office door, the poor fellow had been itching for a walk all morning. The Director grabbed the leash that hung from the hook on the inside of his office door. The same office with the window that overlooked the Gordonston Park and which once had been the fourth bedroom of his Gordonston home. The view of the park was what had attracted him to the property in the first place.

"Come on, Chalky," said the Director as he opened the door and his constant companion bounded into the room. "You and I need to stretch our legs and you need to do *your* business. But we must remember to scoop today. We don't want another letter of complaint from the Resident's Association, no sir, we sure don't," said Ignatius Jackson to his small, white, loyal Cairn terrier, his constant companion and the current thorn in the side of the Gordonston Ladies Dog Walking Club.

CPSIA information can be obtained at www.ICGtesting.com
Printed in the USA
LVOW050434250213

321459LV00007B/247/P